CANDLELIGHT
Ecstasy Supreme

**"YOU WALKED AWAY FROM OUR MARRIAGE
WITHOUT A BACKWARD GLANCE!"**

"You were too old for me," Pip blurted.

"Damn you," Romain said hoarsely. "You certainly
know how to wound me."

"But it's true. I never seemed able to match your sophistication no matter how hard I tried . . ."

"I never wanted you to be any different than the way
you were when I married you. I never tried to change
you." Romain fired the words at her.

"But I changed, maybe that was one of the problems."

"Is that why you left me?"

"That's not the only reason."

"I see."

"Do you?" Pip shook her head. "Excuse me, Romain,
but I stopped thinking about our relationship a long time
ago and it won't help to dredge it all up now."

CANDLELIGHT ECSTASY SUPREMES

DESERT PRINCESS

Hayton Monteith

A CANDLELIGHT ECSTASY SUPREME

Published by
Dell Publishing Co., Inc.
1 Dag Hammarskjold Plaza
New York, New York 10017

Candlelight Ecstasy Supreme is a trademark
of Dell Publishing Co., Inc.

Candlelight Ecstasy Romance®, 1,203,540, is a registered
trademark of Dell Publishing Co., Inc.

ISBN: 0-440-11895-6

Printed in the United States of America

April 1986

10 9 8 7 6 5 4 3 2 1

WFH

I dedicate this book to my father's sisters, my beloved aunts, Sadie, Annie, and Lil, and to my mother's sisters, Helen, Elizabeth, and Kay.

To Our Readers:

We are pleased and excited by your overwhelmingly positive response to our Candlelight Ecstasy Supremes. Unlike all the other series, the Supremes are filled with more passion, adventure, and intrigue, and are obviously the stories you like best.

In months to come we will continue to publish books by many of your favorite authors as well as the very finest work from new authors of romantic fiction. As always, we are striving to present unique, absorbing love stories —the very best love has to offer.

Breathtaking and unforgettable, Ecstasy Supremes follow in the great romantic tradition you've come to expect *only* from Candlelight Ecstasy.

Your suggestions and comments are always welcome. Please let us hear from you.

Sincerely,

The Editors
Candlelight Romances
1 Dag Hammarskjold Plaza
New York, New York 10017

CHAPTER ONE

1978

Attending UCLA was a monumental undertaking for Philippa Tayson. She was an introspective, intelligent eighteen year old, who intended to major in English literature as well as business, with the hope that she might spend one or two semesters studying in England.

She wore very modern spectacles that she really only needed for reading, because she thought they would make her look older. "Instead, you look like an owl and not a bit sophisticated," she often told her mirror. She had boyfriends, whose company she enjoyed, but she had a very serious attitude toward her studies. "Not that Billy Leiden ever accepted that," she mumbled to herself, rounding a hedge on the pathway to the English department and bumping into someone. "Sorry," she blurted, watching her precious journal and other notebooks fly to the ground.

"Tall, willowy, with red curls and turquoise eyes. Are you an Irish goddess peering at me through the Looking Glass?" The man, who was much taller than her five foot nine inch frame, had panther black hair that gleamed in the sunlight, a hawkish nose, and olive skin that gave his piratical face a dangerous look. He touched her glasses with one finger while he gripped her arm with his other hand, "Stop looking at your books, I'll help you with them. Look at me," he commanded.

Philippa did, and felt her insides melt. "I . . . I don't want to be late." She pushed the words from her dry throat.

"Of course." He bent down and swiftly gathered the papers and notes, running his eyes over an open page of her personal journal. "You're a poet, I see." He handed her most of the notebooks and kept the heavy textbooks.

Philippa felt her face turn a fiery red. "I don't let anyone see my journal." She averted her eyes and held out a free hand for the books he had.

"No. I'll carry them for you. That canvas bag must have weighed you down with all you had in it, plus the notebooks in your arms . . ."

"I'm used to it." Philippa walked fast, irritated with him and puzzled at her reaction to him. Why was she so off balance? She was used to being in the company of males her own age and with her uncle's peers. But never had she experienced the shivery uncertainty she was feeling now. Aunt Grace often said she could twist her uncle and his male friends around her little finger. "Your uncle and I are proud of your self-confidence and your ability to get things done." Now she was stuttering and stammering with the dark stranger, feeling both fear and delight in his presence.

"Stop daydreaming. We're at Spruce Hall. Is this where you want to be?"

Startled, Philippa looked up at the building, then at the man at her side. "Yes. Thank you for carrying my books."

"My name is Romain Al Adal." He shifted her books and managed to lift her hand to his lips. "When is your class over?"

Philippa blurted out the time, irked that she had told

12

him, then angered when he chucked her under the chin and told her to hurry or she would miss her class.

She couldn't concentrate on Professor Joles's meaning as he lectured on the Elizabethan concept of morals and how it colored Shakespeare's writing. She loved the course and was carrying an A in it, but during that hour he might as well have been lecturing in Babylonian for all she absorbed.

After class her friend BeBe Linze was at her side. "Trying to blow your 4.0 average?"

"Couldn't concentrate," Philippa said lamely, avoiding her eyes and pushing open the outside door to stand at the top of the steps.

"Right on time." Romain Al Adal was in front of the two girls, taking Philippa's books from her arms. "Shall we go?"

"Go?" Philippa coughed the word from her dry throat, knowing that BeBe's eyes were swiveling back and forth between her and Romain Al Adal.

"I want to take you out to dinner."

"At four in the afternoon?" BeBe interjected, her eyes snapping with curiosity. Her grin widened when Romain looked at her. "Hi! I'm Barbara Linze, Philippa's friend. She never mentioned she was going out to dinner. We usually trade off driving on Wednesday. Today was my day to drive," BeBe chatted. "How long have you known Philippa?"

Philippa fumed silently at her friend, wishing she would close her mouth so that she could tell Romain Al Adal that she had no intention of going out with him. "We'd better go, BeBe," Philippa said and hurried down the steps.

"Wrong way, Phil. The car's parked over in the far parking lot. Remember?" BeBe followed her down the steps, turning the opposite way.

13

"Right." Philippa reached toward Romain, who was still at her side, for her other books.

"She'll see you tomorrow, BeBe." Romain took a firm hold on Philippa's arm, wheeling her away. "My car's right here."

"This is a No Parking zone," Philippa babbled, looking over her shoulder at her agape friend before she was pushed into the plush interior of a Lamborghini. "This is kidnapping—and don't think I don't know you're not an American because I do, and if you figure that diplomatic immunity—" Philippa's head snapped back as the powerful car shot away from the curb.

"I assure you I'm in this country legally; in fact, I have been teaching a seminar on business at this campus." He threw her books in the back, then pressed a button on the dashboard console. A compartment opened, showing papers and two billfolds. "There. Look for yourself, Philippa. Take them." He gestured with his hand until Philippa reached in and took some of the papers, perusing them all, then returning them and studying the billfolds. "Satisfied?"

"Having a passport and credit cards doesn't give you the right to abduct me from UCLA." She cleared her throat, stole a glance at him, then pressed her lips together and stared straight ahead when she saw him smiling.

"Darling, I would have taken you right out of the White House if I'd had to."

Philippa's head shot around and she stared at him.

He glanced at her, not lessening the speed of the sports car. "Your mouth is open, kitten." He put his hand on her knee. "Generally speaking, I never have honorable intentions, but I feel differently with you," he said in a surprised tone. "Would you like me to drive you home so that you can change? I could also meet your parents. I assume you live with them."

"My parents are dead. I live with my aunt and uncle," she told him in measured tones, quite sure she would wake at any moment from this strange dream.

"Stop being so starchy," he told her in his clipped British accent. "I was sure you lived with your family because you didn't direct me to a dormitory."

"And because you think I'm too young to have an apartment of my own. I'm not."

"I'm glad you're not . . . too young, I mean."

She felt the hot, husky tone of his voice from her toes to her forehead and back again. "I have a job. I work in the library for two hours in the evening, seven to nine."

Romain shrugged. "Fine. We'll have a snack first. Then after you get off work, we'll have dinner. How does that sound?"

"Why?" She turned in her seat to face him, feeling a mixture of angst and anticipation.

He looked at her again, his serious mien making his features more hawklike, dark, and sinister, his green eyes looking out of place. "Because you're lovely and I think this is love at first sight."

Philippa inhaled in shaky anger. "I'm not one of your —your kadim . . ."

Romain shouted with laughter.

". . . who comes at your beck and call, and buckles just because you say you're in love." She lifted her chin. "I will not go out with you. . . ."

"You will."

". . . Unless you promise it will be a very casual date. I don't know you. You don't know me—and—and I won't go far from my house either." She waited, hardly aware that she held her breath until she let it go in a *whush* when he spoke.

"All right, darling. Tonight we'll do it your way. You'd better direct me to your home now, though, or do I just keep driving?"

15

"Oh, dear." Philippa focused on their direction. "You'll have to go back two blocks and turn left to get on the freeway." She felt herself blush again as she gave him stilted directions to her relatives' home. Was she losing her mind?

There was a long silence between them as Romain maneuvered the car through the traffic.

Philippa told him where to exit and in minutes they were on the quiet street that led to the cul-de-sac where her uncle, a university professor, lived. "There. Up that drive. Our home is at the end."

"Very pretty," Romain commented as they wended their way along the circular, flower-bedecked drive to the house, totally hidden from the road with a spectacular view of the city.

"Thank you." Philippa held her breath as her aunt came out the front door preceded by Byron, the marmalade cat who thought he was a dog. Her uncle followed them. "Uncle George, Aunt Grace, this is Romain Al Adal. I met him at the university."

"And I'm taking your niece out for dinner."

"Oh." Grace Stonely said, sizing up Romain unashamedly. "Well, she has a job at the library, and I've fixed her a snack as I always do."

"You could join us," Uncle George said in his usual mild voice. "What do you say, Philippa?"

She nodded her head, feeling too shy to meet Romain's gaze when he looked her way.

Romain didn't try to hide his interest in Philippa from her aunt and uncle because he was too intrigued with her to care what anyone else thought, and too bemused by his reactions to her to pay attention to the quizzical glances of her relatives. She was enchanting! He watched her play with the lazy orange cat, her chuckles running over his skin like a caress.

By the time Philippa went upstairs for a quick shower

and to change her clothes for the evening, she was in a quiver about Romain. He puzzled her, repelled yet drew her to him. She felt as though he had thrown a silken net over her that was slowly tightening. She looked into her closet with blind eyes, not really seeing what was there, instead seeing Romain's face. She shook herself out of her reverie and yanked out the deep lilac silk that was her best, her only dinner dress, given to her by her aunt and uncle on her eighteenth birthday two months ago.

She stared at herself in the mirror when she was through dressing, wishing for a moment for BeBe's more generous curves, then shrugged her head. "At least I have long legs." She knew they were attractive. More than one boyfriend had told her so. She untied her hair from the pony tail that usually confined it and let the auburn heaviness of it fall around her shoulders. "I would rather have a complexion that tans than this milk white skin, but what can I do?" she told her mirror image as she outlined her lips with lavender pencil then filled in with a rose-tinted lipstick. "What does it matter? It's just one date." Her heart squeezed in sudden pain and she grimaced at herself. "Don't start building castles with an Arab. He just wants to stock his harem. Stick with American men," she adjured herself, shaking her lipstick at the mirror.

She brushed her hair until it was a flaming gold halo around her, then affixed pearl earrings to her ears. It gave her great joy to slip on her three-inch heels of lavender leather that she had found to match the dress. She rarely wore heels, though, because her dates were generally her height or just a little taller. Since Romain was well over six feet she could wear the three-inch heels with ease.

As she walked along the corridor leading from her room to the sun porch, she overheard Romain talking to her aunt and uncle.

". . . And my family has been in Dharan for centu-

17

ries. Dharan is a good-sized country with a high literacy ratio. My uncle is Haddad Al Adal, the king."

His uncle was a king. Good Lord!, Philippa groaned to herself.

"Interesting," Uncle George replied in his bland voice, then proceeded to ask Romain very pointed questions.

"Yes, part of my education was in the United States, at Princeton. I spent many years in England also. I attended Oxford and Cambridge and went to Harrow in my younger years. Yes, oil has been a principal product of my country, but unlike some of the other countries nearby, our people have the option of education. We have a large oasis where we have substantial orange, lemon, and fig groves. We raise grapes and olives, and we have a fine university, which is heavily staffed with American personnel."

The voices droned on while Philippa stood rooted to the spot, listening to everything that Romain said.

Finally she looked at her watch and saw that she would have to go. She had learned so much about him from the questions her uncle and aunt had asked, but she felt no less trepidation. She took a deep breath and walked into the comfortable room with the large windows overlooking the pool and the vista of Los Angeles. "I'm ready." She shifted the crocheted cotton scarf she carried when she felt Romain's eyes on her.

"So you are."

A frisson of delight traveled from her toes to her eyebrows at his tone. She was scarcely aware of the concerned looks her relatives gave her as she kissed them good night.

Romain led her out to the car, his hand under her elbow, and ushered her in on the passenger side before going round and getting under the wheel. He leaned his left hand on the wheel and looked at her. "So direct me to the library, kitten."

"Huh? Oh, yes . . . at the end of the driveway, turn left and then make the next right toward the business area and the plaza."

"Right."

Even his accent was attractive, Philippa thought, resting her head on the back of the seat and watching him covertly.

"I hope you like what you see, love, because I like what I see when I look at you."

"Maybe I do, maybe I don't."

"Getting daring, are you?"

His silky question wrapped around her. "Yes."

"Good. I like challenge."

"So do I."

Romain laughed out loud, then reached over and threaded his right hand through hers. "I'm going to enjoy this."

"What?" Philippa quizzed weakly. "My working at the library?"

"That, too."

Philippa couldn't remember a time when she felt so at sea while she worked. Generally she enjoyed her short stint at the library, often arriving early to do research for her papers. Most of the time she enjoyed the moments it gave her to study in between checking out books for students. That evening all she could see was Romain. Though he sat at the other end of the room with a newspaper open in front of him, she knew he didn't take his eyes from her.

She's a darling, he thought. Even those glasses she wears don't disguise her wonderful turquoise eyes. It disturbed him more than a little that his pulse beat faster when he looked at her and that the familiar tightening in his lower torso was present when she smiled at him. It made him uneasy that his body was controlling his thoughts at the moment and not the other way around.

19

He was an educated man, a man of culture and learning, but he was primarily a shrewd, hard-driving Arab who excelled and delighted in the world of business. His country had purchased movie studios in Italy, the United Kingdom, and the United States, and it was his responsibility to see that those international cinema enterprises thrived and prospered. Crescent Worldwide Cinema not only showed a good profit, it had purchased some of the hottest film properties anywhere. It was currently negotiating with several world-renown directors, actors, and producers to sew up the deal. Romain had no doubt that Crescent Worldwide Cinema and the other studios would be phenomenally successful. He wouldn't settle for less. He had always been cool and sure of himself in any venture, business or personal. Now he found himself out of stride because of a tall, slender, creature with fire gold hair and outrageous eyes.

Time passed quickly for him because he found watching her so engrossing. She was like a chameleon, taking on the colors of the world around her and the people as well. She was electricity, she was fire, she was laughter. "And you are going bonkers, old man," he muttered to himself, earning the glare of an older woman sitting at the same table.

The library closed at nine o'clock. It only took minutes for Philippa to clear her work away, then she joined him at the table.

"Ready?" He took the scarf from her hands. "It's a little cooler out there."

Philippa felt his hands linger on her shoulders, her body stinging to life in reaction.

The car cocooned them in an intimacy that had her breathless. She wanted to tell him to take her home at once, but she also wanted to drive with him forever.

They pulled into the curving entrance of the Pelican

Club, a place that Philippa had never thought to see except from the outside.

"I don't think I'm dressed properly for this," she said, noting his Gucci shoes and Saville Row slacks.

"If anything, the Pelican isn't grand enough for you," Romain told her, leaning over to kiss her cheek just before the attendant opened her door and helped her from the car.

Romain came around the car and slipped his arm around her waist guiding her into the very exclusive club.

"Good evening, sir." The maitre d' bowed. "Madame."

"How are you, Benoit? It's nice to see you. You have a table for us?"

"But of course, monsieur. Right this way, if you please."

The table was curtained behind some ferns and had a view of the city lights below.

Philippa gasped in delight.

"I'm glad you like it." Romain said at her back, gesturing to the attendant that he would seat Philippa himself, then pulling his chair closer to her so that they were sitting at right angles to each other, *très intime*.

Romain waved away the two-foot-long menus and whispered to the hovering maitre d' who then nodded in satisfaction when Romain smiled. He in turn talked quietly to the waiter.

"Don't we need menus?"

"Not really. Benoit knows the best dishes to be served and those will be brought to us. You would like an assortment to choose from, I'm sure."

"I can think for myself," she blurted in answer to his autocratic manner. Then she bit her lip when he stared at her, his brow creased.

"Of course." He raised his index finger and the maitre d' and waiter were at his side. A few words and the menus were back in their hands. Slender, light as air, willowy, but a tigress, Romain mused, ignoring the pained hauteur of Benoit as they perused the scrolled cardboard in front of them.

"I'll have the paté, the terrine of soup, and the shrimp tournedo," Romain ordered, then inclined his head at Philippa as she hesitated.

"The same please," she muttered, wishing she had kept silent about the menus.

"Beg pardon, madame. I didn't hear you."

Philippa repeated the order, her voice cracking.

When they were alone, Romain lifted her hand to his mouth. "I was not patronizing you. If anything I was placating Benoit. It gives him great joy to surprise me."

Philippa flushed and said, "I'm sorry."

Romain shook his head, then hitched himself even closer to her so that their lips were inches apart. "No. You were asserting yourself." He brushed her lips with his. "You are welcome to assert yourself at all times with me."

She had to smile as she studied the hard-bitten features dominated by the hawklike nose, the wide-set eyes, high cheekbones, firm chin, swarthy skin, and electric green eyes. "You look like a pirate."

Romain felt his blood heat up at her smile, his eyes in lazy assessment of her face. "Darling, how right you are. I'm descended from a most warlike desert people on my father's side, his uncle was one of Lawrence of Arabia's lieutenants."

"You're making that up." Philippa stared at him wide-eyed when he shook his head.

"Truth."

"Tell me about him."

"All right." Romain leaned over and kissed her again, his lips lingering this time.

"Don't do that," Philippa censured, out of breath.

22

Romain stared at her, seeing the fear and uncertainty, feeling his heart thud against his rib cage. "I'm going too fast for you, aren't I, angel?"

"Yes—and I don't know where we're going," she mumbled, not able to move more than a few inches from Romain because of the position of her chair.

"It's high speed for me, too, little one," he mentioned wryly.

"I'm not little. I'm five feet nine inches tall."

"Tiny," he insisted, outlining her face with his finger. "Your bones are delicate."

"Strong."

"Tigress."

"Yes."

"Ahem . . ." The waiter served the paté, then faded from view. In a few minutes he returned with a tureen of clear, greenish soup.

"Do you like turtle soup?"

"I've never had it." Philippa lifted a spoonful of the aromatic liquid to her mouth. "Umm. Nice. Warm."

"Yes." Romain was fascinated by her facial movements. Her eyes were so expressive they couldn't hide what she felt. Her mouth was like a tender messenger. Fool, he told himself, stop behaving like a desert poet. No matter how he silently lashed himself he couldn't stop the river of delight he was experiencing at her enjoyment. Her skin is like the most fragile porcelain but she had no Camille airs about her. "Do you like sports?" The question was a surprise to him even as he asked it.

"Yes, I do. I like to swim and water ski and snow ski. My aunt and uncle and I go to Vail, Colorado."

"It's nice there." He pushed aside his empty bowl and leaned his arms on the table so that he could better study her eyes.

"With my school work and my job, I don't have much

leisure time, but when I'm free, I like to go white-water rafting, too."

Romain grinned at her. "I'd like to go with you sometime. I enjoy that myself."

"I like the theater and the ballet. I like to dance." Philippa knew she was chattering but she couldn't stop herself.

"Do you? I like that, too. Shall we go dancing after dinner?"

"I don't think so." Philippa looked at her watch. "I have an early class tomorrow and I should do some studying."

"Workaholic?" When she laughed, his heart beat out of rhythm.

"Not really. I want to keep a high average so that I can go to graduate school."

"Do you want to teach?"

"No. I want to own my own business."

"You amaze me."

"Many women own businesses today."

"In this country they might but not in mine."

"Well, I don't intend to start a business in your country."

"Now I've stepped on your toes again." Romain nodded his head as the waiter set a pewter plate of shrimp in front of him.

"They're like prawns." Philippa gaped at the succulent fish wrapped around with green pepper and stuffed with water chestnuts.

Romain cut a piece of his and held the fork out to her. "Taste."

Philippa opened her mouth to tell him that she didn't need to taste his since she had the same thing on her plate. Instead, she leaned forward and took the forkful of food. She nodded as she chewed, then swallowed. "It's very good."

24

"May I have some of yours?"

Philippa couldn't speak for a moment, then she carefully cut a small piece of the tournedo and lifted it to his mouth. All of her self-discipline couldn't still the tremor in her hand.

"Wonderful." Romain crooned, wanting to sweep her out of her chair and out of the restaurant and take her to Dharan—to the desert where he would keep her to himself forever.

"The wine is good, but you aren't drinking any."

"Dharanians drink little spirits. It's our way and our religion."

Philippa nodded. "I'm not much on drinking either."

"I noticed." His chest tightened with an unfamiliar constriction when she chuckled. "I do like your laugh."

"Thank you."

"And you're polite, too."

She laughed again. She was having fun with him! She expected to be too tense to enjoy the food or the conversation, but Romain was easy to talk to and the food was —she looked down at her plate, stunned. She had finished the shrimp.

"We were both hungry," Romain whispered to her. "Shall I order a brandy for you? I'm having the cheese board."

"No brandy. I'll have the cheese board, and tea, please."

Romain ordered tea for her, black Turkish coffee for himself.

After finishing the dessert and beverage, they rose to leave. Philippa felt a regret that the night would soon end. She quashed down the feeling of loneliness that assailed her at the thought of not seeing Romain again.

He led her out to the car, noting her sudden silence. He felt a quick anger before he studied her face. "You

25

don't think I'm going to jump at you, do you?" he asked when he entered the car, and began driving.

"No."

"May I see you tomorrow night?"

Philippa swiveled in her seat restrained by the seat belt, happiness flooding her. "Yes . . . but, but I have another early class the following day."

"That's Friday. Do you have classes on Saturday?"

"No, I don't," she told him, her laughter breathy and spontaneous.

"If I bring you home early tomorrow night, will you also spend Friday and all day Saturday with me? Or do you have other plans?"

"Studies," Philippa ventured weakly.

"Do you go to the library after classes?"

"Yes, but I have a paper to complete, and I need to type it." She smiled fleetingly. "Not that my typewriter is any great saver of time. It blanks out the *e* and the *i* unless I'm very careful." Philippa watched as the lights of other cars, silvered and delineated his sharp features, darkening his skin to sinister.

"We'll have an early dinner tomorrow night, and I'll take you to my company's office where I'll show you how to put your paper into the word processor. We'll correct the mistakes with ease, then print out however many copies you need."

Philippa felt her mouth drop. "You'll be bored," she blurted, covering her mouth with her hand when he smiled and shook his head. "I have two papers to complete before term ends. I've finished the research." She hurried the words, blushing at her temerity but very eager to spend more time with him.

He stopped the car and reached over to touch the tip of her nose, his action bringing him closer to her. "Then why don't we kill two birds with one stone?" His lips brushed hers, then he turned away to fire up the powerful car.

"I can't allow you to give up your time watching me work," she said with a sigh.

"Yes, you can. I'll enjoy your company no matter what we do."

Philippa felt the blood boil through her skin. Words stuck in her throat. When Romain reached across the console of the Lamborghini and took her hand, she closed her fingers around his tightly.

Romain's throat tightened and his breathing shut down for an instant. She was a Circe! Philippa weaved a spell around him that caused in him an alien weakness. He fought the urge to beg her to stay with him that night. He didn't want to frighten her nor did he want her to know the power she had over him.

She was sure he would make an excuse about not seeing her again once he took her to the door. None of her rationalizing had any effect on the nervous certainty that when he left her at the door, it would be the last time she saw him.

Once out of the car she hurried up to the door, throwing a quick good night over her shoulder. She had her hand on the doorknob when he caught her by the arm.

"Good night Philippa." He took hold of her upper arms, bringing her close to his chest, his mouth running over her face before touching her lips. "Good night. I'll be there after class tomorrow."

"I get out at three," she said and gasped, her insides turning to fire and ice.

"I'll find you."

"At the library," she whispered, stepping inside the door and closing it behind her. She stood there for a moment, eyes closed, knees weak.

"Philippa. Is that you?" Aunt Grace came from the living room of the adobe one-story house, relief lacing her voice. "I'm glad you came home early since you have an early class in the morning."

"Yes." Philippa tried to focus on her aunt, but all she could see was Romain's face.

"Would you have a moment, dear? Your uncle and I would like to speak to you. It won't take long." She turned away before Philippa could answer and disappeared back the way she had come.

Philippa sighed. They were going to lecture her on going out with Romain. She felt an unaccustomed rebellion filling her. She walked slowly into the room to face the two people she loved most in the world.

"Come over and sit down, child. We're not going to eat you," Uncle George chided her with a smile. He took out his pipe and tamped tobacco down into it, looking at her over the top of his half glasses. "You had a good time this evening, I can see that."

"Yes," Philippa answered warily.

Her uncle passed a match over his pipe, puffing until it was lit. "He's older than you, Pippa, but more to the point, he's a very worldly individual."

"I know."

"Your aunt and I don't want to see you hurt. You've been sheltered, child, by us, but also by your own inclination to be studious and shun the frivolities of your age group."

"I've been happy in school." Philippa coughed to clear the dryness from her throat. "But I like Romain. He was very nice to me. He's asked me out tomorrow night and I want to go. I'll get my work done in the library first."

"It's not just your college work—" Aunt Grace began.

"And Romain says that he will take me to his office and let me put my papers into the word processor."

Uncle George put a hand on Philippa's knee. "We worry about your personal safety, child,—the emotional damage that could be wreaked by your involvement with

28

such a sophisticated person. He has business interests all over the world, not just in oil but in cosmetics, in fashion and clothing manufacturing. He also told me that his conglomerate owns several cinema companies and some television stations."

Philippa was round-eyed. "I didn't know that."

"Your uncle questioned him," Aunt Grace said primly, her brow creased. "We want you to be happy, Philippa. You're like our own child. We would like to see you married with a family of your own someday, but you would be better to choose someone of your station in life, of the same religion . . ." Aunt Grace bit her lip.

Philippa reached out and hugged her aunt. "I'm not marrying Romain, just going out with him on a couple of dates."

"Well, if that's all . . ." Her aunt chewed her upper lip and rolled her eyes at her husband.

He sighed and shook his head. "I see."

Philippa went to kneel down next to his chair. "I'll be fine. You'll see."

Her uncle smiled at her, but there was a look of concern in his eyes.

CHAPTER TWO

The next day when she had just put the last research book back on the shelf and was gathering her papers and notes, she felt a feathery kiss on her neck.

"Don't jump like that." Romain chuckled from behind her. "Do you want the security guard to come and toss me out the door."

Philippa turned and found herself in his arms, not able to stem the happiness bubbling in her. "I didn't expect you for another half hour."

"I've been here for forty-five minutes, watching you study." He indicated a table on the other side of the room where there was an open briefcase and a pushed-back chair. "You were working so hard I didn't want to disturb you. Are you finished with your notes?"

Philippa nodded, totally bemused that Romain Al Adal would have been sitting in the library watching her, waiting for her to finish her work. Hot excitement coursed through her, and she had an overpowering urge to cuddle close to him. It took all her strength of will not to do it.

Romain reached around her and began loading her books into the canvas tote that she carted everywhere with her. "What you need is a camel to carry all this." He wrinkled his nose and grinned at her when she laughed. "I think you perceive me to be your camel."

"Could be." She looked over her shoulder at him as

they approached the front of the library where she was going to check out two books. She felt light as air, but more powerful than a 747 jet. She was Wonder Woman and Heidi all rolled into one. "Hello," she sang to the lady at the library checkout who glared at her and put her forefinger to her lips. "Thank you," Philippa chimed when the books were stamped and handed to her and not all the shushing in the world dampened her spirits or narrowed her smile. She looked behind her when Romain followed her through the large doors to the outside. "Miss Beaney is always that way. She's been head librarian for a hundred years."

"Only a hundred?" Romain wished for a millisecond that he had never set eyes on her when he remembered how he had tossed and turned last night. At any other time he would have known where to go and whom to call to relieve his sexual tension, but he didn't want that. He wanted Philippa and no one else! That bothered him a great deal. He felt as though he had lost control of his life. He, an Arab of royal blood, couldn't admit a thing like that to himself without shuddering.

"Shall we have dinner first?" His voice was abrupt, then he cursed himself as he saw the turquoise sheen of her eyes dim, her mouth leveling out with uncertainty. He shifted her tote bag to the same arm that held his briefcase and caught her around the waist with the other. "Unless you're going to insist on working first and letting a man starve." He exhaled in relief when he saw the smile soften her mouth again.

"No. We'll eat, then work." She leaned against him as they walked, her heart jumping out of rhythm when his hand tightened at her waist.

"Right."

They walked across the quad to the Lamborghini which was parked in one of the No Parking zones.

"You'll get a ticket."

Romain shrugged, then released her so that he could juggle the keys out of his pocket.

"Here, let me." Philippa reached into his trouser pocket, then as her hand came in intimate contact with his leg, she looked up into his face, frozen in embarrassment.

"Just take out the keys, darling. No problem." There was just a trace of huskiness in his lazy voice. Again she was laying him low with just the barest graze of her hand! He felt the muscles of his body hardening in response to her tentative touch. God, she was lethal!

What must he think of her? Philippa agonized. He must think her gauche and . . . and stupid. She didn't look at him as he held the door for her. She wouldn't blame him if he mentioned that he had to go home after they had eaten. She was such a fool!

"I thought you might like to eat the food of my country tonight," Romain spoke over the heavy silence between them. Damn, what was she thinking now? "I have a penthouse at the top of the Pyramid Building. . . ."

"Is that where your company is?" Philippa forgot her embarrassment for a moment. "I've never been in it, but I do think it's one of the most beautiful buildings in the Los Angeles area. It looks like a huge silver harmonica from a distance, studded with diamonds."

Romain glanced her way, pleasure running through him. "Thank you for that description. I helped design that building and I think it's quite beautiful."

Philippa curved her legs up on the seat as she turned more fully to look at him, the seat belt tightening on her body. "You're a designer, too?"

"In a small way. I studied architecture at university but I had a whole team of experts helping design the Pyramid Building." Romain smiled at her excited look, glad they had gotten over the uncomfortable moment. Until now, he hadn't ever worried whether a woman was comfortable with him. He had always assumed that they were and he had sensed he was right. From his teens on he had been well aware of his potency with women, and knew it wasn't only because he was one of the richest men in the world under thirty. But with Philippa he rode the razor's edge of indecision.

They drove the distance into the business district companionably discussing her paper and his penthouse.

It pleased him that she wasn't worried accompanying him to his apartment, and he had every intention of assuring her that she had nothing to fear. He had an overpowering urge to protect Philippa. He didn't even try to plum the reasons.

He pulled down into the underground garage and nodded at the attendant in the booth who had studied them. He drove to the parking place marked with his name, turned off the ignition, then went around to help her from the car. "I'll get your tote bag from the trunk. You go over there and press the elevator button."

Philippa almost skipped to do as she was told, her canvas purse bumping her side.

The elevator door opened at once and she went in and pressed the hold button for Romain who was beside her in an instant.

"Here we go," he said and smiled at her, gripping her tote bag in one hand and his briefcase in the other.

The smile flitted off and on her face like a hummingbird hovering over a wild flower.

Accurately reading her uncertainty, Romain strove to distract her. "It's a good thing I lectured on business at the university and not architecture. I haven't told you about the expensive architectural model my roommate and I destroyed when I was at school in England?"

Diverted, Philippa shook her head. "Oh, you studied architecture in England?" What a complex man he was, she thought when he nodded and continued speaking.

33

"We didn't do it on purpose. The model was in scale to a skyscraper to be built in New York, and it was on show at the university. We were attempting to show our professor the relative merits of a structure imploding or exploding. We set explosive devices on the model to prove our theory of making a building safe in case of a gas or any other type of explosion. My roommate accidentally triggered the device destroying the model."

"Lord," Philippa breathed, laughing.

"You may laugh, but when they phoned my uncle and he ordered me back to Dharan, I wasn't laughing. When he sent me back to school again, he ordered that my privileges be taken away until term ended. I think my professor would have preferred that I be expelled."

"I don't blame him." Philippa nodded, waiting while he unlocked his door, then following him inside to the two-story penthouse. "My goodness, this is grand," she whispered, forgetting all about the conversation they had been having.

"Do you like it?"

"Yes."

Romain was delighted with her answer and a grin stretched across his mouth as he put her tote bag and his briefcase on the round glass table sitting between two monstrous overstuffed camel-colored couches, each one strewn with turquoise pillows. "I hope you'll be comfortable."

Philippa smiled back and nodded, but a thrill of apprehension ran up her spine. "You should use your architectural skills in underdeveloped countries; many of the students do that. Reaching out to help others is the one great peacemaker we have . . ." Philippa bit down on her lip. She was preaching! How awful.

His thoughtful smile had no less heat. "So you are a crusader," he said softly.

Philippa lifted her chin. "Many Americans are." She

couldn't stem the flush she knew was coloring her face. Why was she being so stupid with him?

Romain lifted one of the sofa pillows and approached her. "I really hate to change the subject but your eyes are the color of this pillow and with much much more fire." He leaned down and lightly kissed her. "And when you are excited, they are fresh-mined turquoise from the desert of Mexico." Then he lifted his head and looked over her shoulder. "Ah, here is Abdul. Dinner is ready?"

"As you ordered, Your Highness." Abdul bowed.

"Highness?" Philippa's head swiveled from the servant to Romain.

He shrugged. "It's a title of honor. That's all. In this country I'm mister."

"I see." She didn't understand and wanted to question him further, and Romain took her arm and led her from the spacious living room out into the large foyer again.

"I thought you might want to wash up a little." He gestured across the hall. "There's a bathroom down that corridor. I'll be upstairs. If you want me, come up. My suite is the whole second floor. You won't get lost."

His devilish smile rippled over her skin causing her to back a step and walk in a shaky breath. She stared up at him, but he was already taking the steps two at a time to the second level. She went into the room-sized bathroom that was between two guest bedrooms. "I liked the living room with camel-colored carpeting and couches, but I don't think I like a silver bathroom," she said out loud and grimaced at the stepdown tub and the separate shower enclosure in silver-colored tiles. To her the room was stark and without warmth. She used the facilities and freshened her makeup, dotting her wrist with the sample vial of Joy perfume that she was lucky enough to receive as a gift at her favorite cosmetic counter. Joy was an extravagance she couldn't afford but she always enjoyed the free samples. She made a face at her hair, undid it

from the clips that bound it, and brushed it until it crackled. She lifted the clips again to tie it back.

"Don't." Romain pushed open the door of the bathroom. He gave a rueful grin when she started. "I wasn't
going to disturb you, but I missed you." He reached out
and smoothed her hair with his hand. "When I saw the
door ajar, I couldn't resist opening it further. That's
when I saw you brushing your hair."

"I thought I closed it."

Romain jiggled the lock. "It isn't closing properly. I'll
have Abdul check it." He looked up at her, his lazy smile
widening when he saw her put the clips in her purse.
"Ready?"

Philippa nodded and went past him, feeling his hand
reach out to her waist, making her pause for a moment.

"You have the most wonderful hair." He inhaled the
fragrance. "Like a gold flame, so alive, so curly—so wonderful," he murmured, kissing the reddish mane. "Don't
ever cut it. It's the most glorious blanket any man could
want."

Philippa jumped away from him like a scalded cat,
almost running across the hall.

"Wait." Romain caught up with her in the living room.
"You can feel anything you choose about me, but never
let it be fear. You will control our moments together,
love, not me. I promise."

Philippa nodded again, swaying toward him.

When he held her, his arms were steel bands but his
lips were feather light over her face. "Now it's time to
eat." He grinned at her, trying to control the almost painful thudding of his heart.

"I'm hungry," she told him, surprised that it was true.

Romain kept his arm around her as they entered the
living room again and went down to the far end, up one
step to a spacious dining area with glass doors that led
out to a large terrace. He pulled out a blue satin Louis

Quinze chair for her, then seated himself at the one adjacent to her at the round table. A bouquet of cream and pink carnations gave spicy scent to the first course that Abdul brought them, having place of honor in the center of a fruit salad of dates, bananas, oranges, and nuts, with apples and kiwis dotting the top.

"Umm, that dressing is delightful, a sweet and sour sauce for fruit. It has honey and lemon, but what else?" Philippa ate the mounded fruit with great appetite.

"I'm sure there must be ginger and nutmeg in it. They are two of Abdul's favorite spices." Romain smiled at her and offered her a forkful of his salad.

Philippa took it and smiled back. "I like desert food if this is a sample. I could live my life on fruit."

"I'm glad you're enjoying it." Romain looked up when Abdul entered the room, a spate of Arabic making the huge man bow in Philippa's direction, his hands steepled in front of him. Romain looked back at Philippa. "He's pleased and says he hopes you will like the lamb he has prepared."

Philippa felt her eyes go round. She didn't know if she would like the lamb. Her uncle had lived in England for a time and had come to hate mutton and therefore wouldn't allow lamb cooked in the house. She remembered tasting it once as a child at a friend's house and not liking it, but she was sure some of that was a prejudice engendered by her beloved relative's dislike. "I'm sure I'll like it." She told Romain in what she hoped was a sincere voice.

When Abdul returned to them with a mammoth tray of steaming rice and vegetables with a gravied meat garlanded around it, her nostrils flared in appreciation. "That's saffron I smell, and orange, and mint . . ." Her mouth salivated and some of her dread disappeared.

"I will serve the lady myself," Romain instructed the reluctant Abdul. "He wants to stay and hear you praise

37

his cooking, but I didn't bring you here so that you could discuss recipes with him." He lifted the gold spoon tongs and placed some of the entree on her plate. "You must have some of the orange slices and sauce with it," Romain instructed, gesturing to a boat of orange sauce with pieces of orange in it.

"It looks like marmalade. Is it?" Philippa ladled some of the sauce on a portion of the rice, lamb, and vegetables.

"It's similar to a hot relish."

Philippa looked at the food on her plate and her stomach growled, embarrassing her.

"Time to eat, darling." Romain smiled at her and lifted his fork to her mouth. "Well? What do you think?"

The succulent food was chewed and digested before Philippa answered. "I like the vegetables very much, the sauce is so light and delicious. What is it called?" She didn't tell him that she wasn't overfond of the meat because she determined that she would eat it.

"You'll be disappointed. It's a recipe of my mother's combined with Arabian food. It's simply called lamb ragout."

"It's a wonderful stew."

"It is. Though I think you would have preferred it with another meat such as beef, perhaps." He lifted her hand and kissed the fingers when she blushed. "Darling, don't be silly. We all have likes and dislikes. And I shall remember that lamb is one of yours." He smiled at her. "I assure you there are many things in my country you'll enjoy. Dharanian food is often mistaken for French. Mother, who was born in France, is still a very influential woman in her adopted country, and she insists on haute cuisine. Uncle Haddad defers to her on many things."

"He's wise to pay attention to her on cooking." Philippa said stoutly when he cocked an eyebrow at her. "I truly loved the vegetables and rice," she insisted, not demurring when Romain went to the sideboard and brought the dishes from the hot tray to the table and spooned more food onto her plate, omitting the lamb.

"Does your mother live in Dharan?" Philippa asked, feeling both fascinated and repelled by the elusive female who was his parent.

"She lives in Paris most of the time." Romain gave a hard laugh. "That makes it more comfortable for both of us. My mother is an unusual woman." He saw the shadows in Philippa's eyes and leaned forward to lift her hand and kiss her wrist. "Not to worry, my sweet. Mother is very civilized. I'm anxious for you to meet her. I'm sure you'll find her interesting."

Philippa heard the flavor of satire in his voice and smiled weakly, imagining a wraithlike tigress, ready to protect her son from a foreign woman.

She was too replete to choose from the sweet tray that Abdul brought, but she did try the goat cheese and grapes with black Turkish coffee. She tried to repress a shudder when she tried the coffee.

"It's too strong for you." Romain removed the cup and rang the bell for the servant. "Abdul, bring Miss Tayson some tea, orange pekoe, I think."

They lingered over their coffee and tea.

When they rose, they ambled down into the living room proper and collected her tote bag and Romain's briefcase.

"Are you going to work out of your briefcase?"

"I thought I would once I show you how to put your work into the word processor. Come this way. I've decided we'll use the one in my study. It's more comfortable there, and I doubt you will need any more software than I have here."

He took her hand and led her down another hall and into a room Philippa thought must be under his bedroom until he opened the door. It was a spectacular two-story room with a wide balcony around the second story that afforded access to the extensive library there. A circular stairway led to the second floor. "That door up there leads to my bedroom suite. It makes it easy to hide out here if I have guests. I have the only key."

Philippa looked around her in awe, taking note that though the wide balcony went around the four walls, one of the walls was floor-to-ceiling windows so that a great deal of light came in the room. "It's a wonderful room, so high and clear."

"Most days it is." Romain stood at her side, his fingers kneading her waist.

Philippa turned and found that he was leaning over her, their faces almost touching. "Have to get to work."

"Of course."

Philippa felt like soft gelatin as Romain led her to a chair in front of a computer screen, turned it on, and began explaining the workings of the machine.

"Pardon me. Could you tell me that again? I . . . I was daydreaming." Philippa could feel her face flame when he bent over and kissed her.

"Pay attention, darling. Now, this is the disk drive . . ." Romain went through it with her verbally, then went over it manually showing her how to put in the disks and type in the material.

"I think I have the idea, but you won't go away, will you?"

"I'll be right over there if you need me." Romain kissed her nose, then walked to the large rosewood desk with its back to the window wall.

It was slow going at first, because Philippa had to keep fighting the urge to turn around and look at Romain. She could feel his presence like warm velvet around her. After a while as she began to compose from her notes, she became immersed in what she was doing and started to pick up speed. Romain wasn't completely gone from her thoughts, but she was able to work in his presence.

They had been working three hours when Philippa felt a hand on her shoulder. She looked up and blinked at Romain. "I'm almost done."

"You're almost done in, you mean." He lifted her out of the chair, his arms holding her lightly but closely to him. "I made tea for you and brought some biscuits that Abdul has made."

"You oversimplified your statement on food," Philippa told him, agog at the array of food on the Louis Quinze table set in front of the window. A pot of tea, in its own silver tea cozy to match the finely wrought sugar and creamer, held pride of place. There were fragile cups that were almost transparent and hand-painted dessert plates to match. She sat down in one of the chairs, her legs feeling rubbery after being in one position so long. "I should really stand to eat."

Romain frowned at her. "Why didn't I think of you being stiff from sitting in that straight chair? Come with me." He scooped up the heavy silver tray of refreshments and tea and stalked across the room to the long camel-colored corduroy couch. He placed the tray in front of him on the low coffee table. "Come on. Sit down beside me and relax."

Philippa went over to him and sank down next to him on the couch with a sigh of satisfaction. "This is so comfortable."

Romain smiled at her, then poured her tea and placed an assortment of cheese, apple, and biscuits on a plate and handed it to her. "There. That will refresh you. You're a very hard worker, Philippa Tayson."

Philippa felt a flush of pleasure at his words, hiding her confusion behind the china cup as she lifted it to her mouth and sipped the scalding orange pekoe. "Working on the word processor certainly speeds up the job."

"Yes . . . but I really don't want to talk about a computer's work-saving qualities." He set down his cup and put his arm along the back of the sofa and leaned toward her. She was so wide-eyed and beautiful! So untouched! His mind flashed fire at him. When was the last time he had thought that about a woman, or even cared? What if she weren't as chaste as she looked? Would it matter? Yes! No! Damn it, only Philippa was important, not some clinical conclusion about her, he told himself and knew it was true.

"Why are you scowling?"

His mind zapped his thoughts away and he really looked at her. "Just a flash of stupidity." He let his hand touch her shoulder. "Actually, all I want to do is concentrate on you, tell you you're lovely and—"

"I detest flattery," Philippa said stiffly even as her heart pounded out of rhythm.

"Fine." Romain moved closer to her. "Then I'll just tell you the truth." He dropped his arm around her shoulders liking the feel of her. "You're the most beautiful creature I've ever seen. Truth." He stared down into her eyes, now like a turquoise quartz as they shimmered with tears. "Does that make you sad?"

"No." Philippa swayed toward him, her body throbbing when he embraced her.

His mouth teased hers for a moment then slowly increased its pressure. When her lips parted for him, he felt as though his chest was about to explode. "Darling," he gasped, lifting his mouth and running tiny kisses over her face. "You're a firebomb to me."

"That can't be true. I wouldn't want to hurt you." Philippa managed the words even though she felt drugged.

"I think it's too late. I'm already wounded." Romain muttered to her, rubbing his forehead against hers. His lips found hers again and the kiss seemed to go on to infinity. Their breath mingled in silent commitment. Romain felt as though she had transfused his blood with her own and that he had become a new person.

Philippa tore free of him, her brain reeling. "I have to finish."

"What?" Romain looked down at her befuddled.

"My paper."

"Philippa, how can you think of that damned paper now?"

"If I don't, I'm lost," she said and wheezed, making him laugh even though he grimaced his displeasure when she pulled away from him, sat up, and straightened her clothes. She rose to her feet and looked down at him, the sensual slack of his mouth and sprawl of his body making her heart jump.

"All right, all right, slave driver." Romain rose to his feet, hooked one arm around her waist, and lifted her up against him. "You won't always have the excuse of finishing a paper. I'll see to that."

"Is that so?" Philippa pronounced in a squeaky voice.

"Yes." He kissed her nose. "That's so."

Philippa smothered the moan of disappointment when he released her. Instead, she turned and marched back to the word processor.

Romain took her elbow. "Let me help. I could read your notes to you and dictate the footnotes."

Philippa nodded shyly, her pulse fluttering when Romain pulled up a chair and sat down at her right elbow. It went slowly at first. She was too unnerved by his closeness to react efficiently. Then they began to work well together, his casual manner smoothing over the rough edges. She listened to his advice and the words seemed to flow out of her onto the screen.

In another hour they had finished so they went back over it, checking for typos. Then Romain showed her how to adjust the machine to print the copies on the machine. When they were done, Philippa looked up and found him watching her.

"I liked having you dine at my home. Will you come again?"

She nodded.

"Tomorrow?"

She nodded again, watching pleasure flash across his face.

"Philippa, you've captivated me," he said it with a laugh, but the kernal of truth in the words caused him to be uneasy.

"I'll bet you say that to all the girls." She chuckled.

"Brat."

She lifted her chin when he approached her, knowing he was going to kiss her and wanting it with all her heart.

"I've had a wonderful evening with you."

"And I'll bet you don't have too many when you invite someone to your apartment to use the word processor," she said and laughed.

He leaned closer to her catching her exhalation of breath in his mouth. "Are you calling me a lecher, Philippa?"

"If the shoe fits." The words fell from her flaccid lips.

"You're a darling." He wrapped his arms around her, lifting her off the floor, his mouth meeting hers again.

The kiss deepened, taking them in an undertow of emotion that swept them up into an alien vortex, prisoners of the fire and ice of passion.

When Romain released her, Philippa swayed, not able to stand by herself, her eyes fixed on him and seeing there the glazed, hot surprise that she knew was mirrored in her own. "I . . . I should go home," she said morosely, not wanting to leave him for all eternity.

"I know." Romain's voice was husky, his hands still holding her tightly as though he were loathe to release her.

"I'll see you tomorrow." Philippa didn't move away from him.

"I'll be at the library at two in the afternoon."

Philippa couldn't stem the happy smile that she knew was spreading across her face. He had remembered what she had told him about her class schedule, then her smile faded. "You can't. You have to go back to work. You've finished the seminar."

"So I have. I'll be there at two. Work hard and have your studies done so that you'll be ready."

"Yes." Philippa moved one step back, then turned and walked blindly to the couch where her purse and jacket were. She retraced her steps to the word processor and picked up the neatly collated copies of her paper. She then turned to face Romain, who had not taken his eyes from her. "Thank you for letting me get my paper done."

"Thank *you.*" He reached out a hand. "Shall we go?"

"Yes." She walked to him, her eyes locked to his, but objecting when he took the papers from her and put them in a briefcase that looked similar to his. "But I can't take that. I can put the papers in an envelope, or even if you have a rubber band."

"Not to worry, sweetheart. I have a great many of these. No big deal." He kissed her nose and put the term paper in the leather case. "I have to get you home early," he grimaced his displeasure at the thought of leaving her.

The return ride to her home seemed to be over in seconds even though Philippa knew that it had taken more than forty minutes. Their conversation had been desultory, but their silences had been comfortable, only broken by the sultry music that came from the cassette player in the car.

"Tomorrow night we won't go dancing. We'll save that for Saturday. And then on Sunday . . ."

"Oh, no," Philippa turned to him. "I forgot. My aunt

45

and uncle are going to a lecture weekend with friends. I was going to stay with BeBe."

Romain was silent for a moment, driving down the long curving drive that led to her uncle's house. He stopped the car, switched off the ignition, and turned to her. "Stay with me," he said softly.

Philippa felt as though her chest had turned to a balloon and was expanding so much it would burst. Nothing worked. Her voice had shut down, her throat closed, her eyes felt frozen open, and she couldn't blink.

He reached out one finger to touch her cheek. "Aren't you going to answer me?"

"I don't know how to," she answered honestly.

"I want you to be near me all the time—and I can tell you if you are, I will make love to you. I would like to promise you that I won't but that would be a lie. If you're near, I'll want to hold you . . . and if I hold you, I will want to take you."

Philippa was struck dumb by his admission.

"So? Do you want to tell me that I'm going too fast? That I have no right to speak to you in such a fashion? What?"

"I . . . I . . ." Philippa cleared her throat. "I would like to tell you that I would like to stay with you, but . . . but I'm not on the pill." She rushed her words, glad that they were in the darkness of the car with only the glitter of the dashboard lighting to outline them.

"Sweetheart!" Romain choked, reaching out for her. "I will take precautions. I promise." He inhaled a deep shaky breath, his face pressed into her hair. "Are you sure?"

"Yes."

"Sweet love," he muttered. "How can I wait until tomorrow?"

"I don't know how I'll wait." Philippa meant it. She had never been to bed with anyone. Now she couldn't wait to have Romain make love to her. The thought of it warmed her like fire.

"I had better take you inside now. My imagination is blowing a tube thinking about this weekend." Romain couldn't clear the hoarseness from his voice, nor could he prevent the hand that caressed her from trembling.

She bit his little finger as his hand passed over her face.

"God, angel, don't do that. My insides feel like lava." Romain's voice shook, as he let his finger rove the tender cavity of her mouth. With an effort he gently moved her away from him, taking deep breaths, his eyes touching every pore of her face, taking in the sensuous softness of her lips, the glitter of her eyes. "In the house with you, witch." He pulled back from her and left the car, coming around to open her door.

"I don't want you to leave me." Philippa told him in a matter-of-fact tone, studying the spasm that tightened his features before he looked at her again.

He led her to the front door, opened it, and kissed her cheek, his mouth lingering there. Then he turned and strode to the car, fired the engine, the tires squealing in protest as he wheeled down the drive, not looking her way again.

Philippa walked into the house to the great room in the back where her uncle and aunt were watching an opera on television. A woman with a powerful voice was singing "Die Walküre" and her horned helmet quivered with intensity; yet, Philippa heard not a word. In slow motion she watched her aunt and uncle turn to her, concerned looks on their faces. The pulsations of Romain's loving didn't allow her to hear their words, but she knew they were worried about her. It seemed so silly! How could anyone worry about her when she had been with Romain? "Good evening, Uncle George, Aunt Grace." She bent over the couple.

"You're radiant, dear. You must have had a good

time," her aunt said faintly, seeming to hold her hand longer than necessary.

"Har–umph . . ." her uncle fussed with his pipe, then looked up at her, his usually twinkling eyes needle sharp. "Your aunt and I would like you to reconsider coming with us to Phoenix, dear. You work very hard and the rest would do you good . . ."

"No." Philippa said, and knew her voice was too sharp when her uncle fixed on her in the act of lighting his pipe. "I . . . I mean, I'd rather not."

"Would BeBe mind if you backed out?" Her aunt bit her lip, shooting an anxious glance at her husband.

"She might," Philippa said and gulped, hating the implied lie, knowing that she would see BeBe tomorrow and tell her that she wouldn't be staying with her. "I have to get some sleep." She kissed her beloved relatives again and rushed from the room.

CHAPTER THREE

Romain drove home in a wild state of half fury and half bemusement with himself over the child he had just taken home. "Child is the operative word, fool," he castigated himself, hitting the steering wheel with his fist. "What the hell is the matter with you, inviting that girl to stay with you for the weekend? Are you out of your mind?" he fumed as he recalled the incident involving his cousin Hammet, who had two wives and two children in Dharan. Hammet had committed the indiscretion of getting involved with a starlet who sued him on a paternity suit. The resulting scandal had reached all the way back to the king who had recalled Hammet. It had taken a great deal of money and diplomacy to smooth the matter over. The bad feeling toward Dharanians had extended to the State Department in Washington. "And Philippa is much younger than Hammet's chorus girl," he told himself. "If you had any brains at all you would have Leslie," he lectured himself, referring to Leslie Kebble, his private secretary. "Call Philippa tomorrow and cancel everything."

He drove the Lamborghini down the coast highway at high speed, wanting to blow the cobwebs from his brain. He knew deep down inside himself that he had every intention of seeing Philippa again, no matter what the consequences.

He parked his car in the underground garage and sat

dredging deep into her brain for the concentration she needed. She had to get her work done because she knew once Romain was beside her she wouldn't be able to think of anything. She plowed on, digging into the research materials she needed, filling her notebook. She looked up at the clock at three o'clock, then back at her notes, amazed at the volume of work she'd done.

"Enough." The large, slender hand placed over her notebook was as familiar to her as the voice.

"I did a great deal." Philippa looked up at him, pride in her voice.

"I know. I've been watching you for an hour."

She felt her mouth drop open. "I didn't see you."

"You were too busy driving yourself." Romain frowned at her. "I don't like you to work that hard," he told her as he helped her gather her things together and put them in her canvas tote, which he took from her. "It bothers me." The surprise in his voice made her laugh, sending his lips upward in a twisted smile. "It's a good thing I was working out of my briefcase. Otherwise, I wouldn't have let you work so long. I was tempted to take you away the minute I saw you this afternoon."

As they walked to the car, Philippa explained, "I have to work hard. I've applied for special fellowship next year to study in London, so I have to keep up." She put her overnight case in the back, then moved as close to the console as she could so that she would be near Romain. She felt like jumping out of her skin every time he looked her way.

He lifted her hand to his mouth. "Darling, if you've changed your mind about staying with me, don't worry about it." He glanced at her while he tooled the powerful auto with one hand.

"I haven't changed my mind."

Romain felt oxygen shudder through him, his brain

51

feeling like putty. "I want you very much, Philippa Tayson."

"And I want you."

"God, don't tell me that while I'm driving."

To Philippa the drive was a blur of happiness, and when they pulled into his underground garage, she was both eager and apprehensive. She didn't want to disappoint him!

They were silent as they got out of the car and went up in the elevator, but it was a warm silence with many long glances and soft smiles.

The apartment seemed quiet to Philippa. "Isn't Abdul here?" She turned to Romain, seeing him nod, twisting her hands together.

"Yes. He'll make us our food, but no doubt we won't see him. I told him that we wanted to be alone."

Philippa nodded.

"Having second thoughts?" Romain stepped closer to her, but didn't touch her. "No problem if you change your mind."

Philippa shook her head. "I . . . is it true that . . . well, I mean, I haven't had too much experience and you might get bored . . . or something," she finished lamely, spreading her hands, disgusted with herself.

"Love," Romain said and cupped her chin. "You haven't had any experience—and I will make it good for you." He flashed her a smile. "And it will be wonderful for me, darling."

Philippa exhaled, feeling airy and happy. "Good." She kissed his chin.

Before she could back away, he caught her around the waist, bringing her up his body until her toes barely touched the floor. "You are quite the loveliest thing on earth." He kissed her nose and set her down. "But now we have to decide where we will eat and go dancing." He stared down at her, puzzled when she looked dumb-founded. "No dancing?"

"I didn't bring any dressy clothes."

Romain scanned her frame, tempted to tell her that he didn't want to go out of the apartment anyway. Still, it would be romantic for her to dine in a good restaurant. "Would you believe me if I told you that I had a sister who stays in the apartment with me? Ayada is perhaps not as slim as you, but she is tall. Shall we rummage through her clothes?"

"Could we?"

"Of course." Romain took her tote and her overnight case and put them on a side table. "We'll put these in your room when we go upstairs. Follow me."

Philippa felt her heart turn a slow roll in her chest when he said "when we go upstairs."

They went down a long corridor with several doors. At the last door Romain opened it. "This is the room Ayada uses when she's in town. She always leaves clothes here." Romain strode across the large square room dominated by a king-sized water bed and pressed a button. The mirror wall slid back to reveal a capacious closet and shoe storage area.

Romain looked at her. "Shoes could be a problem. Ayada wears . . ." He lifted a shoe from the rack. "Size seven."

"I wear an eight." Philippa grimaced. She had always hated her feet, thinking them far too big.

Romain shrugged and looked at his watch, walked to the phone and punched out some numbers. He quickly spoke a few Arabic words and hung up the phone. "Abdul will call a few people. Now . . ." he beckoned to her to join him and turned back to the closet, pulling out dresses at random and glowering at them. "These aren't your style."

"I think they're lovely." Philippa stared wide-eyed at

the array of colors and silken fabrics, realizing that the bright cherry, kelly greens, and vivid blues would wash out her own bright coloring. She wore hues and shades rather than vibrant colors.

"Ahh, here we are." Romain reached to the back of the closet and pulled out a silky, light-as-air sheath in aqua blue. "This was the wrong color for Ayada and too tight as I remember." He grinned at her. "She would kill me for saying that." He smiled at her. "This is two shades lighter than your eyes, darling. Try it."

Philippa took the fragile material in two hands, loving the feel of it as it slid through her fingers. "It's lovely but . . ."

"Try it on. I'll wait in the hall. Oh, here, these slippers might fit you. Abdul is seeing to a choice of shoes for you." He left the room without a backward glance.

"A choice of shoes?" She shook her head. "I own one black pair, one beige, and one white. Now I'm to have a choice."

After stripping off her jeans and shirt, she pulled the sheath over her head, slipped the pumps onto her bare feet, and swiveled to look at herself in the mirror wall. "My goodness." Philippa couldn't stop staring at herself. Even without makeup and fixing her hair, she felt she'd never looked better. The dress caught and held her eye color, enhancing and highlighting her pink pale skin, giving it a luminescent glow.

"Philippa? Do you have it on?"

"Yes."

"What?" Romain opened the door. "I didn't hear you," the words died in his mouth. He stared at her as she slowly turned his way in the ill-fitting shoes, the narrow style of the dress falling in soft folds from her one shoulder, the upward thrust of her breasts making the material quiver around her. "Are you real?"

"Yes."

54

"So lovely."

"I like the dress."

"I love it." Romain's hoarse voice frissoned Philippa's spine. He went to her, his hands outstretched, heat building in him when she reached out, the dress delineating every soft curve of her form. "Your breasts are exquisite." Romain lifted her hands, his eyes delighting in the view. "Uptilting, small but full . . ." His voice trailed, his eyes roaming her body like a gentle hot hand.

Philippa felt heat, but no embarrassment. "What time are we going out?"

"Hmm?" Romain lifted his eyes to hers. "Ah, about seven . . . or so."

"Oh. Well, then I had better take this off and get ready." Philippa glanced at her watch. "It's already after five." She turned her back on Romain intending to go into the bathroom to remove the garment when she felt his hands at her waist.

"Wait, darling. I'll remove it for you." Before she could answer, Romain was there lifting the silky garment straight up her body and over her head.

Philippa felt the coolness of air on her back as she stood with her back to him in heels and panties and nothing more. When his lips touched her shoulder, fever tremored her skin. "Romain."

"Yes, darling. I'm here."

"I know." Philippa sobbed as his hands slid round her waist, coming up to cover her breasts and pull her tight to his body. When she felt him kiss the side of her neck, she turned her head, feeling no fear, only a sense of urgency and wonder. When he moved, their lips came together quite naturally with little pressure. Delight shivered through her as his hands whorled over her stomach, then slid down into her panties to touch her gently. "Romain!" she gasped, feeling her body liquefy with pleasure.

His chuckle trembled over her skin. It dismayed and excited him that he was sharing her novice wonderment. It also shocked and delighted him that he was experiencing as new a sensation as she was. He turned her in his arms. "I want to look at you."

"I want to look at you," she repeated, feeling daring but confident.

He stepped back from her, his hands still holding her, studying her face and expression. "No sooner said than done." He released her for a moment, taking one step back and beginning to strip off his shirt and trousers with abandon.

Philippa held her breath when he peeled the briefs from his body leaving his aroused frame naked to her view. "You're quite beautiful." She smiled at him feeling serene when she saw the slashes of red on his cheeks. "You should be in the Smithsonian."

God, she was throwing him out of stride, he thought, staring at her languid body, her silky briefs pushed down to show a tantalizing swatch of reddish hair. He began inching her panties down her legs.

Romain dropped to his knees and lifted her clear of the panties then tossed them away. He pressed his face into her middle, letting his tongue touch the indentation of her navel.

Philippa looked down at the strong head pressed against her abdomen and threaded her hands through the straight, heavy strands of ebony hair, loving the crisp softness under her fingers, feeling a sense of rightness. "I like this," she told him in sensuous tranquillity.

"What, darling?" Romain looked up at her, glazed fire in his eyes.

"I do like what you're doing. My body feels like pudding," Philippa whispered.

Romain surged to his feet, laughing, lifting her into his arms in the same motion. "You are very sweet and beautiful." He was still for a moment. "I'm taking you over to that bed, darling, to make love to you. You only have to say the word and I'll put you down, and we'll go on with our other plans." Romain couldn't clear the huskiness from his throat as he looked at her cradled in his arms, the very faint blue veins in the translucent skin of her breasts seeming the most erotic scene on earth to him.

Philippa stared at him, tightening her arms around his neck. "I want you to love me."

Romain felt his heart thud painfully in his chest as he placed her on the bed and followed her down to cuddle her close to his side, his mouth homing in on her breast driving his libido through the top of his skull. He had never lost control, and he was determined that he wouldn't do it now, but she was driving him closer to it than any woman had ever done.

Slowly he tamped down his own fire and began to minister to her every inch. His mouth coursed her neck and over her breasts then down over her abdomen. When he heard her whimper and her body begin to jerk and move against his, he felt as though he might explode, but he continued to move down her body until he could gently part her legs and push his face against the warmth of her.

"Romain . . . Romain . . ." Philippa arched in surprise.

"Shh, my precious. I'm loving you."

Gradually he sensed the buildup of tension in her body. She began to writhe, her hands plucking at him. In measured care he lifted himself over her, easing his hardened body into her moist cavity.

Philippa felt a jarring pain, then it receded and a rhythm that blossomed like white heat in her began. She felt her body part from her and become a section of

57

Romain's. Like a flash from another planet she knew that she belonged to him and would want to all her days.

Life exploded around them as they gave one to the other and held each other as the stars kaleidoscoped above them.

CHAPTER FOUR

"But, dear, surely you see our view." Aunt Grace wrung her hands, her eyes rolling toward her husband.

"We don't think you know Romain well enough to marry him, Philippa. That's a big step for anyone to contemplate when you've only known the intended three weeks." Her uncle tamped fresh tobacco into his pipe.

The rather stilted, formal way her guardian spoke to her telegraphed his deep agitation with the discussion.

"I know, but I love Romain and he loves me and I want to marry him." Philippa tried to explain, her heart beating faster just thinking of the man whom she had seen every day and night for three weeks, and with whom she was having the most explosive physical relationship that humans could conjure. She had never expected to feel the way Romain made her feel. She had never thought that he would want to marry her. Last night . . . she shivered with the remembered moment, not seeing her aunt or uncle as they stood in front of her citing reasons why they thought she should not make a hasty decision.

Romain had held her after their lovemaking, nuzzling her as he always did. "I don't want separations from you anymore. I hate taking you home. It's wrong. Marry me, so that you won't have to leave me anymore."

Philippa had shot to a sitting position, not at all self-conscious of being naked in front of him. She whirled to face him, noting the appreciative gleam in his eyes as he looked at her. "Marriage? You and me?"

Romain reached up hooking a strong hand around her neck and pulling her on top of him. "Do you think I would let any man ever have you?"

His smile cut a swath over her skin making her shiver. "You have a Lucifer look in your eye."

"I'd feel like him if you were ever with anyone else." His gaze softened. "Marry me."

"Yes."

"Good." He rolled her beneath him and entered her with a gentle violence that had her shuddering. "Look what your affirmative answer has done." His guttural utterances were breathed into her neck. "Your aunt and uncle won't approve, but I'll speak to them tomorrow. No more talk now."

"Romain . . ."

She hadn't waited for Romain to come to the house that day before tackling her guardians herself. She had a feeling that their feelings wouldn't be quite so lacerated if she approached them first.

"Philippa, Philippa, are you listening?" Aunt Grace jerked her back to the present.

"Yes, and I love you both. If you weren't in my life, it would be empty, but I have to marry Romain. I love him."

The concern etched on both faces didn't fade when they nodded their acceptance of the inevitable.

"Oh, thank you." Philippa threw herself at them, managing to hug them both at once. "And you're not to worry about the wedding. We are going to have a quick wedding in a small town in Nevada. Romain will arrange everything."

"But we had always planned that your wedding would be here, at home." Aunt Grace bit her lip, her eyes suspiciously bright.

"But you'll be there with me to give me away and then we shall have a dinner and celebrate together. We won't be going away. I have to be back on Monday for classes."

"What?" Aunt Grace whitened. "You're getting married this weekend?" She pressed her fist to her mouth when Philippa nodded. "You can't. Today's Wednesday." Her aunt sat down in the nearest chair and looked up at Philippa helplessly. "I can't believe it. What will happen to your dream of owning your own business?"

"I'm going to continue school and when I graduate . . ." Philippa shook her head. "I haven't planned that far yet—but I'm so happy."

"Then we're happy for you, child." Uncle George gathered her into his arms, pushing her head into his shoulder.

Philippa had the feeling that her aunt and uncle were using some sort of sign language to communicate over her head.

A little later in the day, after Romain had picked her up from the library and drove her home, he brought her into the house with his arm around her waist. He kissed her, then went right into her uncle's study where the older man awaited him.

The two men were closeted so long that Philippa had to be restrained by her aunt from knocking on the door and asking what was happening.

When Romain and her uncle came out of the study, both men looked a bit tight-lipped. Since Romain took her into his arms at once, Philippa forgot her trepidation.

"All set?"

"All set, darling." Romain smiled down at her before reaching around Philippa's body to clasp Aunt Grace's hand. "Thank you, madame, for your lovely niece. I will take good care of her."

"Then I will thank you for that." Aunt Grace's smile was but no less genuine than his when she grasped

Romain's hand. "I don't suppose you would like to stay for dinner instead of going out this evening."

"We would be delighted." Romain answered for both of them.

Philippa smothered her groan of disappointment and smiled at her guardians. She wanted so much to be alone with Romain so that he could hold her and make love to her.

Her uncle laughed out loud. "I can see this will be a sacrifice for you."

Philippa chuckled when her aunt looked puzzled. "I'll help with the salad, Aunt."

Dinner was fun!

That surprised Philippa. What surprised her even more was that her uncle and Romain had many and varied topics to discuss, including the transport of food to hungry people.

"I don't think giving them food is enough. There has to be the commitment of teaching them new methods, getting water to them," Philippa interjected, disagreeing with her beloved, seeing a frown touch Romain's brow for an instant. "I think there has to be that type of total effort to get the job done, not just a few token experts and a carload of money. We need farmers, agronomists, engineers. Wells need to be dug. Desalination needs to be explored . . ." Her voice trailed when she saw Romain's eyes narrow. She had the feeling that she had unhappily surprised him.

"I see." Romain looked at her politely.

"Don't be too incredulous," George said and chuckled. "She really does have the facts to back up her arguments. Philippa was raised to be a reasoning and thinking adult."

Romain sank back in his chair, a smile playing about his mouth as she joined further in their discussions.

After dinner they all played bridge and when Philippa was partnering her uncle, she managed to defeat Romain roundly in one game. After that, he paid close attention to his cards. She was soundly trounced the next two games to lose the rubber. He grinned at her when she poked her tongue at him.

Later when Romain was leaving and she walked him to the door, their arms around each other, she sighed and said, "I hate that I'm not going to be in your apartment with you tonight."

"You can't hate it more than I do. I'll be in the shower all night."

"You won't." She turned to face him at the door, chuckling.

He nodded, lifting a hand to thread through her long hair. He leaned forward inhaling her scent. "You have the perfect body fragrance, darling. It's in my head now." He hugged her for a moment, then released her. "You're quite a little competitor, aren't you? I'll have to be on my mettle to keep up with you."

Philippa blinked up at him. "Oh. You mean the bridge game. Well . . ."

Romain's mouth fitted to hers taking all her words into his. He lifted his head, then left.

Philippa forgot what she was going to say to him and ignored the needle of anxiety deep inside her.

Her wedding day dawned bright and sunny, and they flew to the desert area not far from Las Vegas with Romain piloting the Lear jet.

When they landed, a chauffeured Rolls-Royce met them, but Philippa hardly noticed. She was too busy looking at the beautiful round emerald, larger than Romain's thumbnail, that graced her left hand and refracted the sun like green fire.

"You look lovely in your silk suit, darling. That deep

gold color enhances your turquoise eyes." Romain held her close to him as they sat on the middle seat of the limousine, her aunt and uncle in the rear seat.

The ceremony in front of the judge was brief and uninspiring, but Philippa was thrilled, and when she kissed her aunt and uncle, she couldn't stem the tears that flowed down her cheeks.

"No crying today, silly." Romain was there wiping her cheeks gently. "Isn't it bad enough your aunt cried through the whole ceremony?"

Philippa nodded, giving a watery laugh.

The dinner, held directly after the wedding in a private room of a Las Vegas club, was delicious.

After dining, the four of them returned to the airfield to the waiting plane and made the journey back to Los Angeles.

When they landed, there was a limousine to take her aunt and uncle back to their home while Philippa and Romain would take the Lamborghini. Philippa said good-bye to her guardians, seeing the sadness behind their smiles, but it didn't dim the ecstasy that held her in thrall. She was Romain's wife!

"Are you worried about your aunt and uncle?" Romain asked her as they sped down the freeway toward his apartment.

Philippa shook her head, then pressed it back against the plush upholstery. "No. I was thinking how happy I am." She turned her head, without lifting it, to look at him. "I do love you."

"My angel. You'll be happy."

She was. They both were. They developed a routine. Romain managed to keep his work hours to when she was in school, then most of her free time, they were together. She scheduled all her study periods directly after classes so that she did most of her studying then. When she was home with Romain, she could concentrate on him. It had only taken her two days to discover that he didn't like it when she studied or did anything but be with him when she was at home.

Little by little they began to see other people, but a good share of their time when they weren't alone or working was spent with her aunt and uncle. Both her relatives had come to like Romain, and though Philippa sensed a little reserve on her uncle's part, she was convinced that he, too, would come to be as relaxed with her husband as she and Aunt Grace were.

As a couple they had occasional arguments, a few even flaring discussions, but all in all they were content with one another and sought each other's company all the time.

Trouble began when she noticed how unwelcome she was whenever Romain's relatives visited them. One by one she met them, even formed a wary friendship with his sister Ayada who had moved into her own place. It was when they began to come in droves to see Romain about every facet of their lives, not just the business, that Philippa became resentful. "They don't want me around," she fumed one evening after his cousin had left. "I'm supposed to disappear into the harem, am I?"

"They are my family, and I am my uncle's representative in this country. As his heir, it is my job to see to the care of his people and that includes their personal problems. They just feel more comfortable talking to me alone."

"To the exclusion of your wife?"

"I never exclude you," Romain shot back.

"No? What do you call it when your cousin Halid asks the women to leave the room so that he and his relative can have a discussion. I was the only woman, for God's sake."

Romain reddened. "I'll admit that he was gauche, but in my country . . ."

"This is my country, damn it." Philippa whirled away from him and went up the stairs two at a time, cursing herself if she dared to cry.

That night when they made love it was with an even deeper intensity, as though the anger they'd had had fired their passion.

Romain felt that she held him even tighter, but that a part of her was aloof from him. He sensed a fear in her that he swore to himself he would scotch.

Four months after their marriage Romain had to travel to Washington and New York, and because she had term papers, Philippa couldn't accompany him. He found that he ached for her and that the twice daily telephone calls were not enough to assuage the pain of separation. "What's wrong?" He noticed the coolness in her voice the evening of the fifth day they'd been apart.

"I—nothing. I'm going to stay at my uncle's until you return."

"What? Why? Abdul is there to care for your needs."

"Romain, I want to stay with them. They're my family. I'll come home when you return."

Romain felt all at sea, threatened in a way he couldn't fathom. When he hung up the phone, he stared at the instrument as though it were a snake about to strike, then he punched some numbers into the system, barking some orders in Arabic.

Striding through the apartment he snapped more staccato orders to others who appeared like magic in his wake. In minutes he was downstairs in the limousine that would take him to Washington International. He was used to the smooth VIP way he was ushered through the airport to the first-class seat on the jumbo jet that would take him to California and Philippa.

Working in his briefcase was the only way he had of getting her out of his head. He had the feeling if he thought about her too much he might jump out the jet and try to fly himself.

He called the Stonely home from the limousine carrying him to their house.

"Yes?"

"George? It's Romain. Tell Philippa that I will be picking her up in twenty minutes."

"It's after midnight. She's sleeping . . ."

Romain broke the connection and stared out the window at the glittering blackness that was Los Angeles at night.

When the limousine pulled down the curving drive, Romain had the door open before it stopped. He was out and issuing a sharp order even as he walked up the steps to the cedar door.

It was flung open and his wife stood there. "I didn't believe it when Uncle George woke me." Then she flung herself into his arms. "Romain, I didn't think you would be coming back so soon."

"Neither did I," he spoke dryly not able to resist pressing his face into her fragrant hair. "I want to know what's wrong, but first we'll say good night to George and Grace and collect your things."

"But . . . but . . ." Philippa sputtered behind him as he went into the kitchen where her aunt and uncle were having a hot lemon and honey drink before returning to bed.

Romain made all the excuses and in minutes they were outside and in the car.

"I don't know if I have all my books." Philippa felt flustered all at once, sensing an anger coming off Romain.

"I have your books."

"I . . . I know you're mad at me for something, but I don't want to fight when you've just come home."

Romain gathered her into his arms, knowing he held her too tight. "Then we won't fight, we'll make love."

"I'd like that." She took a deep breath. "Tell me why you're upset."

"I will." Romain looked down into her eyes and felt as though he'd been set adrift. She had too much power over him!

Philippa sighed, putting her arms around his neck, welcoming his hot caresses on her neck, putting the unpleasant reflections of the last few days behind her. Without him she'd been fearful, lost, and the sensation had scared her!

Once home they raced up the stairs and into the bedroom, tossing their clothes every which way, impatient to hold and love each other.

Later, when they lay entwined, panting and replete, she turned to look at him and smile.

He leaned up on an elbow and looked down at her. "Now tell me what set you running home?"

Philippa looked away, only to have him take hold of her chin and turn her toward him again.

"Tell me."

"I don't know if I can. You'll think it's picayune."

"From the beginning, Philippa." He leaned down to kiss her left nipple.

"Not if you do that. My mind goes blank."

Romain chuckled. "Didn't Abdul take care of you?"

"Of course he did, but that damned family of yours kept dropping in and your cousin—Halid—"

"Did he come on to you?" Romain's voice was like an electric charge.

"No, of course not. They know better than to cross you," Philippa said matter-of-factly, making Romain laugh. She wasn't fooled. She heard the lacing of steel in his voice. She stifled the quick shudder she felt when she thought of what Romain would have done to his cousin had he dared accost her. "It's just that they all consider me stupid. I know this isn't my home—"

"It is," Romain interrupted. "You're my wife. This is my home, ergo it's yours."

"Then why don't they ask my permission before they come here and take over the study, practically ordering me to leave because they are going to discuss business."

Feeling uncomfortable, Romain shrugged. He could imagine what must have happened. Philippa would have been studying, and his cousins, who were his business associates, would have come for a meeting because it was so private in his apartment, and they would have asked Philippa to leave the library. "They are the original macho men," Romain began.

"Don't explain them to me. I saw it for myself." Philippa sniffed. "I realize it seems a very small thing to you, but I felt uncomfortable and out of place here when you were gone. I really felt I was the alien that they think I am."

"You're my wife." Romain's hands convulsed on her. "Do you know how I felt when I discovered you weren't in my—our home? I wanted to throw things." Romain didn't voice the words that tumbled in his core. He had feared to find her gone! It was a fear that weakened him and made him vulnerable. He ground his teeth at the acceptance of such a thing. "You are not a stranger in your own home, and I will not allow you to think that." He kissed her fiercely.

"Umm," she responded. "I do like to make love with you, husband."

Many times they buried the differences between them by a physical union, but it disturbed Philippa more than she cared to admit that there were so many gulfs they had to bridge. It wasn't until Romain began pressing her to accompany him back to Dharan to meet his uncle, the king, and stay in the country for several months, that they really began to quarrel.

"Surely you can see it my way, too," Philippa wailed at

69

her husband one Saturday morning before she was to attend class. "If I leave with you, I'll lose the entire semester and maybe the year. I've worked very hard to get through university, and I don't want to throw away something so precious."

"You have plenty of money of your own. You know that. You can afford to attend any university you choose . . ."

"I want to get my degree here. My heart's set on it." She lifted her chin, the tears that she always felt when she was at odds with Romain drying up in the face of his determination.

"Shouldn't you be at the side of your husband when he goes home to report to his chief of state?"

"Couldn't you wait until I finished my semester, then we could take the whole summer and go to Dharan? That way I would be back in time for fall semester."

"My uncle wants to see my new wife, and I have things to discuss with him. I should go in two weeks. Please try to be ready." He spun on his heel and left the room while Philippa was opening and closing her mouth, angry but floundering.

"I won't," she panted. "I have a good mind not to go to that foolish dinner with you tonight, too." But she knew she would accompany him.

That night, as she readied herself, she dwelt on her husband. "Bullheaded, opinionated son of a camel, that's what he is," she grumbled, reaching for a towel to dry herself. She slathered the varied rich emollients that Abdul supplied for her and that he assured her caused the women of the Near East and Far East to have perfect, translucent skin.

She staggered out to the bedroom, swathed in one of the heated bath sheets rather than donning her robe. She had every intention of just closing her eyes for a moment as she fell face first on the bed. Then she would get up and get dressed. Her eyes were like lead. They closed before she had the chance to pull the coverlet fully over her nude body.

She felt the soothing strokes on her back before she opened her eyes or registered what they were. "Ooh. You're giving me a massage. I love it."

"Isn't that what husbands are for? To be the slaves of their beautiful wives?" Irony laced his voice at the truth of that.

"You would never be anyone's slave," Philippa murmured through a haze of delight.

"Aren't I yours?"

"If you are, you're a wonderful one, but I still think it would be well-nigh impossible for you to be."

Romain's hands stilled for a moment, then resumed their rhythmic pulling and stretching of her muscular yet softly feminine form. Was it possible that she really didn't know the power she had over him? "You're quite beautiful." He leaned down and kissed her one rounded buttock, letting his teeth nip.

"Biting," Philippa drawled. "Umm, lovely. Have we time?"

"We will always have time for this." Romain pressed his face to her spine and began moving his mouth from her neck to coccyx, causing her to spasm in joy. He flipped her over onto her back and began the same foray up the front of her. "This is the most important part of us . . . our togetherness."

"Yes, yes." Philippa arched herself against him, locking her arms and legs around him. He's my life, she thought, and then wondered why she didn't say it out loud to him.

Romain felt his body and soul break apart, then join with hers as they became one in the only way that man and woman can. It transcended earth and melded with the stars. The moon was the base on which their love

71

built, and they were gone on that special journey that only lovers take.

"We do have to get dressed," Romain muttered in her ear, willing himself to come out of the love aura that held him. His sensuous wife had cartwheeled him into another dimension of living, one that he had never known before. Each day she had tied him tighter with her very special silken rope so that every moment he was more bound to her. The subconscious thought that he would get used to her lovemaking, that it would become the norm fled in the knowledge that his feeling for her had grown each day, that not having her would be like dismembering himself. The thought of being without her shuddered through him like a war wound.

"What is it? You shivered. Are you coming down with a cold?"

"It's nothing." Romain rolled from the bed and to his feet, avoiding her eyes. "I just need a quick shower." He strode across the room and into the bathroom, shutting the door behind him and turning the key.

Philippa sat up in bed and stared at the door. "I thought you'd just had a shower," she mused.

She reclined again, puzzling over Romain for several minutes, then rose and ambled over to the mirror wall that housed the walk-in closet for their clothes. She pawed through the numerous dresses and suits with the fashionable labels, trying to choose something for the evening.

"Wear the Chanel silk suit," Romain said at her back, his hand patting her naked backside.

"That was the fastest shower on record." Philippa leaned back against him, feeling the coolness of his skin. "And a cold one at that. I thought wives were supposed to be the answer to the cold shower syndrome."

"You are, angel." Romain slipped his hand around her waist. With the other he reached for the two-piece suit in

72

pink silk satin with the brown satin lapels and pocket trim with the Chanel signature jacket. "I love this on you with the brown patent leather pumps and clutch purse."

Philippa shook her head, not moving away from his body. "You have the most definite taste in women's clothes . . ."

"Not all women, but with your beautiful coloring I admit to having preferences." He bit her neck softly and released her. "I will dress in the other bedroom; otherwise, we won't dress." He backed away from her, holding her eyes in the door mirror for a moment. *"Au revoir, chérie."* Romain left the room.

Philippa exhaled. "No man should have as great a hold on a woman as Romain has on me," she said with a sigh. "But why fight it? It's not going to change."

She donned pink silk underthings, eschewing a bra for a camisole with a matching slip. She fastened dusky rose stockings to the silk garters attached to her pink briefs.

She whirled in front of the mirror after she put the milk-chocolate-colored patent leather shoes with three-inch heels on her feet. "Romain says high heels make my legs look sexy," she said and laughed to herself.

She studied the effect of the exquisite evening suit and approved. The pink and brown enhanced her red hair and gave her skin even more of a glow.

She twisted this way and that to get the full effect of the outfit, as she tried to choose the jewelry she should wear with it. She was going to wear her engagement ring, which she never removed, the green fire a macabre complement to the pink and brown, but she hesitated on the earrings.

She saw Romain approach her in the mirror and paused in her movements to watch him. "You're a very beautiful husband in your silk suit." She whirled to face him, pleased that he had worn the ebony brown evening suit with the palest cream shirt and sewn-in pleats

threaded with cocoa. "We look like twins . . . almost."
She laughed out loud, feeling freer than she had in days.
Maybe all their troubles would evaporate! She smothered
the cynical laugh of the voice deep inside her and went to
meet her husband, arms outstretched.

Romain pulled her to him, gently nipping at her ear.
"I'm glad you didn't put your earrings on yet. I have
something for you."

"You give me too much," Philippa protested weakly
even as she leaned back and took the leather case from
him.

"Impossible." He touched the gold lock and snapped
the case open when Philippa continued to hold the box.
"See? Pink diamonds. They belonged to my grandmother." His smile twisted. "She gave them to my father
so that he could give them to my mother, and she's given
them to me so that you can have them. She told me she
hoped that we were as much in love as she and my father
were. I told her yes."

"You sound as though you're close to her."

Romain shrugged. "I am. I don't see her as often as I'd
like. But she's remarried to a Frenchman, and she's very
happy. One day I'll take you to Paris to visit her. She
would like you. She always told me that I'd meet someone who would bowl me over and the thought pleased
her. I'll have to tell her how prophetic she is."

"Romain." She lifted her hands to clutch his neck,
warmed by his words.

He eased her back from him. "I think you should wear
her jewelry. Her coloring was similar. Her hair was never
as red as yours, but it had highlights and she has green
eyes, not turquoise . . ."

"That's where your eyes come from." She ran a finger
over his brow, staring into the green depths.

He nodded. "Now let me put on the diamonds."

"Just the earrings, please. That necklace, and bracelet

. . ." Philippa lifted the heavy encrusted pieces, shaking her head in awe. "They demand a strapless pink gown with lots of skin showing."

"Your skin." Romain took his time affixing the crescents of diamonds that fitted the curve of her ear, the perfect stones large and sparkling. He stepped back and stared at her. "I think I made a mistake asking you to wear such an outfit. I thought you would be so covered, but you have managed to be as exotically beautiful and desirable as one of my great grandfather's favorite and very naked kadim."

Philippa laughed out loud, knowing all about the long deceased Emir who had had over a hundred wives and twice as many houri, the kadim being the most favored of those. "I should be wearing a veil." She undulated and hummed Eastern music, loving it when Romain's bright eyes darkened to a hunter green glitter.

"We had better go." His reluctance when he led her from the room, and his constant contact by kissing or holding her, caused a surge of heady sensuous power in Philippa.

CHAPTER FIVE

Romain drove the Rolls instead of the Lamborghini so that Philippa could sit close to him on the bench seat and not be separated by a console.

They were to dine with other members of his family at a restaurant called Oasis and owned by a distant cousin of Romain's. Philippa looked forward to the gourmet meal that Dassar, the owner of Oasis, would prepare because it was always a combination of French haute cuisine and Dharanian. He had trained in Paris, and was an expert in the choicest desert fare.

Dinner was a gourmet meal, beginning with golden Beluga caviar so rare that it was once kept for the delectation of the Shah of Iran only. The caviar was followed by sole amandine nestled in a bed of fresh spinach to tease the palate, with the entree being a boned breast of chicken stuffed with fresh apricots and dates and broiled over hickory.

Philippa loved the dish with the accompanying tiny boiled potatoes crisped with parsley. "I am enjoying the food very much."

"So I noticed." Romain laughed at her when she grimaced at him, then he touched the corner of her mouth with his napkin. "I wanted to kiss it off."

"What? And shock the family?" Philippa shot a glance down the table trying to smother the lacing of bitterness in her voice. She and Romain had argued too much about

76

his macho relatives who thought women had brains the size of a pea!

"Cousin, pay attention," Halid spoke to Romain but glowered at Philippa. He had made the concession of having a woman with him, but he didn't want anything to interfere with his man's talk. "We were discussing the merits of purchasing that horse farm in Kentucky—"

"I think having horses would be wonderful," Philippa began, then cut herself off when Halid looked at her horrified.

"I listen to my wife's opinion." Romain stared at his cousin, taking Philippa's hand into his.

"Yes," Halid observed, grinding his teeth.

The conversation continued after an awkward moment, but despite Romain's efforts to include her, Philippa felt excluded.

At dinner's end, Romain looked at her. "There is a cabaret in the next room with a very good dance band. Shall we go there?"

"Please. Anything to get away from the scowling Halid."

Romain chuckled, but Philippa saw the frown crease his brow. He was so very loyal to his family!

Romain watched the athletic sway of Philippa's body in front of him as she preceded him to the dance floor. She floated, not walked. Grace was innate in her, both physically and spiritually. No woman had ever been able to capture the core of him as Philippa had done! It angered and titillated him that far from being bored with her each day he wanted and needed her more and more. It bothered him that she found his family so objectionable that she couldn't understand the threatened masculinity of Halid's machismo. He pushed the unwelcome thoughts away and concentrated on his wife as she turned to face him, her arms outstretched, the silk suit hugging her body.

"You're too beautiful." Romain enfolded her as they swayed to the love ballad.

"You, too."

"What a way to talk to your husband." He pressed his face into the fragrant hair. He didn't like it twisted on top of her head. He preferred it loose and sexy so that it would tickle his face, but he had to admit that she looked cooly sophisticated that way and that the ivory column of her neck was very erotic.

The music changed and she flowed away from his body in a beguine rhythm that seemed to become part of her.

He watched her a moment, having the strange sensation that they were alone on the planet, then he joined her in the pulsing beat of the latin music.

"Romain, I love to dance," Philippa breathed, her eyes half closed. "I wish we could do this all the time."

"We will, darling."

"Please."

"Yes." He felt out of breath and off keel by the turquoise fire in her eyes. He vowed to have more time for her, that their life together would somehow overcome the many obstacles that were constantly thrown their way. Damn the world for interfering with his love! He pulled her closer so that their bodies touched in throbbing rhythm to the music.

"Umm. Are we making love?" Philippa quizzed in heated wonder, her eyes closed as her hands flowed over him in a feather touch that torched him to her.

"I think we are." Romain's laugh choked in his throat as he became aware that some of his business associates had joined them on the floor and were now watching them as they moved in a more sedate pace to the theme.

"Halid doesn't seem to have benefited as much as you from the French dancing master employed to teach you the finer arts of ballroom dancing." Philippa chortled, the heat in her body not lessening as she became aware of the stares around them. "I have the most overpowering urge to poke my tongue at him."

"Not at him, darling. At me." Romain pulled her close, feeling a thrust of jealousy that Halid could demand so much attention from her, even as his common sense told him she disliked his cousin.

"Could we leave, do you think? There are quite a few things I would like to do to my husband." Philippa felt a boundless excitement while Romain was touching her, holding her. She tamped down the helpless anger she felt at Halid's attempts to put her in her "woman's" place and instead concentrated on how much she loved Romain.

"Yes." He didn't give a damn for any of his family when his very blood was pumping Philippa's name. He gently steered her from the dance floor, heading for the table in the corner where their party of stiffly seated males was now interspersed with chattering females who spent their time craning their necks to speak to each other.

"What is the matter with them?" Philippa fumed at her own sex as they approached the table. "Can't they see that they're not thought of as persons?"

"There are houris in all countries, my love, who really don't care what people think of them as long as they are well taken care of, and I assure you these are." Romain's hard laugh fueled Philippa's anger.

"Damn it, they should care. They're women." She stalked ahead of Romain to the table and faced Halid who didn't rise to his feet, but instead looked up at her haughtily. "Get to your feet in the presence of a lady, you clod." She heard the hiss of Romain's breath behind her and the muted indignant roar of Halid.

"You dare talk to me . . ."

"She does." Romain pulled Philippa back to him, stepping around her and glaring down at his cousin. "As my

wife, she demands your respect—and she'll get it."
Romain stared at his cousin and the other men at the
table. One by one they rose to their feet, the chattering of
the women fading away. Halid was the last to rise, and he
did so with his jaw locked and blood filling his face. "We
are leaving now," Romain told his family, rigid with anger.

On the way home there was silence between them.

"You're angry with me, I know, but—"

"I'm angry, Philippa, with you, yes, but also with my
cousins. They know how to behave with a woman; they
have been taught to rise in the presence of a lady. If any
man had not done so in the presence of my mother, my
father would have had them flayed alive, and my cousins
know this . . . but I still feel that you attack them too
much, that you don't try to find a common ground where
you can converse with them in a civilized manner."

"I'm civilized." Philippa shot back, stung.

"I know that, but when we go to live in Dharan, you
will have to curb your . . ."

"We don't live in Dharan. We live here." Philippa felt a
flutter of fear. "I don't want to live in a country where
women are things. We're happy here."

"Yes, we are, but Dharan is my home. And I could be
heir to the throne one day . . ."

"No. How could you?"

"The accession will be the king's choice either in his
lifetime or in his will, plus the favorite of the many tribal
sheikhs who wield a great deal of power in Dharan."
Romain knew that he sounded formal, but he had to
make Philippa understand. "I have a duty to my people
. . ."

"Your duty is here, you told me yourself. The biggest
centers for Dharanian investments and industries are in
London and in the United States, and you own land and

mining interests in Mexico and Central America, which you control from the United States."

"That's true." Romain pulled into the garage under their penthouse. "But I must go where I will do the most good for my people."

"But you've told me that you feel like an American much of the time."

"That is also true. I have American interests and my country is very much an ally of yours, but my first duty is to my people." He lifted her out of the car, holding her to his side as they walked to the elevator. Once in the enclosure, he turned her toward him and kissed her tenderly.

"I know we have much more to discuss," Philippa managed the words through lips gone flaccid.

"We will always have much to discuss, desert flower." Romain knew deep down that he was trying to avoid the issue, that he was trying to coerce her with his body. Emotional and sexual blackmail, he mused, even as his mouth was pressed to her neck as he held her to him.

The elevator stopped with a swish of opening doors.

"Abdul isn't here," she muttered to her husband, her head lolling on his chest as they stepped into the marble parquet foyer.

"He has his orders not to be around when I bring my lovely wife home just in case I would like to make love to her in the living room in front of the fireplace."

"You must admit that it's more conducive to that now that I've had them remove all that modern furniture and put in the oriental carpeting."

"Indeed. It's like a harem now," Romain said and chuckled when she pulled the hair on his chest after unbuttoning his shirt.

"Trust you to picture that."

"My darling, I carry around an image of you in a harem in my head—all by yourself, of course."

Philippa laughed, too, but she couldn't bury the uneasy

81

feeling that assailed her. She couldn't be imprisoned, not even by Romain. And it would be a form of incarceration to live the way many of the women lived in the Middle East. The freedom to make choices, to come and go as she pleased, would be curtailed. It would be difficult just to visit such a place. She would be stifled if she had to live in a country like Dharan. Purdah was not for her even if it would be in the figurative sense. She knew from what Romain had told her that his country was very strong on educating its citizenry and that women were included in that. Even so . . .

"What are you thinking, my love?" Romain saw the play of emotions across her face. He knew what she was going to say before she opened her mouth.

"About your country."

"Are you, indeed?" Romain drawled, his churning insides tamped down behind a lazy smile. She was building walls! Damn her, she wasn't going to put up barricades between them. He would have enough to contend with when he introduced her to his uncle. He didn't need the angst of knowing his wife was trying to be as divisive as his uncle!

"Yes. I don't think I'd fit very well in Dharan."

"And I thought we were making love." Romain pulled the jacket from her shoulders, aware that he was being rougher than he usually was.

"Anxious, aren't you?"

"Very."

As always it was good between them, heat building like a furnace that threatened to burn all before it, but there was something so elemental to surviving this time that it had both of them breathing in ragged painful starts. It was as though they said a painful good-bye and then came together again.

Something in the core of Philippa seemed to give way as she gave herself to her husband. She felt at the instant of joining that she could never break free of him from that moment, that a celestial glue cemented them and made them one.

"Darling, darling," Romain crooned to her, "you pulled me apart, limb by limb, joint by joint. There was a feeling . . ."

"Yes."

He leaned back from her and looked into her eyes. "You are my half."

"And you're mine." She repeated the ancient desert vow that some of the nomadic tribes in his country used in their wedding ritual.

"Allah has made you mine."

Philippa chuckled as he buried his face in her throat. "Just because we repeat those vows almost every night doesn't make us any more married."

"Of course it does." Romain's voice was muffled as he pushed his face into the velvet of her abdomen. "We will be married into the next millenium, my pet."

"And only you saying 'I divorce you' three times can nullify that. Correct?"

Romain lifted his face, flushed from renewed lovemaking. "And that I will never say."

"Romain, we'll argue. You might want to say—"

"No." He slid further down her body, his tongue intruding in the most intimate caress, arching her body, his own tremoring in the sensuous satisfaction of giving her pleasure.

Philippa had the sensation of flying, her body exploding, all the sensible things to talk of melting in the heat of love.

Romain held her, willing all anxiety away from him as he melted to his wife and soared with her to the lovers' place where they belonged. It was so beautiful with her.

"It was as though we built a mountain . . . all on our

own." Philippa breathed into her husband's chest, her body lifting with each ragged breath he took.

"It might be something more elemental than that, my angel. I didn't take precautions." Romain couldn't keep the disgust from his voice. The last thing he wanted was to impregnate Philippa now. They had enough problems without taking on the care of a third person at the moment.

Philippa turned over to lean on his chest, her eyes alight. "Are you saying that the great Romain Al Adal, descendant of the mighty desert sheikhs and kings, made a boo-boo? That he doesn't want his kadim to have a lusty son?"

"Stop laughing and you are not my kadim. You're my wife." He kissed her, nipping at her lower lip with his teeth. "Of course I want us to have children some day, but not for years. You're only eighteen. Maybe when you're twenty-five we'll talk again." He lifted her free of him, kissing her nose. "Shall we take a shower together?"

Philippa felt the smile freeze on her face as he leaped from the bed, yawning and stretching. It was on the tip of her tongue to ask if she didn't have some say when she should have a child. It was true that she hadn't wanted to have one until she was in her twenties, but to have Romain state a time when they should think about it, rankled. She shook her head, burying yet another annoyance and let him pull her to her feet when he turned toward her.

Later he carried her upstairs, her eyes already fluttering closed even though she mumbled words to him. She smothered the niggling realization that there were too many things between Romain and herself that weren't discussed. It was far too easy to put them aside for another time.

"Wonderful."

"What's wunnerful?" She quizzed her husband, sleepily happy to let him tuck her under the silk sheets.

"The way we are together." He gathered her close to him.

She fell asleep.

Romain watched her for a long time. "How will you take it, I wonder, when I tell you that we're going to Dharan next month, and that it's a command performance, my love." He felt his face harden as he looked at her every pore. "You are beautiful, my darling, and very young, but you must realize that a man's work is important, too, that his duty sometimes has to come first." His hold on her tightened. He needed her! He wanted her, but she had to make concessions!

Later that week he broke the news. When Romain told her that they were going to Dharan in just a little over three weeks and that he had known they were going for the past six weeks, she flew into a temper. "And when were you going to tell me? When we were getting on the plane?"

"I'm telling you now. Damn it, that's why I didn't tell you sooner. You refuse to listen to reason. I have to go back. It's business. I don't want to leave you here. I want you with me."

Philippa watched his face wanting to rail at him, seeing the shuttered look of those green eyes. "I don't want you to leave me, but what will I do about my classes?"

"Darling." Relief coursed through Romain at her answer. He hardly heard her other hurried words about not wanting to be shelved like harem women, that she wanted say in their lives. It was enough that she would be coming with him without a terrible struggle. "We have a fine university in Dharan City. You can transfer there." He leaned back from her. "I've already spoken to the university, here and at Dharan. They see no problem with you fitting right into the class schedule there. The classes are primarily in English with some Arabic, but English is the second language of my country along with Spanish and French . . ."

"You have been busy." Philippa laughed but she felt that uneasiness once more.

The next day she went to see her aunt and uncle directly after her classes, before she went home to their apartment. "So you see I won't be missing anything . . ."

"You don't sound too thrilled about going to Dharan." Her uncle pressed down his tobacco into his pipe, watching her over his half glasses. "As you know your aunt and I will be going to New York when I take my sabbatical. You are welcome to come with us if you feel that Dharan is too much for you, just until Romain's return, of course." His mouth widened in a macabre smile as his pipe was clamped between his teeth.

"Of course," Philippa said and smiled at him. "It's tempting, but I had better go to Dharan. I understand the king wants to see me even though I feel he doesn't approve of me."

"Fool," Aunt Grace said tartly. "I would match our blood lines against any desert sheikh."

"Up the rebels," her uncle said mildly as his wife harumphed and rose to her feet.

"I'll make dinner. You did say that Romain would be late tonight?"

"Yes. He's picking me up here after his meeting. I'll be doing my homework here, if that's all right?"

"This is your home," Aunt Grace sniffed, then left the room.

"All is not *gemütlich* in paradise, eh?"

Philippa sighed. "I love Romain and he loves me, but Uncle George, I don't want to live in another country away from you and Aunt Grace." She swallowed. "I have the feeling I would be in nominal purdah. Sometimes the men and women don't even eat together at banquets. I couldn't live like that."

"Romain is your husband."

"I know."

"But I also want you to know you have a home with us."

"I know that, too." Philippa rose and went over to her uncle's chair to kiss the top of his head. "Can a marriage survive if two people seem to pull in different directions much of the time?" She knelt at his feet leaning her head on his knee. When she felt his hand on her head, she closed her eyes, feeling the peace she had always experienced with her aunt and uncle.

"A good marriage can survive anything but lack of love, and you say you have that."

"We do. That's the only thing I'm sure of, but I still feel uneasy about Dharan. Romain seems to feel that everything will work itself out . . ."

"Maybe he's right."

Philippa sighed. "Maybe. I don't mind going to the university in Dharan. In fact, it sounds as though they have a very modern program." She paused, all at once confused about how she really felt. "I don't know what it is, but I feel threatened," she blurted the words, lifting her face when she sensed her uncle's uneasiness as he shifted position.

"Romain is kind to you?"

"Oh, yes." Philippa laughed. "He's gentle and very loving. It's just that I realize that Romain has tremendous responsibilities as the probable heir to the king. He's told me that many times." She inhaled, staring up at her uncle. "Sometimes I think he's two persons, and I'm pretty sure I know only one."

"A man's work must be important to him, even more so when he has the lives of other people in his hands."

Philippa nodded. "Romain feels very strongly about

his people." She pressed her face to her uncle's leg again. "Romain also feels that he has to orchestrate our lives, sometimes without asking me. I'm young but I'm not a baby. I think a decision to have a child should be made by both of us not just him."

"Oh."

"Yes, I know what you're not saying, uncle. That I'm nitpicking, but there are so many things that bother me."

"And have you discussed them with Romain?"

"No!" Philippa's head shot up. "I . . . I don't like to argue with him."

"And you think it's healthier to bottle things up and develop a sour attitude about your marriage? In a marriage is it better to tell an uncle or discuss differences with a partner?"

"I know it's better to talk to my partner instead of my uncle." Philippa's head dropped back to his knee. Then she looked up at him and smiled. "How come you're so wise?"

"I've had you and Grace fooled for years."

She rose to her feet, stretching. "I had better hit the books. That English lit course is throwing me."

Her uncle chuckled. "You always did get angry when you couldn't whiz through a subject."

"Smarty." She left the room and went up to her old bedroom, hauling her tote bag filled with books behind her, feeling better after talking to her uncle but not totally reassured about her life with Romain.

After studying for a couple of hours and then having dinner, she and her uncle sat around playing cribbage, one of his favorite games, while her aunt picked out tunes on the piano.

When Romain arrived, the three of them were laughing about a move her uncle had just made. They didn't notice him at first.

"Hello." His voice sounded stilted even to his own

ears. Damn it, she never seemed that carefree when she was with him!

"Hi." Philippa jumped to her feet and approached him, reaching up to kiss his cheek.

At the last second he turned his face so that their lips met. "I like that better," he murmured.

"So do I." Philippa laughed up at him, feeling tension in the hard body pressed to hers. "Had a bad day?"

"You could say that." Romain knew he sounded stiff, but he didn't want to tell her what his problem really was. He was jealous of the open, easy relationship she had with her aunt and uncle, and he wanted her to have the same type with him. He wanted to be all things to her!

Philippa stepped back from him, seeing the familiar shuttered look. He was closing himself off from her again, as though she wouldn't or couldn't understand his business. Irritation curled through her. She was as bright as his cousin, Halid, and she had to bite her tongue to keep from saying it right in front of Aunt Grace and Uncle George.

Romain hooked his arm around Philippa's waist as she started to move away from him. "I didn't know you played cribbage, darling."

"Yes." She didn't look at him.

"Do you play, Romain?"

"I used to play when I was Oxford, George."

"That's where I learned to play." Uncle George grinned, glancing from his wife to Romain and back again.

"How are you, Romain?" Aunt Grace said and coughed behind her hand.

"Fine, thank you. How are you?" He asked in the same formal tone as Philippa's aunt had used.

Damn him! He was being patronizing to her aunt, Philippa fumed anew, gesturing for him to take her place at the cribbage board opposite her uncle. When he sat down, she tried to move away from him.

Romain looked around at her, searching her face, then reaching out a hand. "Here, darling, it's your game."

"No. You play it." She turned and walked over to her aunt where she sat on the piano stool. "Want to play a duet?"

Her aunt beamed at her. "We haven't done that in a long time."

The two women played and sang a repertoire of songs that they had done many times when Philippa was practicing the lessons her aunt had given her. Her aunt had been her teacher and rather than insist on prescribed exercises, she had developed with Philippa the habit of playing with her and singing. It had made Philippa's interest wax, and she had continued tutoring from her aunt until she entered university. Though she'd never had a desire to pursue music as a career, she enjoyed the freedom and solitude that playing the piano gave her.

"Is Romain an arbitrary person?" her aunt quizzed hesitantly.

"I would have to say yes."

"But he is loving?"

"Yes, again."

"Child, marriage is difficult with the best man, like your Uncle George. You have to work so hard at it." Her aunt hit a flat instead of a natural, then grimaced. "I want to encourage you in your marriage, but at the same time I don't want to discourage you from coming to us if anything goes wrong."

"I know." Philippa kissed her aunt.

Grace sighed. "I think I'll make some tea. Would you like lemon or orange spice?"

"Lemon, please."

When she and Romain left that night, Philippa made up her mind to speak to him when they reached home.

"Say what you're thinking, Philippa," Romain said in clipped tones, firing the car down the freeway.

She sucked in her breath, still not used to the way Romain sensed any change in her. "I think we should make decisions together about our life."

His head shot her way. "Don't we?"

"No. I think you make a dictum and expect me to go along."

The car rocketed ahead for a mile then slowed. "And I think that you would rather our marriage existed in a vacuum of no discussion, so that I'm forced to make decisions for us. Then you can complain."

"That's not fair." Philippa felt tears clog her throat.

"But true. So, why don't we change that? Speak up. What's bothering you now?"

"I don't really want to go to Dharan."

"Would you rather I went alone?"

"I don't want you to leave me. No."

"Then we have to go." She didn't object and the relief that surged through him almost deafened him to the next thing she said. "What?"

"I said we should both decide if we want or don't want children."

Romain put on his signal and drove down into the underground garage. "You don't want children now. Do you?"

"No, but I think it shouldn't be your decision alone that we won't have them."

"All right. Do you want children now?"

"No."

"Neither do I."

"End of discussion," Philippa muttered.

"Not so." He parked the car, then turned to look at her. "Was there something else on your mind?"

"I can't live in purdah, Romain. I need to express myself."

Romain was silent. He, too, had been pondering what his uncle would have to say about his wife and her liberated ways, but he nodded slowly. "I wouldn't want you to change."

"Thank you."

CHAPTER SIX

Dharan surprised her. It was not just the flatness of the area or the intense heat. It was the amalgam of old and new, seeing camels alongside Mercedes, women in business suits coupled with those in obvious purdah. Dharan City was a study in contrasts, a thriving metropolis hand in hand with a five-thousand-year-old marketplace. Bicycles and autos warred for space, and hawkers were everywhere. The homes were blinding white and set on winding streets with gardens and fountains. Children were everywhere, laughing and playing and looking well-cared-for. Many of the women were driving cars or bicycles.

Romain laughed out loud when she continued to crane her neck as they were driven from the very modern airfield into the center of town. "Were you expecting an oasis with date palms swaying in the breeze?" At her smiling nod, he said, "Well, you won't be disappointed. We have those, too, and I hope to take you to one of them before we return to the States."

Philippa's head whipped his way. "The States!" she echoed. "I don't refer to my country that way," she murmured, her eyes sliding away from his. It struck her that Romain was home. He was a foreigner in her country as she was one here. She had always known that, but somehow the knowledge had never really surfaced until this moment.

Romain pulled her close to him, his mouth at her ear. "Yes, my sweet wife, we come from differing cultures, but that does not change my feelings for you."

She sighed and lifted her arms to circle his neck. "Nor mine for you." She closed her eyes and let herself sink into the pulsing lethargy he always engendered in her. She didn't want to ponder the nagging doubts that seemed to assail her more and more.

The palace was huge and seemed to be made up of a conglomerate of buildings, all domed and white.

Philippa stood in the large courtyard after Romain helped her from the car, and looked around her at the high walls. The clanging of the gate closing behind them made her jump.

"Our house is over here, darling." Romain gestured to an archway that led to a smaller courtyard with its own fountain and a profusion of flowers surrounding it. "See? That's the seraglio. It's not used anymore, even though my uncle has had three wives." Romain leaned over and put his finger on her bottom lip. "Your mouth is hanging open."

"Where do the wives stay?" Philippa whispered, moving closer to him.

"There are four other households in the complex besides mine and my uncle's. Three of my aunts live there. The fourth lives with my uncle." He grinned at her when she nodded slowly. "She was actually his first wife, but since she could have no children, he took others. But none of them produced a son, so I'm the ostensible heir," Romain explained. "But as you know much depends on the opinions of the sheikhs. They could very well choose someone like Halid or one of the other cousins, though they are farther removed from the throne by blood." Damn her, he thought, she was withdrawing from him again as she always did when she was upset.

"I see."

They entered the lovely coolness of the house to the obeisance of the many servants who appeared silently.

Romain gave some orders in Arabic and a young woman stepped forward and steepled her hands in front of her, bowing to Philippa. "This is your maid, darling. Her name is Yasmin. Go with her so that you can freshen up. I must see my uncle." Romain strode down another long corridor, a man wearing a djellaba and carrying a rifle stepped at once to his side.

Philippa's protests that she could change and bathe herself did not deter the smiling Yasmin. "We will have to figure out how to communicate with one another, I suppose, until I learn the language," Philippa said, as she sank down into a pool-sized tub filled with bubbles and essence of attar of roses.

When Romain returned and saw her standing in the shadowy, cool room that had both a garden and lily pad pool, he was struck by her beauty. She was dressed in the silky garments of a woman of the East. "You're too lovely. I may have to keep you in purdah." Romain didn't realize he'd spoken aloud until she turned to look at him, smiling ruefully.

"I must say it's a very cool garment."

Romain took her in his arms, feeling his heart beat quickly as he looked down at her veil-framed face, the turquoise silk almost the same color as her eyes. He kissed the corner of her mouth, feeling her body quiver against him. He had come to tell her that they must hurry because they were dining with his uncle, but the feel of the silk whispering over her skin was more than he could take. His aroused body gently bumped hers.

"You don't have to ask, my sweet husband. The answer is yes," Philippa murmured, wanting to tell him that having him hold her was her security. It was when he was away from her she was prey to the quicksand feelings of doubt about their marriage. She shook away her doubts, trying to gasp at the pain that the thought of losing him engendered, her hands clutching him tightly.

"What is it? Are you ill?" Romain leaned back from her, his one hand coming up to press her forehead. "You've only had bottled water, haven't you?" he glared around him, looking for Yasmin.

"Yes, yes. It's nothing." She turned his face back to her again, her lips fixing to his. Romain, Romain, her darling man! When he held her, he banished the plaguing thoughts of how unsure she was in his country, how alien she felt.

They made love with a desperation that almost hurt them. Philippa dug her fingers into him as though she would nail him to her. He embraced her until she was breathless.

They fell away from one another, knowing that the world would intrude again. Each of them looked up at the silk-swathed ceiling of the room, cocooned in their own disturbing thoughts.

Yasmin didn't turn a hair when she was called by Romain to gather up madame's clothes from the floor and bring her fresh things, but Philippa blushed. He pointed to the clothes with a spate of Arabic, then he smiled at Philippa when the woman left carting the clothes. "I told her I wanted the same color because it matches your eyes."

"She knew what we were doing," Philippa said uncomfortably.

Romain shrugged. "So?"

"I can't be that offhand."

"Don't be silly." Romain kissed her then went through to the bathroom.

After dressing, Philippa could feel her trepidation returning at the thought of meeting the king. By the time she and Romain were ready to leave their home and go along the intricate hallways leading to the center of the palace, she was quaking.

"Darling, don't. You wouldn't be this nervous meeting the President of the United States."

"He only has one wife."

Romain chuckled, trying to mask his own fears about the meeting. He wasn't as nervous about his uncle as he was about Philippa. Why couldn't she see that nothing was going to separate them? Why didn't she know that his uncle wouldn't even try to change Romain's mind about his wife, even if he despised her? She both annoyed and dismayed him as he sensed that she was closing him out again. He turned her in his arms just before they entered the palace, and kissed her. "You know I love you."

"Yes. And I love you." Philippa gave him a grateful but somewhat shaky smile. "You read me too well. You know I'm nervous."

"When the hand I'm holding has tremors, that's a good clue." Romain kissed her again.

It wasn't a throne room! Philippa sagged with relief when they entered a mammoth room covered with costly oriental rugs, both on the walls as well as the floor. A man seated at a high-backed chair behind a desk was listening to a man standing at attention in front of it. When he noticed them, he waved them forward at the same time excusing the other person.

"Ah. So this is your wife, Romain." The silver-bearded man rose, his hawklike features bland, the only life seeming to come from a pair of black, glittering eyes. "Welcome to our country, Philippa." King Haddad of Dharan stretched out his hand to her.

Philippa stared at the hand as though it were a snake. What was the protocol? Kiss it or shake it?

The decision was taken from her when the king caught

her hand, shook it, then leaned over and kissed her cheek. "You are as charming as Romain said you were."

"Thank you, sir," Philippa said shyly.

"Tell me about yourself." The king indicated a couch adjacent to a low table that held a carafe of iced orange juice.

A servant appeared as though by magic and began pouring the juice and dispensing small sections of oranges and plump dates.

"I, ah, there's not much to tell. I'm still at university."

"Studying business, my nephew tells me." The king bit down on a date.

"Yes." Philippa shot a look at Romain, who nodded encouragingly. "I was hoping to start my own accounting firm when I graduated, but—"

"But now you are married."

"Yes."

"American woman often work after they are married," King Haddad stated.

"True." Philippa wasn't sure how to answer him.

"And do you think you will do that?"

Romain leaned forward to spear an orange slice with a toothpick and pop it into his mouth. "My wife hasn't quite decided."

"I see." The king looked from one to the other.

Dinner was the same as the cocktail hour with the king asking provocative questions.

Sometimes Philippa answered, sometimes Romain interjected.

At the end of the evening when they were making their way back to their own quarters, Romain felt as though he walked on coals waiting for her to speak.

When they entered their own rooms, Philippa turned to Romain, her hands threading together. "He's a very intelligent, and sensuous man. Yet, talking to him was like trying to read a book without opening it. He's a very controlled individual."

Romain exhaled and pulled her into his arms. "I'm sure he's very taken with you. My uncle is a man who does not like to be in the company of those he dislikes, or those who bore him. He would have cut short the visit long before he did if that were the case with you."

"Love me." Philippa clung to him, not letting him see her face which she knew mirrored the many fears she felt despite his encouraging words. Dharan and its people were enigmas to her and she had felt rather strange vibrations coming from its leader.

Days stretched into weeks. Philippa had no trouble getting into classes at the university. She welcomed the work as it helped fill the lonely times when Romain was away, seeing to his country's business.

"Not that I know what that business is," she muttered to herself, sitting in their patio room, the cool greenery providing its own air conditioning. She enjoyed studying there. "There must be more to it than rug weaving and oil." She threw down her pencil and stared around the walled courtyard, wishing she had gone with Romain, but knowing it would be boring for her to tag along after him when he spoke to the exporters and workers. The few times that Romain had taken her she had found that a woman's opinions in business were not appreciated.

"It's not like that in the city . . ." Romain had told her one night when he held her in his arms in the huge tent that was larger than some of the homes she visited in the United States. The tent was situated on the edge of the oasis and was used by the king or his representative whenever one or the other was in the area. "Women have many jobs in the city. It's just out here in the country where they cling to the old ways."

"I hated being stared at as though I had two heads when I offer an opinion." She turned in his arms, not wanting acrimony between them, eager for the passion that blotted out their differences.

The next day when Romain had gone to a meeting with some of the sheikhs who had joined him at the oasis, Philippa had walked from the tent to the marketplace. Abdul was at her heels, his red and white djellaba proclaiming him a royal guard. She stopped to watch bartering that was going on between a group of camel drivers. She shivered when she noticed some of the bad-tempered beasts bellowing and snapping at the young boy who was attending them. At first Philippa only gave scant attention to the toddler who staggered away from his mother and was weaving in and out of the grownups around him. When he wandered closer to the camels, Philippa wanted to scream, but she feared to stampede the creatures. Instead, she started to run toward the child, barely hearing Abdul's Arabic oath. She threw herself forward almost under the hooves of an angered beast, snatching up the child and whirling away again. She felt the breath leave her body when she felt a blow at her back, instinctively knowing that one of the beasts had struck at her. Then Abdul had her in his arms, child and all, and mayhem had broken loose. The shouting camel drivers and nomads were loudly cursed by Abdul who told them her royal highness had been in danger and that she had risked her life for the child.

A short time later Romain had burst into the tent and lifted her bodily from the bath she was taking. "Don't you ever endanger yourself like that again!" he shouted, not releasing her even when she'd explained about the circumstances. "You are now the angel of the desert tribes, my darling, but don't do that again." He chuckled shakily, his face pressed to her hair.

Since the incident Romain had not taken her into the desert. Now as she paced the courtyard, trying to concentrate on her books, she could have smacked him for his stubbornness.

That afternoon his mother, who had been visiting the king's palace for a week and whom Philippa had met the first day, came to visit her. She even complained to her mother-in-law. "I could have stayed at home and worked at the university and seen him as much as I do now."

"He's very fearful of your welfare, my dear," his mother said, soothingly, her French-accented English most charming.

Philippa stalked around the fountain, paying cursory attention to the flashing jeweled movements of the large goldfish swimming there. When she lifted her head, she saw a hint of sadness in her mother-in-law's eyes, which was quickly masked. Philippa was puzzled, then she forgot about it when Abdul brought a tray of cool fruit juice for them.

She made friends at the university. Some were Dharanians, but most were Americans or British. The Dharanians became cool when they found out her name and who her husband was. Though the king and his family were much loved, they couldn't be relaxed with a woman who was a royal princess by marriage. Philippa felt more alienated and pulled closer to her other friends.

Peter Lands, an associate professor of Middle Eastern studies at the university became a particularly close friend. They spent long hours discussing his course and a variety of topics over coffee in the vast university union. More often than not there were others involved in the discussions, but sometimes she was alone with Peter at the table, which didn't bother her. She'd had many friends who were instructors when she'd been at the university in California.

When Romain questioned her about it, she was taken aback, then angered. "You have spies, do you?"

"People talk. My uncle mentioned it to me," he answered her stiffly.

"I won't be kept like a hothouse flower," she cried. Her nails curled into the palms. "I was born free and I want to live that way."

"I haven't curtailed your activities." Romain shot back, stung by her remark, and jealous that she was spending so much time away from him.

"I feel smothered."

"Don't be ridiculous." He raised his voice, angry with her that she didn't see how hard he worked, how he strove to be with her as much as possible.

The arguments increased, often over nothing at all. They seemed to pull farther apart.

Philippa was in Dharan six months when she told Romain she was going home.

"It's not possible at the moment," he told her in the stilted tone he used with her lately.

"For me it is."

"I see. Then I'll see you when I return to the States."

"Don't count on it," she yelled after him, tearfully, when he strode from the room.

Her tears turned to fury when he immediately returned to the desert area of Dharan where he was supervising the Dharanian Oil Company's sinking of another well.

Shortly thereafter, she represented the king at a scholarship ceremony at the university, presenting scholarships and congratulating the three students who were to go to England to further their studies.

The king called from London where he was conferring with a British trade group to congratulate her. "I heard that you did a fine job, my dear."

She felt warmed by his call.

Romain, however, did not call.

After a week of silence, she made her own arrangements to go home, wrote a long letter to the king thanking him for his hospitality, and assured him that she thought his country was beautiful. Biting the end of her pen, she added to herself, "Even if I was never quite comfortable with you, I like your country and admire you. At least you called me on the phone. Romain never did."

Drying her eyes, she packed her things, ordered a place on the next flight to London where she would spend a few days with some friends whom she met at Dharan University. In London she was sure she would hear from her husband, but again he didn't call even though she had left a number and told him where she would be.

She returned to the United States, hurt, angry, bewildered, and disillusioned.

"We would still like you to accompany us when we go on sabbatical, darling," Aunt Grace told her when Philippa called her on landing in the United States. "I think you'll like New York and you can continue your studies there."

At first she hesitated, but when she didn't hear from Romain, she decided to go with her uncle and aunt to New York. They would be living on Long Island, but her uncle would be teaching at Columbia in the city.

She buried herself in her studies, trying to blot her husband from her mind. Each day she told herself that what she thought she had in her marriage was just a figment of her romantic imagination; none of it was real.

It was sometime after she had begun her classes at Columbia that she discovered she was pregnant. "I am not telling him about this." She pressed her hand against her middle and cried in her aunt's arms that evening.

"You'll feel differently a little ways down the road and want to tell him," her uncle told her.

She was half convinced he was right. Then she had a miscarriage and she was too heartsick to tell Romain or let anyone else tell him. She became more insular, more restrained as she tried to deal with the terrible pain of loss she was experiencing. Romain became all mixed up in her ambivalent emotions until she felt totally alienated from him.

Six months after the miscarriage she instituted divorce proceedings without ever having seen him or talked to him.

CHAPTER SEVEN

1986

Eight years later Philippa was twenty-six, had graduated from the university with a business degree, and had changed her name. She was Pippa Stonely, adopting her uncle's name, and dropping the Al Adal name completely. She was a successful model in New York, with a half interest in the agency called Rafkin and Stonely. They had six other full-time models and a host of part-time help.

Pip lived in Manhattan now, even though her uncle and aunt had long since returned to the Los Angeles area, her uncle resuming his post at the university.

She called her uncle and aunt once a week to chat, feeling an intense gratitude to them for the loving support they'd given her through the divorce and the long mental and physical rehabilitation she'd undergone after the miscarriage. Even the time she'd spent in the private rehabilitation center in Upstate New York was unknown to anyone but her uncle and aunt and her partner, Lou Rafkin, whom she'd told before they'd signed partnership papers.

She was close to few people, even though she corresponded sporadically with Romain's mother, who wrote to her once a month whether Philippa was able to answer or not. Once or twice she'd even heard from the king.

She'd heard nothing from Romain and never tried to get in touch with him.

She felt her life was full with the agency and had no real desire to seek the company of other men. She buried those feelings in hard work.

"I may be coming back to California for about a month or two. Would you like to put me up?" Philippa asked her relatives one evening when she called them after work.

"For a small fee," her uncle responded, chuckling when his wife gasped on the extension phone.

"George!" Grace admonished when both her niece and husband laughed. "When are you coming, dear? You know your room is always ready for you."

"The end of the week. I need the weekend to prepare. We're going to be involved in the big show at the Lotus." Pip mentioned the exclusive hotel up in the hills overlooking the ocean that had a gold-star clientele. "Some of the movie people are doing this as a benefit for the Sudanese and Ethiopian Relief. They're expecting to make maxi dollars for the fund."

Her uncle whistled over the phone. "I'll have to see if I can scrape up the money to attend. I certainly believe in the concept."

"Not to worry. I've already arranged tickets for you. Good-bye. See you in a few days."

It gave Pip a wrench to see Los Angeles as she steered the rented compact car through the wild traffic of the freeway to where she turned off and drove up into the hills to her aunt and uncle's home.

Romain! He was there in her mind again, she thought resignedly. "So what's new?" she asked herself. "Doesn't he pop up now and then anyway?" She yanked the wheel of the Ford Escort in too sharp a turn up the hill road and earned an angry blare of a horn from another motorist, who had to swerve around her. She shrugged. "Sorry, fella, I was thinking about my bête noire." Bitter humor touched her as she recalled the many pleasant evenings she spent in the company of very interesting men until she would look across a dance floor and think she'd spied her ex-husband. It would jolt her so much that she would make some excuse to get home as soon as possible. The hurt of separating from him had stayed with her, growing more painful in the long months before the divorce was final. In all that time he hadn't attempted to contact her once except through lawyers.

Her aunt and uncle were still in the East at the time of the divorce and George Stonely had cajoled and urged his niece to call her husband.

"Shouldn't he call me?" she'd shot at her uncle.

"You left him," he reminded her gently.

"And I left him a note explaining why."

They had gone round and round, her Aunt Grace watching them worriedly. Pip had not made the call, but it hadn't stopped her from jumping every time the phone rang, thinking it would be Romain. That went on for months even after the divorce was final.

"But not anymore." Pip hit the steering wheel with the flat of her hand as she turned into the curving drive that led to the house. She parked her car in front of the garage and stared blindly at the steel door in front of her. "I'm dealing well with my life, and I will never let another Romain Al Adal into it." Pip turned her head as the front door burst open and her aunt and uncle ran toward the car.

She was out and into their embrace in seconds, burying thoughts of Romain in the recesses of her mind. "It's wonderful to be home."

The next day she was up at five to get to the Lotus Hotel to rehearse for the much publicized charity event.

"Hi, Lois." Pip walked back to change into a sport outfit.

"Hi." Lois hardly noticed Pip. "Did you ever see so many celebrities in your life? What gorgeous men!" she groaned, dragging Pip forward so that she could look through the curtains of the makeshift changing room near the staging area. "Look at them." She pulled Pip in front of her, urging her to look.

"Umm. Yes, you're right. They are good looking, but remember most of them are married and the rest—"

"If you're going to tell me that the others are gay or bisexual, forget it. I won't listen," Lois informed her cheerfully. "I haven't had this much fun since I found most of the chocolate eggs on an Easter hunt when I was ten."

"Enjoy," Pip chuckled, moving back to the long racks of clothing. Lois was one of the models who had been with her since she had bought into the agency with Lou Rafkin, and she was also one of the persons, besides Lou, who Pip was close with. They didn't socialize very much for the simple reason that Pip didn't date as much as her ebullient friend, though Lois had been seeing Lou steadily over the last few months, rather than flitting from boyfriend to boyfriend.

By the time Pippa returned to her uncle and aunt's home, she was bone tired and dragging. "Not to worry," she told her fretting aunt as she sprawled on a lounge next to the pool. "I'm tired but pleased, too." She took a glass of iced lemonade from her aunt with a smile. "It went well. Our girls were really the best and moved through the work well. I think all will be ready for Saturday, despite a few chaotic moments."

Saturday dawned bright and sunny. Even the ever-present smog seemed to be cooperating by disappearing for the day.

The usual tizzy of lost apparel and frantic search was going on when Pip arrived at the Lotus. She had taken a taxi instead of driving because her uncle and aunt would be driving her home.

"Help me," Lois groaned. "I'm doing the 'Blue Moon' number first, and they can't find the belt. I'm dead." Her hands flapped against her sides, her white face testimony to her agitation.

"Not to worry. We'll find it. You were wearing it yesterday for the fitting," Pip said soothingly, taking Lois's limp hand and leading her toward the more solid dressing rooms that had been finished for them the night before. Pip tried to mask her own uneasiness behind a smile. There were minor catastrophes at every show, and each time, though they seemed unsolvable, they were dealt with and handled.

Finally, after searching through three huge bins of accessories, they found the errant belt and some of the color came back to Lois's face.

"I don't know how you and Lou do it," Lois said with a sigh, hugging the belt to her. "You're both totally unflappable."

"Speaking of the Bear, have you seen him?" Pip asked her, knowing that her partner had been scheduled to arrive that morning with their cameraman Ben Hastings.

Lois nodded and pointed to the stage. "He's out there, being important again." She rolled her eyes.

Pip went out and spoke to her partner briefly, knowing that she had to get her own costumes ready before the show as she was in the big overture number with nine other models. "So you and Ben are set for the *Day Magazine* shoot?"

"All set." Lou's heavy ginger-colored brows came together over his nose, his burly body hunching as though he were going to throw a tackle rather than talk. Lou "Bear" Rafkin had been a running back for Georgia Tech and had a short run as a pro before an injury retired him and he turned to his love of photography to make a living. "I changed Melanie for Lois on the shoot," he told her, his mouth tight.

"Oh?" Pip watched her friend. "Why?"

"Because she fits the job," he shot back, his face relaxing as she chuckled. "And don't try to be so damned smart." He leaned forward and kissed her cheek. "Break a leg today."

"Thank you." She looped her arms around his neck and hugged him.

When they heard the crash behind the huge stage backdrop, they both jumped apart and turned to look.

"What the hell is going on?" Lou shouted to Ben who was at the other end of the stage.

"Beats me," Ben shrugged, raising his voice. "Some guy went crashing through the equipment and left in a damned big hurry, knocking things over. Good luck today, Pip."

"Thanks. See you later." She made her way back to the dressing rooms, stepping carefully over television cables, furniture, dress caddies, and sundry equipment needed for the afternoon. It was difficult for her to believe that all would come together for the opening.

Pippa forgot the small annoyances the moment she entered the dressing room and began checking on her girls and their clothes, then taking charge of the four numbers and finale costume she would be wearing.

Her overture outfit was a turquoise silk by the Greek designer, Andrus. It was a swath of material, draped from one shoulder around her body to the ankles, and edged with gold cord. With it she wore gold flat slave slippers. The number was called Greek slave and the gold cording that wrapped the dress to her body was coiled in a top knot in her hair. Her tall slender body seemed to shimmer with gold fire when she moved, the dramatic coloring of her eyes enhanced by the material. Her makeup was a deep turquoise eyeshadow that made her

110

already large eyes seem twice their size. The gold clip on the shoulder and dangling gold hoops in her ears were her only adornment.

"My goodness." Lois came into the closet-sized dressing room. "You'll knock 'em dead, Pippa. You look like a turquoise goddess. You'd better watch out or some of those Arabs in the audience will spirit you away to a harem."

"Arabs?" Pippa felt a ripple of alarm.

"Lou said they were Arabs. Most of them are wearing business suits, but there's one older man wearing a djellaba, who looks very important sitting out there at a table right in the middle. You won't be able to miss him when you go down the runway."

"Older?" Pip coughed to clear the huskiness from her throat.

"Oh, you know, about sixty or so, I guess, with rings on his fingers."

Pippa hadn't realized that she had been holding her breath until she exhaled with a shaky sigh. She tried to smile at her friend when Lois gave her a puzzled look. "Oops. There's the music for the overture."

"Good luck." Lois gave her a thumbs-up sign. She would be on in the second segment of the show with four other models.

Pip stood at the back of the curtain waiting for her signal to go on. She was the last. The curtain lifted and she stepped forward to applause, the model's smile in place, her chin up as she moved in the forceful grace of the model's walk. Swing to the left! To the right! She was in control and enjoying herself. She had done this many times, and though she preferred the business end of the agency, she still enjoyed modeling, and it was sound economics for the firm that she do so. She made a full turn in a controlled energy swing that almost brought her to the tip of the runway. Her smile broadened when she heard

111

the rise of applause, and as she swung back to face the audience, the silk whispering about her legs, she was almost laughing.

Pip looked down into the faces of the audience and froze. King Haddad was smiling up at her and nodding. Her eyes slid left as though they controlled themselves. She felt Romain's presence before she saw him. The menace was a solid mass coming at her. She felt that she could lift her hand and push against it. His hawklike countenance was the same only sharper, thinner, crueler-looking. The glitter of gray in his ebony hair surprised her, then she swung away in a fast turn, forgetting to take the final pirouette in front of the audience. She was almost running as she made her way back to the curtain and through it.

Lou almost caught her in his arms. "Hey! What's up? You hurried that last segment, but they loved you." His eyes narrowed on her. "Something wrong, Pip? Headache?"

"Romain." She tried to smile but her face felt frozen.

"You're kidding! Damn it! You're not." Lou had a sketchy knowledge of her marriage as did Lois, even though few others knew about her disastrous alliance with the Dharanian.

"He's sitting out there with his uncle." Pip tried to stem the tremor that ran through her. "I never expected to see the king here," she murmured inanely. "How stupid. I should have realized that he has business interests here." Her words dribbled away as Lou led her into the dressing room, gesturing at Lois to go on and that he would take care of Pip.

"You need a drink, kid, but since you don't drink, how about some strong tea?"

"Please. I have to go on in the fifth segment," Pip pushed the words through plastic lips.

112

"Hang on. I'll be back as fast as I can." Lou stared at her for a moment then rushed out of the room again.

"He can't be here," she said to her mirror image. She put her hand to her forehead, her skin feeling cold and clammy. "Why do things have to get complicated? My life was moving along nicely. I stopped thinking of him once a day—now it was only once a week or so." As she said this, she saw him appear in the mirror. She blinked as though he were a mirage that she could dissipate by wishing him away. She didn't have the strength to face him.

"Philippa." The silky hardness of his voice was the same, except for the threat that vibrated in the air between them.

"What are you doing here?" She'd had to clear her throat twice before she could force the words from her throat.

"We have a vested interest in the continent of Africa." The cold dictum was like a censure to Pip's lacerated nerves. "Therefore, we want to be part of a charity benefit for it."

"Business, no doubt."

"Ah, how like you to think that the Arab has no heart." His words flayed her. "Surely you remember some warmth?"

"Don't lecture me." She reached down and grabbed the oversized powder puff, willing her hand to cease its shaking. She dabbed at the dampness of her face with the puff, not only to dry it but to mask herself behind the puff. "You'd better leave. We have a tight schedule and are not allowed visitors backstage."

"Your husband can hardly be construed as an ordinary visitor."

"Ex-husband," she said in a strangled voice.

"In my country we are not divorced," Romain shot

113

back, his face twisted with a fury she had never seen him show.

"Then . . . then say the words 'I divorce thee' three times—"

"Don't dictate to me." The words ricocheted around the room.

In the silence that followed Pip tried to repair her makeup, but despite the fact she worked slowly, she had to redo her lip gloss three times. Her eyes kept flashing up to his face in the mirror. "Stop staring at me that way," she said in a choked voice.

He shrugged and lifted a thin, black cheroot from his pocket and lit it with a gold lighter, his eyes roving the room and coming back to her.

It struck her as an hysterical absurdity that he had stopped smoking after they married because she had told him it bothered her that he put his life at risk in any way.

Lou bounced back into the room, balancing a steaming foam cup, the tea bag still in it. "Here you are, Pippa." He kept his eyes on the cup as he approached her, not noticing Romain who had stepped to one side and was leaning against the wall. "Wait. I'll take that out." He dripped the tea bag onto a napkin, then handed the cup back to her, leaning down to give her a quick kiss on the mouth. "Drink that up. That will bring some color back . . ." Lou whirled around in midsentence as he became aware that she was intent on something behind him. He straightened. "Hello." He put out his hand. "I'm Lou Rafkin." Lou watched open-mouthed as Romain jammed his cheroot into an ashtray sitting on the small dressing table, glowered at him, and stalked out the door.

"Whew! Can I assume that was Romain?"

Pip nodded, drinking the scalding brew greedily, almost welcoming the burning sensation on tongue and lips. "Thanks. That helped." She handed him back the empty cup, trying to smile at her partner.

"He looked like he was readying a human sacrifice."
Lou grinned at her, but there was sympathetic understanding in his eyes.

"Both of us, probably." Pip tried to smile, but failed miserably, her hands ice cold as she threaded them together.

"It won't be easy going out there again. Shall I cancel your segment?"

Pip was tempted, but she stiffened her spine. She was not about to let Romain Al Adal and his uncle put a damper on an event that was not only important for charity, but also valuable exposure for their company. "And damage the name of Rafkin and Stonely? Not on your life."

The door opened and Lois stood there, staring at the two of them. "Are you all right, Pip? You looked like you might faint."

"I'm all right now."

"Romain's out there with the king," Lou informed Lois as Pip rose and went behind the screen the girls used for changing.

Lois sank onto the chair Pip had vacated, staring up at Lou, then over at the screen that hid Pippa. "That's awful. Did he recognize her?"

"He just left here, looking as though he were going to firebomb the mayor's office," Lou remarked dryly.

Lois leaned back with a sigh. "You didn't tell us everything about your ex, Pip, but you're not worried he'd be violent, are you?"

"Of course not." Pip was glad the screen hid her face. She really didn't know what Romain would do. In the short time they had been together, they had quarreled about different things and always made up, but she had never witnessed the palpable rage she'd seen in his eyes a few moments ago. She took down the stark black outfit she would wear next and studied it, not really seeing the tiny black bugle beads that made the dress heavier than mere fabric. It was strapless and form-fitting, reaching the ankles. A slit that opened when she walked, exposed her thigh. She would wear four-inch black patent slings with it, her hair to be twisted in a very tight chignon with no side curls. She would wear no jewelry, just a rope of jet twisted into the chignon.

She put on a thin robe and went out to do her hair before she donned the dress.

"Here, let me do your hair," Lois offered, pushing her friend into a chair. "Don't worry, kid. Lou and I will run interference for you."

Pip smiled at her friends, letting Lois brush her hair, then twist it into the stark knot at her neck. No one could block Romain in anything he chose to do, Pip wanted to tell her friends, but she knew, somehow, they wouldn't believe her.

When it was time for the fifth segment, she couldn't seem to keep her hands dry. Her body felt cold and clammy, not just her face. When the curtain swept back, she stepped up, a smile pinned to her lips, her chin up as she went automatically into the moves and walks of the routine.

She reached the end of the runway, pausing for a moment, letting herself smile at the king, who was beaming and nodding at her. Her eyes slid past the brooding, slouching Romain, aware that he never took his eyes from her. She turned with a sigh of relief and retraced her steps, approaching the curtain as though it were sanctuary.

After what seemed like hours of torture, the finale, with all the models in costume, doing a short routine of singing and dancing, had begun.

Pip felt wrung out, flattened. She managed the high kicks in the brief black net costume, and she smiled with the others at the applause and the curtain calls, but she felt boneless with shock and fatigue. She even stood there while the master of ceremonies told the audience the astronomical sum they had collected. After the applause died, he invited everyone to a party in the Lotus ballroom that would be funded by some of the wealthy sponsors that he began naming.

The only names that struck Pip were King Haddad Al Adal and the Dharan Interests, Ltd. Romain was president of the firm. She knew from what Romain had told her that the company funded almost all jobs for Dharanians and provided scholarships to the best schools in the United Kingdom, France, and the United States for boys or girls who chose to attend.

Lois put her arm around her and led her to the dressing room. "Are you going to the command performance?"

"I'm tired. I think I'll just go home with my aunt and uncle. Since I'll be here such a short time, I would really like to visit them."

Lois nodded. "Right." Her eyes said she understood why Pip might not want to go to the party.

While the girls were dressing, there was a knock on the door. Pip was still dressing behind the screen, but Lois was finished, so she answered the door. "Hi. You must be Uncle George and Aunt Grace. I recognize you from the picture Pip keeps on her desk."

"I hope you ladies are ready for that party this evening. I'm looking forward to dancing." Uncle George beamed at an open-mouthed Lois.

"Oh, but I don't think Pip wants to go to the party."

"Lois is right, Uncle George." Pip stepped from behind the screen, smoothing her hands down the front of the silk dress she was wearing.

"Don't be silly, child. This will be a golden opportunity for me to meet your co-workers and your aunt wants to go, don't you, Gracie?"

"Well, if Philippa would rather not . . ." Grace Stonely looked at her niece. "She does look pale."

"Of course she wants to go and unwind, don't you, Pip? You want to dance with your uncle, don't you?"

Pip stared at her relative. She couldn't remember the last time her uncle had asked anything of her. "Of course I want to dance with you. Do you think we'll be able to get them to play a waltz?"

"We'll insist."

Aunt Grace smiled but looked searchingly at her niece. Lois looked relieved that the awkward moment was past.

"You look lovely in that sundress, child. It matches your eyes," her uncle told Pip as he squeezed her arm and led her from the room.

"That sundress, as he calls it, is a very expensive raw silk that the designer Andrus gave Pip to wear," Lois whispered to Grace. "He did mine, too." She indicated the lavender shirtwaist with the short sleeves she was wearing.

"You both look lovely," Grace answered, her brow knit in a frown. "I can't imagine what has gotten into George. It isn't like him not to notice when Pip is tired."

"He did say he thought she should unwind."

"Yes, he did say that," Grace said with a sigh, the worried look not leaving her face as she and Lois followed behind the other two. They traversed several long corridors before they reached the main lobby of the Lotus. They crossed the lobby to a very wide, fan-shaped staircase that led up to the ballroom.

"Come along, child," her uncle urged her through a large archway into the mammoth room already filled with people. Some were seated at tables, others were dancing to the music of the ten-piece band that, at the moment, was playing a soft rock tune. "We'll wait for something more my style."

118

"Yes." Pip tried to smile, but her face felt frozen.

"Here you are. I've been holding seats for you at our table." Lou came up to them. He reached down to kiss Pip's cheek. "Godzilla is here," he whispered against her skin. He moved back from her a bit. "Not to worry. We have our army to protect you, three of the girls and their escorts and Lois and me. We'll see that he doesn't bother you." He didn't see the disbelief on her face as he turned and shook George's hand. "It's good to see you again, sir. I wish you would come to New York more often and visit." Lou then smiled at Grace and Lois.

"Grace and I might do that this year," George answered blandly.

The four of them followed Lou.

Pip didn't look left nor right, and she exhaled in relief when she saw that their table was partially screened by potted plants. She spoke to the models, Lori, Petra, Sue, and their escorts, and sank down into the moderate anonymity of a chair behind one of the palms, between George and Lou.

"I'm glad you're here so that we can get some food. I'm famished." Lori rose to her feet. "It's a wonderful buffet."

"Can we get some for you, Pippa?" Lou looked at her as he helped Lois to her feet.

"I'm not too hungry." Pip meant it. Her mouth was dry with tension, her insides twisted into knots. "Some fruit juice would be nice."

"We'll get you a plate, too." Lois said firmly, earning a grateful glance from Grace.

"We'll be back shortly," her uncle informed her cheerfully as he shepherded his wife and the others before him.

The relative privacy of the table let her relax a bit as she looked out of the window wall at the panorama of clouds and sky. She felt a prickling up her arm. She steeled herself before she turned to look at Romain standing at her elbow, an attendant following him with two plates. She watched silently as the waiter put the food and a bottle of champagne on the table, arranged cutlery and glasses, and left.

Romain seated himself next to her, inhaling her perfume. "The buffet is excellent but the line is very long. Your friends and aunt and uncle won't be back for at least half an hour, maybe more. You need some food. I told your aunt and uncle that I would bring you something. Eat." He speared a small wedge of pineapple with his fork and put it to her mouth.

She took it, chewed, and swallowed it before she reacted. "I can feed myself."

"Good. Do it."

She lifted the fork and picked at the fruit, all at once realizing that she hadn't had anything but fruit juice all day. She worked her way through two rolls, fruit salad, prawns doused in lime juice and served with hot sauce, and two tiny roulades, the wafer thin steaks rolled and wrapped around thin sticks of carrots and onions. She slowly wiped her lips on her napkin, aware that she hadn't yet spoken to Romain. "Thank you. It was very good." She sipped the champagne in front of her, wrinkling her nose.

"It won't hurt you to drink champagne for once. It's a very good year." His silky tone shivered over her skin. Romain lifted his glass to his mouth.

"Your country doesn't approve of drinking alcohol."

He shrugged. "Habits change when one is in another land." His civil smile did nothing to mask the glittering menace of his green eyes. "You're too thin, Philippa," he said abruptly.

She jumped at the harshness in his tone, anger at her own reaction coloring her words. "I'm called Pip now, and I am not too thin to be a model."

"I'd heard that you changed your name to Pip Stonely

and that you were moderately successful in your business," he said in an expressionless voice.

"Through your personal CIA, no doubt."

"Actually my uncle told me."

Pip felt her mouth sag. "Your uncle?"

"He has a very efficient network of information." He shrugged, then gestured that the table be cleared. In seconds it was done. "Would you like a sweet?"

Pip shook her head, then stiffened, when she felt herself lifted to her feet.

"I'm sure you'd like to dance."

It angered her when her pulse fluttered as his arm slipped around her waist. "Forget the Genghis Khan imitation. I'm not impressed." She tried to wrench her arm free, but felt his fingers dig tighter into her flesh.

When they reached the floor, he turned her into his arms, and the beguine music the band was playing seemed to become a part of him. It angered him that his body responded to her swaying nearness at once. His arms convulsed on her, bringing her even closer to him.

"Not so tight," she gasped, pushing at his shoulders. "What are you doing at this gathering anyway?"

"My uncle issued a royal command and said that he was coming, and that he wished me to attend. Many of our people work in the Sudan and Ethiopia, and despite what you think of us, we are not blind to the misery of Africa."

"I'm sorry. I didn't mean to imply that you or Dharan would not help the unfortunate," Pip mumbled, looking at his ruffled shirt front, knowing that the slightly curling hair on the chest had always been an erotic stimulant to her emotions. No! She jerked back from him, trying to blot the runaway thoughts of Romain.

"Stop trying to pull away. I'm not letting you go. Relax. You can't deny that we always danced well together."

"I'm not trying to deny it." She shot him an angry look, then looked back at his shirt. No, she couldn't do that. Lord, there was nowhere to look when Romain held her.

"Ah, this is the rhythm you like." Romain gave a hard laugh and swung her free of his body as the music changed, the swing rhythm chasing some off the dance floor.

A giddy sense of release filled Pip as she felt the freedom that dancing always engendered in her. She couldn't mask the smile as she watched Romaine gyrate in controlled motion in front of her.

When they came together, their bodies had a sinuous friction as they touched one another. Romain felt as though his blood had truly begun to boil. Her bones were so fragile that he could have snapped any one of them with one hand, but there was strength in her face, challenge in her eyes, and even a wariness that had not been there before. He had wanted to blot her from his mind, but nothing had worked. It had bothered him more than he thought it would when his uncle's operatives, investigating the show for the safety of their ruler, had told him the names of all the persons involved with the show at the Lotus. Only fierce pride and sense of duty to his uncle's dicta kept him from balking and refusing to come. He had known where she was and almost every move she made from the time they'd separated. Yet, it hadn't occurred to him that he would see her here. He had been flummoxed at seeing her, all the ease of manner he had with other women withered to bumbling idiocy with Philippa. He had been tempted to confront her more than once, but he had always held back. Other women he had found boringly easy to handle. With his young wife he felt sliced open and bleeding to death.

"It's a rock tune, not a slow one," Pip whispered to

him, bringing him out of whatever reverie that was making him frown.

"So it is. Shall we sit this one out?" His steely sophistication ran over her skin like a cattle prod.

"Fine." She cleared her throat, lifting her chin as she preceded him back to the table. Black humor assailed her as she watched the women in the room turn and stare at Romain, many openly assessing him and predatory. They're welcome to him! Bitter resentment that he had come back into her life seemed to drown her for a moment.

When they reached the table now occupied by the rest of her group, Pip felt out of breath and feverish.

"Gosh, don't you like that beat, Pip?" Sue quizzed her, her eyes running over Romain. "I'd love to dance to that."

"Good. So would Romain. Dance with him." Pip dared the stars, feeling the phosphorous coming off Romain as he turned to the model, inclined his head toward the dance floor, and smiled.

"I don't mind you pulling the tiger's tail, but don't be too ambitious. He might bite your friends," Lou said from the side of his mouth.

"Make up your mind. Is he Godzilla or a tiger?" Pip snapped, reaching for the champagne and gulping a mouthful, then coughing.

"Lord, he really got to you, didn't he?"

Pip nodded, her eyes watering as she continued to cough. Her uncle began to pat her back.

"Are you all right, dear?"

Pippa nodded, waving at her uncle to stop.

"All set?" Her uncle beamed at her.

What was making Uncle George act like the Good Humor Man this evening? Pip wondered, sipping water slowly.

"Romain looks wonderful, doesn't he?"

"Wonderful, Uncle George?"

"I invited him to brunch tomorrow after church." He beamed at his agape wife and horrified niece.

"George . . ." Grace's voice faded. "He'll want quiche. I planned scrambled eggs and broiled tomatoes."

"Fine."

"Make sauteed toadstools," Pip muttered, shooting suspicious glances at her uncle.

Grace looked at her blankly for a moment. "Oh, I don't think so, dear. Even if you cooked them very well, I'm sure they aren't good for you."

"Pippa made a joke."

"I did not." She glared at her uncle. When had he become so insensitive?

"You and Lou must come, too, Lois," Uncle George said grandly. "You'll enjoy talking with Romain. He's a very cosmopolitan man."

"Viper," Pip said under her breath.

"Even if you baked them, I shouldn't think it would help." Her aunt pulled her napkin between her fingers and rolled her eyes at her husband. "I'll make tomatoes instead."

"Good idea." Uncle George patted his wife's hand.

"Let's have our dance, Uncle, and then it's time to go." Pip rose to her feet.

"Not yet." Romain was behind her chair. "I think you should speak to my uncle."

"Of course she should," her uncle concurred.

Uncle George looked like a Cheshire cat when he smiled, Pippa thought.

"I would like to speak to the king," she said woodenly, aware that Lori and Petra were looking at her quizzically. She wanted to shrug off the arm Romain put around her waist, but decided not to make a fuss.

"Wise of you." Romain could feel the tense struggle of her body beneath his hand.

Philippa lifted her chin as she approached the royal table, seeing an aide whisper to the king so that he turned and smiled at her.

He rose to his feet and opened his arms. "My dear, how happy I'll be to have you under my roof again. I am flying to New York to have some tests made at Cornell Medical Center." King Haddad leaned over and kissed Philippa's cheek, startling her because he had never done that. "I've taken a home on Long Island for a month, and I want you to stay there with me so that we can visit."

Philippa knew her mouth was hanging open and that Romain had stiffened at her side, but she was too stunned by what his uncle had said to react to anything else.

CHAPTER EIGHT

Philippa flew back to New York two days after Lou and the other models, unable to cure the headache that had nagged her since the royal invitation. She groaned silently as she recalled the king's insistence, how he had overrode every suggestion and argument that she and Romain had made until she acquiesced. She had been stymied when King Haddad had beamed and announced to Romain that he expected him to be there as well, then turned to an aide and informed him that they would be leaving for the hotel at once.

"Why didn't you refuse?" Pip had tackled Romain at her uncle's house the next day when he arrived shortly after Lou and Lois for the brunch.

"He is my uncle and Dharan's leader. As such I must obey him," Romain told her, furious with her that she had posed such a question. He had intended seeing her again with or without his uncle's order. Damn her! He was going to make her explain why she had left him. He tamped down the voice in the core of him that told him to let go. The fury he'd felt when he'd been served with divorce papers threatened to swamp him now. He'd tried to lose himself in other women, but Philippa was always there.

It was left to Lois and Grace to converse with Romain at the brunch. Pip was too irked and frustrated to even look at him. How dared he come back into her life! She

126

would have nothing to do with him. She'd seen the way he'd held Sue when they had danced last night. She'd watched the way Lori coiled her arms around his neck and the amused knowing look on Romain's face, his hand rubbing the model's lower back. Lecher! She had hated the feelings that seeing him had engendered in her. She'd wanted to hit him. She was a better person than that, she adjured herself. She had never wanted to hit another person, not even Romain when they had lived together and argued, but now that he had come back into her life, she felt like grinding her teeth and throwing things. Philippa had engaged Lou in conversation about one of their accounts. An hour later she couldn't recall one thing they'd discussed.

Now, here she was in a plane descending to La Guardia Airport, still trying to figure how she was going to get out of staying at the king's home on Long Island.

She deplaned and went directly to the baggage pickup. She'd sent most of her things back with Lou and the models, but she still had one heavy case to cart. As she leaned down to retrieve it from the movable pickup, a hand was in front of her.

"I'll take that," Romain said in flat tones. "Don't bother asking what I'm doing here." His hard mouth curved cynically as he looked at the hordes of people around him. "Since I don't enjoy shouting to make myself heard, perhaps it would be better if we talked in the car." He strode away carrying her heavy case easily, almost disappearing in the crowd before Pip could react.

"Damn you, Romain Al Adal," she panted as she ran after him, her purse banging against her leg. "Wait," she called as he moved up the escalator and toward the door. When he didn't even turn around, she ended up running. "Oops. Sorry, madam," she apologized to an older woman she'd just bumped into on the escalator.

"I should think so." The woman yanked at her purse and glared.

When Pip looked up, Romain was holding an outer door for her, and a liveried chauffeur had just taken her bag and stowed it in the trunk of the limousine at the curb. "What are you doing to that poor woman?"

Stung, Pip inhaled a deep breath. "Nothing would have happened to that woman if you hadn't run off with my bag. I was chasing you and bumped her."

"Ridiculous." Romain took her arm and all but threw her into the vehicle.

"Stop being a caveman."

"Good afternoon, my lady." The chauffeur touched his forehead in obeisance to her before he shut the door and went around the car to slide under the wheel.

"How are you, Abdul? Is your family well?" Pip recognized one of Romain's bodyguards who had been her own personal guardian when she became Romain's wife. She had always liked the huge, burly man, his intelligence masked by an expressionless mien. She pointedly ignored Romain, sitting as far away from him as she could on the plush upholstery of the Rolls-Royce.

"We are all well, my lady."

Romain leaned forward and closed the glass.

"How do you know I was through speaking?" she asked him frostily.

"I shouldn't think you'd want to distract a driver especially in such heavy traffic as this." He waved his arm at the snarl of autos honking their way toward the tunnel leading into Manhattan.

"There was no need for you to pick me up. I was going to take a cab as I always do."

"My uncle wants you to move out to the Island at once for the three weeks of your stay."

"I never said I'd stay three weeks. I need time to think," she answered in fading accents.

"I'm sure you don't want to upset him. He goes in for a few tests tomorrow, and he would like to speak to you this evening."

"But wouldn't it be more efficient if I stayed at my apartment, then I could visit him in the hospital right here in town?"

Romain shrugged. "He did want to see you tonight. I'll tell him you won't come."

"No! Don't tell him that." Pip wanted to smack him. She couldn't be in his company five minutes without feeling that way. She inhaled deeply and sat in silence for several minutes. The king had never been a demonstrative man when she'd lived in Dharan, but he had been kind to her. The flashing red lights of the tunnel seemed to telegraph the danger she would be putting herself in if she went out to his house. "I was just trying to figure things out. I have to work every day, the king will be in the hospital . . ."

"My uncle has arranged for you to work at the house. There is a charity benefit he wants to put on in New York like the one at the Lotus. He thought you could lay out the bare bones for him, for a fee, of course . . ."

"Of course," Pip said woodenly. Her hand itched to slap him. "I'll have to talk to Lou."

"It's all been arranged with him," Romain said blandly.

"I see."

Romain could feel anger crackling across the space between them and it gave him a black satisfaction to have jolted her. Damn her! She had left him! What was worse he had seen her face every time he had tried to make love to another woman.

He didn't even know why he had made that statement about their divorce not being final when they'd met in California. They were divorced, despite what he had inferred about the religion of Dharan. He had embraced no faith, not even the Christian faith that his mother had instructed him in. Philippa made him crazy! He glanced at her as she sat next to him lost in thought. She was still gloriously beautiful, her raw beauty now refined to a sophisticated loveliness. If her profile was too finely etched, if her hip bones showed through the cotton skirt more than they should, her very fragility was enticing to him in the extreme.

The car broke through the lines of traffic heading down Fifth Avenue.

"You have a very fine address in Manhattan," Romain drawled, not wanting to hear her answer.

"Lou Rafkin's uncle left him one of the small apartment buildings not too far from the museum. I rent from him."

"How convenient," Romain observed silkily, wanting to shake her for letting herself be compromised in such a fashion.

"Lou is my partner and my friend. I'll give you that information for free. Nothing else about my personal life are you entitled to know," Pip snapped, opening the door of the limousine before Abdul could come around to help her and heading toward the steps that led up to the old-fashioned foyer of the building. There was an apartment in the basement that the custodian and his wife occupied. There were five floors above, each floor being an entire apartment. Pip lived on the third floor, Lou on the fifth.

She didn't realize that Romain had followed her until she turned and faced front in the elevator. "There was no need for you to come with me."

"Could you carry all the things you'll need for your stay at the house?"

She sagged tiredly. "I would much rather face the packing tomorrow."

"Fine." Romain held the elevator door for her in the small hall in front of her door, his hand out for the key.

"Just pick up your mail, read your messages, and I'll send Abdul and Ersa to fetch your things in the morning."

Pip handed him the key, feeling off balance. "You don't run my life."

"Do you have a better idea?" He followed her in the door and shut it behind him.

"No." Her chest felt tight with anger.

At the slight tap on the door, Romain opened it and let Abdul enter and bring in her bag. The chauffeur smiled at her and left at once.

She warred with herself for a moment, then shrugged. "If you'd like anything to drink, the cabinet is in the corner, or I could make you coffee."

"Nothing." Romain looked around the roomy apartment, knowing full well that she could never have afforded such luxury if Rafkin hadn't provided it. Rage twisted his lips.

Pip went into the bedroom and closed the door and leaned back against it closing her eyes. "Lord, how am I to stand it for three weeks?" She pushed away from the door and went to the bathroom off the bedroom, cleaned some of the travel grime from her face, and stared at her image in the mirror over the sink. "Why did I let myself be stampeded into this?"

She walked back into the bedroom, seating herself at the Chippendale desk that had come with the apartment and began a list of the clothing she would want Abdul to bring. She left it propped against the mirror on the dressing table and went out into the other room.

Romain was standing in front of her bookcase, an apple in his hand, studying the books.

"I'm as ready as I'll ever be."

"Here's your mail." Romain indicated a few letters on the table near a chair and one in his hand.

"That's private." She crossed the room in long strides,

scooping up the things from the table, then pulling the letter that she could see was from BeBe Nestor nee Linze, her friend from university days, from his hand.

"Bite?" Romain held the apple out to her.

She bit into the apple without thinking, the action taking her close to him. It struck her with the force of a gale wind that that was one of the things they had often done together. They had shared food, fruit, sandwiches. Pip could feel her body reddening as she stared up at him, the unchewed bite still in her mouth, his mocking smile telling her that he knew what she was thinking.

She stepped back and chewed the offending bit of apple, her stomach growling in protest at not having been properly fed for several hours since she could not bring herself to eat airline food.

Romain put his hand on her abdomen, setting down the apple. "You're hungry. I could make you something."

"You? Cook?" Pip wheezed, feeling as though she should run but that all her faculties were on shut down.

"I make a fabulous omelet." Before he even thought about it, he'd leaned down and kissed her mouth, a feather touch that shot his blood pressure through the roof. He whirled away from her and went to the kitchen.

"Abdul," Pip said, once she'd found her voice again. "He'll be waiting in the car."

Romain shrugged. "He doesn't mind. I'll call him." He picked up the wall phone in the kitchen aware that she had followed him and was listening as he gave terse orders in Arabic to the chauffeur. "There." He turned to look at her, the wide turquoise eyes making his heart thud against his chest. "You chop the vegetables. I assume you have peppers and onions."

"No." She didn't want him cooking in her apartment. She didn't want him touching her utensils and plates. She had the feeling if he did he would put his mark on them and she would never rid him from the apartment. "Don't

132

cook," she told him, recalling the times when they had gone on safari into the desert when Romain had cooked for them. Despite the incredulity she'd shown before, she knew that he was rather adept in a kitchen. She didn't want that intimacy with him. The kiss he'd just given her had been shattering to her spirit. She had to get him out of her home.

Romain stared at her for a long moment. "All right. Then I'll take you to a little supper club I know. You won't object to that?"

She did, but since she preferred that to having him in the apartment, she shook her head.

She took a few more toiletries with her, stuffing them in a canvas carryall.

They returned to the car where Romain gave instructions to Abdul.

"I'm not really dressed for cabaret."

"There's a very quiet French place with a strolling violinist and delectable food that I know."

"Fine."

When they reached La Paysanne, it looked closed, but when Romain opened the door the subtle odor of French cooking assailed Pip's nose and she began to salivate.

Romain ordered in excellent French. Then he looked up, his eyes narrowing on her. "Perhaps you would have preferred to order yourself."

"No. A cheese omelet is fine, thank you."

He felt a smile touch his mouth. "I see you've kept up your French."

She laughed, feeling out of breath as his lazy grin ran over her skin, more relaxed than she'd been since she talked to him in California. "Not as much as I would have liked, but I can still understand most things." She recalled the long hours Romain had spent with her trying to teach her Arabic, French, and Italian. Her high school French and Latin had been a little help, but Romain, who was fluent in many languages, had been a patient and loving teacher. She didn't want to remember the number of times the tuition had taken place in bed or in the hot tub when their bodies had rubbed against one another in velvet abrasion, the love words issuing from his mouth in many tongues.

Pip looked away from him trying to concentrate on the couple who were on the postage stamp-sized dance floor, swaying to the strains of the "Anniversary Waltz."

"Shall we dance?"

"Ah, no. I imagine our food will be here in a moment." She had no intention of letting him hold her as he had in California. She hadn't been able to sleep that night for thinking of it.

"As you wish," he responded tightly.

In the long minutes that it took to be served the fluffy entrees, Romain offered no other conversation.

Pip felt as though her tongue had cloven to the roof of her mouth. Conversational openings ran like loose marbles around her head, but she remained mute.

The omelets were airy, redolent of herbs, served with thick slices of homemade bread and a crisp green salad.

Pip felt so uncomfortable with Romain she was sure that she wouldn't be able to swallow a mouthful, but at the first taste her hunger took over. She couldn't stem the satisfied sound when she bit down on the fresh mushrooms and sliced almonds in the salad laced with a subtle sweet and sour dressing.

"You haven't changed. You still are very vocal about your food." The smile changed his face, softened it, blurred the harshness of his mouth.

"Yes," Pip said and laughed back, relief flooding her that he was no longer angry. It gave her such joy to see him like that! He had always looked that way when they were first married—carefree, with the sensuous droop to his mouth that was wildly erotic to her.

134

He stared at her. He had been wrong. She wasn't as beautiful as she once was. She was far more stunning, the life force like a rampage in her. She was a flame! Her hair captured all the light in the room and refracted it from the shining depths. He felt lyrical, poetic as he gazed at her. Her eyes were a turquoise glitter that burned and froze everything in their gaze. Her skin was like a fiery pearl, luminescent, soft, alive. He remembered how she had looked to him when she had lain next to him, nothing but a fine gold braided chain around her neck. It had been his first gift to her and she had never removed it.

As though his hand had a life of its own, he leaned forward and pulled the neckline of her blouse away from her skin. He caught a glimpse of the creamy swell of her breasts and the rich gleam of the gold chain. "So you still wear it. No! Don't pull back. You'll break the strand. It's very delicate. Actually, this is ten strands of gold chain so fine that you could thread the eye of a needle with each one."

Pip looked into the green glitter of the eyes so close to her, her mind turning blank from their power. "I didn't know that."

"I thought I told you." He wasn't sure what they were really saying, but the warmth pulsing through him at her nearness was so welcome that he didn't want to break the spell. She was a Circe!

"No."

The strolling violinist neared their table, smiling. When he saw the barbaric look Romain shot his way, he melted away from the corner table.

Romain threaded his fingers through hers, his other hand touching the third finger of her left hand. "You've taken off your rings." His eyes lifted to her face. "You sent me back your engagement ring. You shouldn't have done that. It belongs to you."

"No." Pip tried to clear her throat of its huskiness.

135

"You told me that it had belonged to your mother and was part of your family's heritage."

"True, but it was given to you, so that you might pass it on to your own son one day."

Pain so sharp she caught her breath lanced through her. She had wanted a child! Not a day passed that she regretted not having Romain's child. She lifted her coffee cup and sipped, trying to mask the feelings that were gushing through her.

"What's the matter? What is it?"

"Coffee was too hot."

"Oh?" Romain frowned at the cup that had sat for minutes at the side of her plate.

"Shall we go? I'm tired." Pip shot to her feet, startling the hovering waiter and making Romain's eyes fix on her.

He signed the bill, still watching her. Then he rose and helped her on with the embroidered cotton knit sweater she'd worn as a buffer to the coolish spring night.

She walked ahead of him, feeling his eyes like a prod on her spine. She knew from experience that Romain didn't like mysteries, that he would poke until he unraveled it.

Once in the relative anonymity of the dark car, she moved as far to the opposite side from him as she could and stared out the window. When she felt the seat depress with his weight as he slid closer to her, she stiffened.

"Tell me." His breath whispered against the back of her neck.

"No." She didn't pretend to misunderstand him. Her hands threaded together tightly. She had the feeling that if he said one more thing she would split down the middle into two pieces.

He turned her in his arms, holding her so that the passing lights flashed in her face. "Something's hurting you." He folded her to him, holding her tightly but

136

gently. "I can't allow that." His voice was harsh. He felt as though he were bleeding from every pore, as though his life blood was leaving him in a steady stream. He couldn't bear her to be hurt. He felt as though he'd lived in a maelstrom since his marriage to Pip. Not once in the early days, when she'd left him, did he doubt she would return. When she didn't come back, he had begun drinking to sleep at night. His uncle had chided him, not only for breaking the laws of his country that forbade drinking, but because of the bad effects it was having on his health and on his duties as his uncle's minister throughout the world.

Now she was back in his arms and it felt as though she had never left. He pressed his mouth into her hair, closing his eyes. He would analyze his foolish behavior later. At the moment she needed to be comforted, and he needed to hold her. When he felt her one hand slide around his waist, his breath went out of rhythm and his heart thundered in his chest.

Pip wanted to scream at him to release her. He would tear her life apart if she didn't keep him at a distance. If only he didn't feel so good, so warm, so right. She closed her eyes in fatigue, promising herself that she would only stay in his arms a moment, then she would ask him to sit in his own side of the automobile.

"Philippa," Romain whispered, not wanting to disturb her as the big car purred up the circular drive leading to the front door of the house on Long Island. "Pip. Wake up."

"What?" she lifted her head from his shoulder. "Oh. I fell asleep. I'm sorry."

"Don't be. You were exhausted. You work too hard." He told her gruffly, reluctant to release her.

"Oh, lord. The king is waiting on the steps." She pushed at her hair, knowing that her face was flushed with sleep and she had very little makeup on.

137

"You look fine." You look beautiful, Romain amended in his mind as she turned stricken eyes up to him just as Abdul opened the car door. "Just fine." He slid out of the car and leaned in to take her hand and help her to stand. He turned and stared up at his uncle, challenge in every line of his body. "Here she is."

"I can see that." The older man chuckled at the thunderous look of his nephew. "Come in, child, and see our new home." The king extended his arms to her.

Not hesitating, Pip walked into the embrace, hugging the older man and sighing. "It's a beautiful home and so big," she said.

"Yes, my aide told me that I really needed one hundred and thirty rooms not merely eighty," he said and laughed when Pip did.

"Hakim will take you to your wing, child. I'm sure you are tired from your flight."

"Thank you, sir. I am."

"Would you like a meal sent to your room?" The king accompanied her to the foot of the staircase that rose from the center of the hall. It split in two directions on the first floor which had a smaller staircase running to the third floor. The huge foyer was three stories high.

"I'll take care of her," Romain interrupted abruptly.

"Good," his uncle said easily, his eyes dancing, not seeming to notice the smoldering look his nephew had fixed on him. "Then you get a good night's sleep, my dear, and we'll talk tomorrow about the plans for the charity benefit, shall we?" King Haddad's clipped British accent had a thread of amusement.

"That will be fine. After breakfast?" Pip felt ill at ease, aware of Romain's anger and his uncle's seeming ignorance of it.

"Fine." The king turned away followed by his secretary and bodyguard.

Romain looked up at her. "I'll have Abdul bring up

your overnight bag. Tomorrow all your things will be here. For tonight, look in the closet. Some of your things that you left in Dharan are there and you can use them." He spun on his heel and strode to the back of the house before Pip could respond.

"This way, madame. My name is Ersa and I'm to be your maid."

Pip followed the young woman up the stairs, and wondered if she could be a relative of Abdul's. She knew from her days in Dharan that many of Abdul's fellow tribesmen were servants to the Al Adal family and had been for centuries. She was too tired to question the girl, just grateful to get to her room.

"I will run a bath for you, madame."

"A shower will be fine."

"Lord Romain said that you are to soak in a hot bath. He left orders for us before he went to pick you up from the plane."

Pip was too tired to argue. She nodded. "All right. There's no need for you to remain, Ersa. I'll take my tub, then I'm going right to bed. Good night."

Ersa salaamed. "I'll put your night things on the bed."

"Thank you." Pip smothered a yawn behind her hand and watched as the girl left the room.

She stripped off her clothes, tossing them on a chair, and walked to the bathroom dressed only in panties and bra. These she removed in the bathroom that was the size of her apartment, the floor and ceiling in peach-colored tile with a recessed tub in the same shade and a separate shower stall. The tub was all ready steaming with fragrant water as she stepped down into it.

She wriggled her head against the satin-covered neck pillow and stared around her. "If I had the strength I would laugh at you," she told the gold gargoyle faucets. She closed her eyes, feeling the smile on her lips.

When she heard the door open some moments later,

she was halfway between sleeping and waking. Her eyelids fluttered open.

"Hello." Romain looked down at her, seeing the intriguing outline of her uptilted breasts through the frothy cloud of bath bubbles. "Comfortable?" he questioned throatily.

"Yes. I thought we'd said good night."

"Did we?"

"Yes." Pip felt out of breath, fearing to move.

"That looks inviting." He closed the door behind him and began unbuttoning his shirt. In seconds he'd stripped the clothes from his body.

Pip watched him. "You can't"

"I can."

"Sleepy," she managed in fading accents.

"I'll hold you while you sleep. I did in the car."

"Romain."

"Stop. Don't bother with reasons why I shouldn't. I'm not listening."

Pip watched as he stepped down into the tub, the water forming a mini tidal wave as he settled his big frame next to her.

"Hot."

"Yes." Pip said in a choked voice, feeling his muscular leg as it brushed hers.

"Are you comfortable?" he slid an arm around her.

"Yes. Romain, I don't want . . ."

"Shh. Just relax."

"How can I?"

"Close your eyes."

She fully intended to tell him to get out of there. Instead, she closed her eyes, her weight sinking against him.

"Nice." His breath ruffled the curling tendrils of damp hair at her temples.

"Yes."

Her skin was like cream as he tightened his arm so that their bodies were touching hip to hip.

"We'll turn into prunes."

Romain shrugged, his mind so drugged with her nearness that he didn't want to speak.

"What will the maid say?" Pip said with a sigh, her body floating and weightless.

"Nothing, if she values her job." Romain's voice crackled with the arrogance that Pip remembered.

"Ruthless man."

"Not with you."

Pip's eyes flew open as his words penetrated. Hadn't he been ruthless with her? No! The answer spilled through her blood. She had always expected he would. When they had courted, he had ridden roughshod over every reason why she shouldn't marry him, not that she had really wanted to thwart him. But after the ceremony he had been gentle with her. If, perhaps, he was a little overprotective at times, she realized now that much of the problem could have been mitigated had she talked to him about it. She had given too much of her life over to him, a voice reminded her. Yes, she had done that, but without any urging from Romain. She should have been more open about her feelings. Instead, she had allowed irritations to simmer and fester until they grew into resentments.

"Who are you wrestling now in that convoluted mind of yours?" Romain had his mouth pressed to her forehead, but he could feel the tenseness in her body. It telegraphed to him the inner struggle she was having about something.

"You." Pip whispered the word, surprising herself by admitting that. She had spent so much time hiding her feelings from Romain, burying the doubts, trying to be the person she was sure he wanted her to be that at the end of the marriage she had found it hard to be straight with him on anything. Over the years there had been many revelations about her life with Romain that she'd had to face, and with it a bitter acceptance of her childish attitude.

"It's obviously not good."

"Soul-searching is uncomfortable at any time, and I've done my share . . ." she hesitated, not sure what she was going to say.

"If I understand you correctly, you are thinking about us in the past, of course, and maybe questioning your actions or mine?"

"Both. Mostly mine." She shrugged. "Silly thing to do in a hot tub."

"I can think of things we did that were more enjoyable . . . but this might be more important to us. Tell me what you were thinking."

She shook her head. "I don't want to do that."

Romain tightened his hold. "All right. Then let's make idle conversation." He wanted her to tell him what she was thinking, and yet there was an angry part of him that wanted to tell her to go to hell, that she'd discarded their marriage like an old coat, terminated their union, that it had taken him long months to even function at his job after she left him.

She twisted her head to look up at him. "I can feel a little tension in you. I would have to assume that your soul-searching is irking you."

"You walked away from our marriage without a backward glance." He fired the words at her, feeling her stiffen and pull away from him.

"We should get out of here," Pip said in a stricken voice.

"Let's talk first."

"You were too old for me," Pip blurted, then gasped as his hands dug into her flesh.

"Damn you," he said hoarsely, his fingers kneading the

skin he'd just bruised. "You certainly know how to wound me."

She felt as though her nerves had jumped through her skin, but the words kept coming. "I never seemed to be able to match your sophistication no matter how hard I tried." She cleared her throat, keeping her eyes on him. "I didn't like being relegated to the back room, figuratively speaking, when important matters were being discussed."

"My country used to be that way, but we have made great strides," Romain said stiffly. "My mother still heads a relief organization that has received citations of honor from countries in need. She sits on the board of directors of our company," Romain fired the words like missiles. "I never wanted you to be any different than the way you were when I married you. I never tried to change you."

"But I changed. Maybe that was one of the problems." She looked up at him, shivering at the emerald hardness of his eyes.

"Is that fear I feel in your body?" he seemed to exhale sulfur.

Pip watched him for a moment, her eyes running over his face as though she wanted to review every bit of him. "No. At least not the kind of fear that made me think you'd strike me." She closed her eyes for a moment. "I think we should end this conversation and get out of here."

"Tell me." He shook her gently, the water lapping around them.

"I was never afraid of you, as such, but I did fear your contempt, the icy rejection I had seen you levy on persons who displeased you. I was never knowledgeable enough to handle that side of you and"—she paused and looked around the steamy room—"I was afraid that same disdain would be turned on me one day."

143

"Is that why you left me?"

"That's not all of it, but yes, that was one of the reasons."

"I see."

"Do you?" Pip shook her head again. "Excuse me. Romain, but I stopped thinking about our relationship a long time ago, and I don't think it helps to dredge it all up now. It's better to leave—"

"Don't say it." He lifted her chin, his mouth coming down on hers.

She braced herself, expecting his hard mouth to crush hers.

Instead, he let his lips brush hers in a soft quest, his tongue touching her bottom lip, urging it to part for him. When he felt the softness open, his tongue pierced the warm depths, his heart thudding against her. He rolled her body on top of his without releasing her, letting the softness of her slide down his hardened body. He wanted her! "You're tired," he said, harsh regret in his voice.

"Romain." She sighed, her eyes fluttering closed.

He let his mouth slide across her cheek so that he could nip at her ear. "You still taste very good, Pip."

"Thank you." She swallowed, her wet hands sliding over his shoulders. She tried to smile at him, but her eyes didn't quite meet his. Nothing had changed! He kissed her and she folded. "Tomorrow comes very early if I am to speak to the king before he leaves for the hospital."

"Of course." A hard laugh escaped him as he saw the surprise flit over her features. "If you were not so tired, my dove, you wouldn't have escaped tonight." He pressed his one finger on her lips when she opened them to speak. "And not all your sputtering to me that it wouldn't have happened means a thing." He stood, bracing himself as he pulled her upright beside him. "But tonight you're tired, and as much as I would love to rediscover your body, it can wait until a more opportune time." He set her on the tile surrounding the tub and reached for a warm bath sheet, which he wrapped around her.

"Sure of yourself as always," Pip blustered, knowing that she would have let him love her even if she was dead on her feet, and angry with herself for feeling that way. "That must have been one of the other things about you that chased me from Dharan . . . your arrogance."

"Not so." Romain stood in front of her naked, removing the towel and rubbing lotion on her shoulders. He backed away and handed her the bottle. "On second thought you had better do this, or all my good intentions will disappear."

Pip wanted to smack him because she hadn't wanted him to stop. "You aren't the only one who makes decisions about . . . about that sort of thing."

"About making love? No, certainly not. We both do." He touched her nose with one finger, then let his eyes rove her body. "Lotion yourself tonight. Tomorrow night I'll do it, and we'll continue our delightful interlude when you're rested." He caught up a towel and strode from the room.

"That's what you think," Pip said with a shaky breath. "How do you know I won't be busy tomorrow night?" she raised her voice in the empty room.

CHAPTER NINE

Pip was appalled when she woke and found that she had slept through the breakfast hour she was to have spent with the king. Jumping out of bed, she rang for the maid, then galloped to the bathroom to hurry through washing, shampooing, and toothbrushing. When she returned to the room, the maid was there smiling at her.

"Madame, his royal highness sends his regrets that he could not wait for you to waken, but that he will see you this evening."

"The king must have been furious," Pip whispered, sinking down onto the dressing table stool, a towel swathed about her head and one around her body.

"The king? Ah, but no, madame, it was Prince Romain who told me this. He accompanied our great ruler into the city."

"Oh? Oh, yes, of course he would." Pip looked around her at a loss for a moment. "Um, let me see. Yes, I'll get dressed." She stood, her enthusiasm for the day pricked like a helium balloon.

She donned a pair of aqua cotton slacks with a long vest that went over her hips. With it she wore a white and turquoise striped shirt with a boat collar. She excused the maid with a smile after donning low-heeled suede ankle boots that just reached to the hem of the pants.

When she was alone, she dialed the office. "Lois? Yes, it's Pip." She gave a half laugh. "No, I haven't been

146

served up for breakfast with an apple in my mouth. Is Lou there? Yes, please." She waited for a moment.

"Pip. How are you, baby?"

"Fine. No scars." She made a face at the mouthpiece of the phone. "Now tell me what the king has in mind for the benefit."

Lou laughed. "Do I hear vinegar in your voice?"

"Yes."

"All right. No chatting about the illustrious heir of Dharan." He cleared his throat.

Pip could hear shuffling papers on his desk.

"Ah, here it is. I have the rundown on the Lotus show in front of me, and I thought that since the king's benefit will be held at Trainor's we could modify our Lotus plans to pick up the horse decor of the club."

"I've never been to Trainor's. Come to think of it, I've never even seen anyone play polo except on television."

"No? That is strange. Your ex will be playing in the benefit, and as I understand it, he's one of the best, not that I know a chukker from a base hit."

"Romain?" Chalk up another item she hadn't realized about the man she was married to, Pip thought.

"You've never seen him play?"

"No," Pip answered dully.

Lou talked for several minutes and Pip knew she must have made the appropriate answers, but nothing really penetrated the dull shock of knowing that there was yet another facet to Romain, however unimportant, of which she had no knowledge.

She hung up the phone and walked down the hall to the wide staircase leading to the second floor and then down the larger set of stairs to the ground floor.

Abdul appeared as though by magic, his slight smile and deep salaam letting her know he'd seen her start of surprise. "My lady would like to go horseback riding to-day."

His firm statement that brooked no argument made her laugh. He had spent many long afternoons in Dharan trying to make her an equestrienne, believing that the wife of the Lord Romain would take to horses easily. "You must remember the caliber of rider I was in Dharan, Abdul. How many times did you stop me from trying to mount on the wrong side? I was barely able to post, let alone gallop."

"Your highness was quite good for an outsider and you improved greatly from your lessons," Abdul averred, considering anyone, including other Arabs, an outsider who was not a Dharanian.

All at once the thought of fresh spring breezes was most appealing. "Perhaps I will go. Will you go with me?"

Again the deep obeisance. "Of course I will, my lady. His Royal Highness and Lord Romain would flay me alive if I did not guard you well," Abdul said serenely, accepting the gruesome fate as his due if duty were not done.

"I assure you I wouldn't let them do that," Pip muttered, retracing her steps back to her room, mentally making the choice of jeans and a long-sleeve cotton shirt to wear riding.

"Your highness will find her riding outfits in the closet. I will send Ersa to help you." Abdul's voice floated up to her on the second-floor landing.

She nodded, not bothering to question how riding clothes could be in her closet when she didn't own any. She remembered how garments would appear in her rooms when she'd lived in Dharan, perfect sizes, in colors and styles that were the most flattering to her.

She opened her huge closet and saw the large assortment of sports clothes and knew that she wouldn't wear half the things there. She chose a very attractive outfit and Ersa appeared to help her with the short riding boots

148

she decided to wear with the tight-fitting stirrup pants. The clothes were in a hunter green and beige check, the boots were brown suede. A pheasant feather was affixed to a cockade on the bowler-type riding hat that matched the outfit. The hat had a brown suede chin strap.

"I'm not wearing the hat, Ersa. I'll just twist my hair on top of my head."

"It is not good for her highness to be seen riding without a hat," Ersa said and sniffed, inclining her head. ". . . But I'll say no more." She bowed and left the room.

"I'm not 'her highness' anymore." Pip said to the empty doorway before she left the room herself.

She retraced her footsteps back down the stairs to the main hall. She went out the front door and stood under the portico watching Abdul, dressed in the flowing robes of a desert tribesman, at the head of a bay mare who tossed her head, more in fun than bad temper.

"Ah, my lady, this is Tempura, one of a long line of speedy gentle horses that the prince has bred himself. She has won prizes at horse shows in Ireland and England."

"I don't need a champion to ride, Abdul," Pip said lamely. Even to her untrained eye, the mare was special.

Abdul looked affronted. "But you must ride on the best, my lady."

"Good Lord," Pip muttered to herself, approaching the adamant Abdul and the beautiful mare.

Pip stepped into Abdul's cupped hands and let him toss her gently into the saddle. She loved the feel of the beautiful, soft desert saddle and took the reins.

At once Abdul grabbed the pommel of his saddle and swung himself aboard in one graceful motion.

Pip was amazed at the smooth gait of the horse and her ability to adjust herself to it. "You are a beauty, Tempura." She patted the horse's neck.

Abdul took her over hilly meadows and through

woods blooming with crocuses, the limbs of the bushes beginning to swell with spring growth.

They had been gone less than an hour and Pip was feeling relaxed and refreshed, the damp air putting color in her cheeks and a sparkle in her eye.

"Well, well, trying to get away from me?"

The silky whip of his voice curled around her. Pip whirled in the saddle, causing the mare to sidle in agitation and Pip sway out of balance. "Romain!"

"Be careful." He was at her side, controlling his own mount easily with his knees, his strong hand steadying her.

Abdul melted away like a wraith.

"When did you get back?" Pip asked, out of breath.

"About twenty minutes ago. Ersa said you had gone riding with Abdul."

"Why are you angry?" Pip watched the muscle jump at the side of his mouth, recalling the many times she had kissed it to make the sign of anger disappear.

"Am I?" Romain forced a smile to his lips as he indicated an upward curving narrow path and that she should precede him. Damn her! She went riding with Abdul! If she had waited, he would have taken her. How many times when they had lived in Dharan had he begged her to ride with him and she'd refused.

Pip could read his mind. He was furious because he was remembering the times she had told him that she wouldn't ride with him. She could imagine his towering rage if he ever learned that the reason she had chosen not to ride with him was because she had secretly been taking riding lessons to improve and become the equestrienne his wife should be.

Pip let the horse go at her own pace along the narrow path that began to widen as it circled through a thick undergrowth. She stopped at the crest of a hill and looked down into a shallow valley of evergreens. "It's pretty here." She turned to look at him, noting the stiff set of his jaw. Romain had never been a moody person when they had been married, but he seemed that way now. "Lou told me today that you will be riding in the benefit polo game at Trainor's. I never even knew that you played polo."

"You never asked many questions about me, personally. You asked about my family, my country, my people. We talked of theater, the arts, even the sciences, but I don't think you ever questioned my tastes on anything." Gall laced his words.

Pip caught the acerbic tone in his voice. Stung, she faced him. "You weren't that forthcoming with me. I was expected to accept whoever you were and whatever you did and not question, wasn't I?"

"No," Romain thundered, his horse rearing in surprise for a second before he brought the animal under control. "You had free rein to be yourself always."

Pip opened her mouth to retort angrily, but closed it, struggling to check the fury that gripped her. Hadn't she dealt with the anger and frustration and shelved it where it belonged? "There's no need to go over old ground. I admit that my inhibitions were of my own making. I shouldn't have been intimidated by you, but I was."

"I know," he rasped.

Silence spread like a thick blanket between them.

Pip shivered.

"You're chilled." Romain reached over and grasped her reins, turning her horse. "We'll go back and get you a hot drink."

She wanted to tell him that she'd shivered because of remembered pain. That, even now, she could recall the tearing arguments that had begun over similar simple and uncomplicated conversations.

They rode side by side after leaving the woods, the horses moving in a comfortable trot.

151

Pip began to feel some soreness after the unaccustomed time in the saddle and thought longingly of the hot tub in her suite of rooms.

"Tonight my uncle has invited a few of the persons involved with the benefit to dinner so that some of the initial planning can be discussed over cocktails."

Pip's head swiveled his way, biting her lip in contrition. "I didn't even ask how your uncle's tests went. How is he?"

"Fine. He's back here now because he wouldn't stay overnight. He'll have to stay in the hospital tomorrow night, then we'll have the results of all the tests at the end of next week. The doctors were very encouraging this morning when I spoke to them."

Pip nodded, seeing the relief on his face. "I'm glad."

They were silent again, but with less strain. They rode down the winding paths toward the barns at the back of the property.

When they stopped in front of the door of the stables, two young men came out with Abdul at their side. Before any of them could help Pip dismount, Romain was lifting her from the horse.

"Stiff?"

"A little." She winced. "It's not the mare's fault. She is marvelous to ride."

"She is a most valuable animal. My uncle has been offered a million dollars for her." He kept one arm around her, keeping her weight on him.

"Really?" Pip's hand lifted from the satiny neck of the mare, surprise holding her still. She watched as the horse was led away to be rubbed down.

"Really, but I won't have her sold. She is the perfect mount for you, and so I told Uncle Haddad. He agrees."

"I don't know if I like riding such an expensive investment."

"You needn't worry. She belongs to you."

"Me? No! That was not in the divorce settlement
. . ."

"You never took anything from me," Romain interrupted, harshly.

"That's because I was able to support myself and
didn't need anything."

"Your jewelry was a gift," he fired at her.

"I wouldn't have worn it," she answered him in a
strained voice. How could he think that she could have
worn anything that reminded her of him? She had tried
so hard to forget!

"I won't argue over such a stupid thing. As my wife
you are entitled to a great deal of money and property."

Pip stopped, facing him, arms akimbo. "Why do you
do that?"

"What are you talking about now?" He took her arm
and led her away from the stables toward an outdoor
complex of swimming pool, tennis courts, and a patio
with umbrellas, tables, and lounges.

"Whenever we had an argument, you'd make a point
and then say that you didn't want to discuss it," she
fumed. "But you always made the last remark before you
closed the subject." Her hands curled into fists as she saw
his hard mouth quiver. "That drove me crazy."

"And it still does."

"Yes." She inhaled an angry breath.

He reached for her before she could back away. His
arms pinning her to him so that the struggle she made
had no appreciable effect. He leaned down so that their
lips were touching. "I'll try to mend my ways if you do
the same."

"What do you mean?" Pip fought hard to keep the
quaver from her voice. She tried to blank out the sensuous hardness of his body so close to hers.

"Don't hide from me. Tell me if something bothers you
of if you would rather have things done in a different

153

way." He pressed his one finger over her lips when they parted to speak. "And please don't tell me that this isn't your house and that you are a guest here."

"Well, it's true."

"You are a princess of Dharan by order of his royal highness, King Haddad of Dharan. My people think of you as my wife still because it is common knowledge that we did not have a Moslem divorce."

"Romain, you aren't a practicing Moslem."

"My people see it differently."

Pip could feel herself melting at the soft insistence of his massaging hand on her spine, his body shielding her from the cool spring breeze. "Are we going to play tennis?"

"If you like. First tell me if you are going to cooperate in this venture."

"Venture is rather an expansive word for it, I think."

"Pip!"

"All right. I'll promise to speak up if you promise not to try and have the last word when we disagree."

"Done." His mouth settled once more on hers, the pressure gentle, yet insistent, his lips coaxing her to let his tongue enter in tender exploration. He felt the blood thunder in his ears and only the strongest will kept him from putting her on the ground and taking her at that moment. Shock froze him as he realized she had as much sexual power over him as she ever did, and he held her away from him.

"Romain? What is it?" Pip saw the pain flash across his face as he continued to look down at her.

"Nothing." He took the hand she'd placed on his cheek and pressed his mouth into the palm, his eyes veiled from her. He couldn't tell her that a kiss between them had almost shattered his control, that he wanted her so much he would have taken her in his uncle's

154

flower bed. Disgust filled him as he buried his face in her hair. He didn't want her to look at him.

"Tennis anyone?" She laughed shakily.

"I'll wager a lunch at a country inn I know not far from here that I beat you straight sets."

"You're on." Pip grabbed his proffered hand and shook it, relieved that the emotional moment had passed.

They went into the large, heated changing rooms and donned the cotton sweat suits that were there for them.

On the tennis court Pip had to concentrate. As in most things he did, Romain was a hard, cool player, and he had a punishing serve.

Pip put everything she had into it. In minutes sweat was coursing her body as she strove to return his shots.

Romain wanted to win! He had every intention of beating her, not only because it gave him extreme satisfaction to whip her, but because he wanted to take her to lunch at the country inn and keep her there all day, making love in a small romantic room.

Pip struggled mightily, hating the glint in his eyes telling her that he was very aware that he was winning and she was flagging.

Romain won! Pip's teeth ground together when he leaped the net easily and came to her side.

"Cheater," she said unfairly, out of breath.

"Fair and square." Romain's wide grin showed all his even teeth.

"How would it be if I rapped you in the mouth with my racket?"

"Sore loser."

"Yes." She exhaled the word, feeling reluctant amusement at the satisfied look on his face. "Someday I'm going to beat you, and you're going to land square on your backside, not knowing what hit you." She inhaled a shuddering breath.

"You've done that." His voice was a silky steel, but his

155

eyes were warm as he stared at her moist, shining face. "You still play as hard as anyone I know."

"With you I have to," she said, out of breath.

"As though your very soul was on the line?"

"Maybe it is." She watched him warily when he threw back his head and laughed out loud. She couldn't miss the triumph in his voice. "About the bet . . ."

"No hedging. The bet is won, by me. Which day would you like to go to the Camellia Inn?"

"Ah, I do have a very busy schedule . . ."

"Name a day or I will."

"Thursday," Pip said through her teeth. "I need a shower now."

Romain's laughter trailed after her, coiling around her, making her whole frame stiffen.

He could see the tension in her, and it gave him immense satisfaction, but it didn't lessen the delight he felt at the thought of having her to himself in two days time. "We'll be leaving at nine in the morning," he called after her. Before she could answer, he turned and jogged back toward the stable area.

She paused and turned to stare after him. "He is insufferable. I don't know how I tolerated him as long as I did." Pip watched his disappearing figure, wishing she could shove him in the ocean. She felt mocked by her own voice as she heard the frustration in it. Trying to win against Romain at anything was like trying to reach the moon in the Wright brothers' plane. She walked through the kitchen, trying to smile at the cook and the kitchen staff and emerged from the spacious cooking area to the main hall.

"Ah, there you are, my dear. Do you have time for me now?"

Pip spun around and saw Romain's uncle standing in the doorway leading to the library. "Your highness," Pip inclined her head, "If you could allow me fifteen minutes to shower, please?"

"Of course, child. I shall see you here in fifteen minutes." The king smiled at her, retreated into the room and closed the door.

Pip raced up the stairs. "Fifteen minutes! Good Lord! How like a Dharanian to take me literally." She shot into her room, ripping off her clothes, aware that Ersa was right at her back. "Run the shower, please. I have an appointment with his highness."

Ersa nodded and hurried in to the bathroom, then scurried out again to get fresh clothing from the closets and built-in dresser.

Pip didn't even bother to check what the maid had chosen for her. She rushed into the shower, grabbing a bottle of shampoo and scouring her scalp and body in minutes. Ersa was there to rub her wet body with emollients before she dried Pip with a fluffy bath sheet.

Ersa frowned at Pip when she insisted on donning her own clothes. Before she could say anything, the thin-lipped maid slipped the dress over her head.

Pip gasped at the gold raw silk dress, styled deceptively like a shirtwaist, the striking color and material the only drama of the dress. "This might be something to wear to the theater," Pip said lamely, sinking onto the dressing table stool and letting Ersa push the antique gold leather slides on her feet. Everything fits perfectly. Didn't it always? Pip thought grimly, trying to smile. In Dharan she had been horrified to see how things were discarded if they were the slightest bit off the fit. When she had complained to Romain about such waste, he had patiently explained that nothing was thrown away. Instead, the unused clothing and shoes were donated to the poor. Lost in thought of her former husband, she barely noticed when Ersa began to fuss with her hair.

"Does my lady like the way I've done her hair on top of her head?"

Pip's eyes flew to the mirror, amazed at how deftly the woman had managed her long, thick red hair into a chignon with loose curls about her face. "Yes, I like it very much."

Pip hurriedly left the room and retraced her steps back to the main foyer at the front of the house. She paused in front of the library door and took a few deep breaths before knocking. At the muffled answer, she opened the door. "Sir?"

"Come in, my dear." The King stood and gestured to her to take a seat.

"You look well, your highness. It must mean that the tests are going well."

"Thank you, they are." He smiled, then grimaced. "I do not like the idea of spending two days in the hospital for further tests but my nephew is adamant. I'm sure you'll agree he can be quite forceful when he chooses," he said with a twinkle in his eyes.

"Yes," she said and grinned at the tall, smiling man, his gaunt good looks telegraphing his kinship to Romain.

"Yet in many ways he is a proud fool and has lived with a cancerous pain rather than excise it." He steepled his hands and watched her thoughtfully.

"I . . . I don't know what you mean."

The king shrugged. "The ravings of a doddering old man."

"We both know you're not that," Pip replied shortly.

"Do we?"

"Sir, are you laughing at me?"

"Child, I would not do that. My foes will tell you that I have no sense of humor. Your uncle seems to think that I fit the name the desert people have given me. Lynx." He laughed out loud.

Pip laughed with him for a moment, then his words sank in and she stared at the king. "My uncle?"

"Ah, yes, did I not say that we have chatted a few times?"

"No, sir, you did not. More to the point my uncle never mentioned it either."

"No? Ah, well, the meetings were few." The king flapped his hand effectively ending the discussion. "Now, as to the benefit, I think that we should have an assortment of performers plus the modeling, and I want music —big bands—I think."

Pip forgot her uncle in the enormity of what the royal personage was saying. "Sir, you can't mean that. It would take months to line up the sort of entertainment you're suggesting. Surely you know that it isn't possible in four weeks' time."

"Well, then we'll let Romain line up the entertainment. He has a way of getting what he wants." The king looked over his glasses at her. "Most things, anyway." He looked back down at the pad of paper in front of him. "You can settle on the models and what they will be doing."

Pip spent almost two hours trying to dissuade King Haddad from charging two thousand dollars a ticket for the evening, and from trying to hire an entire circus and perhaps even the Marine Corps Band.

The king rose to his feet, signaling the end of the meeting as he walked Pip to the door. "Sometime, my child, you should talk to my sister-in-law. She and I have decided that there are a few things about my nephew you do not know." He kissed her cheek and gestured to an aide to close the door.

Pip stared at the wood paneling for a few moments trying to fathom the king's cryptic remark. She turned away, shrugging it off. He just would like you to call Romain's mother, and you do owe her a call, she thought

159

to herself not quite able to shake the uneasy feeling that assailed her.

By the time she'd returned to her room, she shoved the thoughts to the back of her mind as she went over the list that she and the king had compiled for the show.

That night, when she was freshening up for dinner, she decided she would wear the same antique gold silk she'd worn for her interview with the king. It was still fresh and she knew that the color was flattering to her, enhancing the gold flecks in her turquoise eyes and giving her skin a luminescent glow. She thought it was more a dress for evening anyway.

At the given time for cocktails, which would be nonalcoholic according to the king's wishes, she descended the stairs.

"You look lovely."

Pip spun around midway down the staircase and looked up at Romain. "I didn't know you were in this wing."

"Yes. You and I have the only bedrooms on this side of the house. My uncle and his guards and secretary are on the opposite side."

"Oh." Her heart flip-flopped at the thought of Romain being in a room so close to her.

"Yes." He came down toward her, looping his arm around her waist and bending to plant a quick kiss on her lips. "You're like the statue of a golden goddess I once brought back from Mexico. Your eyes are turquoise just like hers, though yours have tiny gold flecks to match the dress."

Pip tried to ignore her quivering body. "Do you still join the digs down there?"

"When I can, but I've also been going on digs in my own country. There have been some interesting finds. Would you like to join me on one?"

"Me?" She felt her soul reach out to him and tried to

steady herself. Join him on a dig? Wasn't she trying to be rid of him? "I . . . I have a tough time getting away from the business . . ."

"I see." His voice was bland, but the hand at her waist convulsed on her soft flesh, bringing a start of surprise from her. "Sorry." He released her.

Pip felt his fury crackle around her and was glad to precede him into the huge living room. Safety in numbers!

"Ah, here, you are, my dear." The king held out both hands to Pip, kissing her on both cheeks. "Ah, yes, the lovely gold dress that matches the tiny flecks of gold in your eyes. Your coloring is exquisite with it." He turned and smiled at his nephew. "Philippa wore this dress when we spoke this afternoon, and though I applaud your taste in choosing her dresses, I'm surprised that you did not provide your wife with a variety of clothing. But then I suppose it is the new way to teach a wife to be saving on her sundries while the husband spends the money on necessary things like polo ponies . . ."

"Uncle!" Romain's face reddened. He stared at his relative as though he were seeing him for the first time. "I would deny my wife nothing."

"We're not married," Pip managed in a strangled tone, bringing the eyes of both men her way. "Not married," she repeated.

Romain glowered at her.

The king inclined his head in a bland smile. "Dharanian wives have always had the loving care of their husbands. It has always been our custom," he stated in benign ambiguity.

Romain sucked in an angry breath, baffled and irked with the man who had been his mentor and closest friend since childhood. "Philippa will always have every advantage."

"I'm single," Pip said from the side of her mouth as

161

Abdul came up to her with a tray of fruit juice. She chose orange juice.

"I should think so," King Haddad answered his nephew, then chose a pink grape juice, sipped, and smiled. "She drives a rather shabby car, I'm told."

"It runs well, and I get twenty-five miles to the gallon," Pip tried to explain.

"More economy?" The king's smile was pained.

Romain glared. "Her Maserati is in Dharan," he spat the words, his knuckles showing white where he held his glass.

"Ah, yes, the car you liked so well, Philippa! I was sure you would miss it, so I had it shipped here."

"You what?" Romain grated the question.

"Oh, no," Pip said at the same time, closing her eyes. Why was everything getting so complicated?

Romain was ready to bite through steel. He'd fully intended to bring Philippa's car to the United States, but he had wanted to discuss it with her first.

"I will have to place it in storage, sir," Philippa began.

"Nonsense, child. Abdul has already seen to garage space for you, and you will be much safer than you have been in that other vehicle. Abdul says it is rusty."

"A little around the rocker panels and doors, but the tires are new this year, and . . ."

"I'm sure you'll get a good price for it then when you sell it."

"Sir, if I drive around New York in a Maserati, people will think I've been dipping into the petty cash at my company." She looked at Romain. "You explain what I mean."

"The car is yours," Romain said stiffly. Damn his uncle and Pippa! He felt adrift! The reins were not in his hands! "I think dinner is being served, uncle."

"Ah, yes, we are having baby lamb, child. I remember that you loved it with rosemary and basil, but we'll also have crab legs. I know how partial Americans are to them." He signaled to the hovering guards and assistants who had been standing some distance away, seemingly deaf to the conversation between their master and his family.

"He knows that you dislike lamb," Romain growled, frustration filling him. "And that the only seafood you eat are lobster and shrimp."

Pip smiled weakly. "There's always the salad."

"I don't know what's gotten into him." Romain put his hand under her elbow and led her back into the hall and across to the dining room. He seated her, fuming, waving his hand at one of the hovering waiters. "You will get the princess a lobster and cook it at once," he spoke through his teeth.

"At once, lord."

The king was seated, smiling at Pip. "Ah, my dear, you will enjoy this."

Pip felt as though she'd stepped through the Looking Glass. The king was gleeful, Romain was livid. Pip expected the Queen of Hearts to come through the door at any time and join in the macabre game.

She didn't know how they got through the meal. She had cringed when the two huge lobster tails were placed in front of her, but when she looked at the king, he had smiled sweetly and asked her if she was enjoying her food.

She refused the honey cakes that the king was partial to and chose the cheese and fruit board for dessert.

Later when they were back in the library, the talk was desultory. Romain kept shooting sharp looks at his uncle and the king smiled benignly and asked Pip if she had an active social life in New York.

"Reasonably." Pip foundered under Romain's baleful stare and the king's twinkling curiosity.

At the end of the evening Pip collapsed into her bed,

exhausted by the strange dinner and the growing suspicion that the king was baiting Romain, exacerbating him and certainly not trying to calm him.

When she woke the next morning, her eyes felt sticky with lack of sleep, her body stiff with the tension of the tossing and turning she'd done.

She stumbled from her bed, yawning, barely listening to what Ersa was telling her.

". . . And Lord Romain says that you will enjoy it." Ersa beamed at her.

"Enjoy what?" Pip held up her hand, palm outward. "Never mind, don't tell me until I get out of the shower."

She scrubbed her head and body feeling more refreshed, wishing for a moment that she had jogged for a few miles around the property before showering. She needed the loosening up that exercising would have given her.

She stopped short when she reentered the bedroom, her head and body swathed in towels. Romain was stretched out on her freshly made bed, his hands cupped behind his head. "What are you doing here?" Surprise sharpened her voice.

"I thought Ersa told you what we were doing today."

"Ah, she did, but I wasn't paying attention," Pip admitted, hitching the towel up higher on her body as his green eyes glinted over her in sensual assessment. "I am not cattle to be sized up that way," she told him tartly.

"So, as usual, when you got up this morning, you were too bleary-eyed to catch the meaning of anything said to you. Correct?"

"Bleary-eyed!" she glared at him. "As I recall you weren't all that sharp in the mornings . . ." her voice trailed as she caught the amused glitter in his eyes.

"Tell me more about our mornings. I'd like to see if it agrees with my memories of that time." He settled back and gazed up at the ceiling. "Let's see. I recall the pinky cream color of your skin when it was flushed with sleep, how you always wiggled your bottom to get as close—"

"What was it that you wanted?" Pip interrupted, her voice more strident than she wished.

He sat up in bed, his body indolent, belying the watchfulness of his eyes. "We're alone in the house. We're going to spend the whole day together . . . and the night. Nice, huh?"

CHAPTER TEN

They went horseback riding. Pip felt as though every tooth in her head was jarred loose from the unaccustomed galloping. "And I was bemoaning that I hadn't jogged," she muttered to herself.

By the time they'd changed into tennis clothes, she was sure that she wouldn't be able to play well, but she refused to let Romain see that she was uncomfortable. To her surprise she won a game.

"I didn't have as much at stake this time," Romain told her after he leaped the net and noticed the look of triumph on her flushed, moist face.

"That's hedging," she shot back.

"Yes." He leaned down and kissed her, his tongue touching hers.

"You said we were going swimming," she managed, out of breath.

"So I did."

It was when they were lying by the pool that she felt the most quivering awareness of Romain, a cloud of feeling that seemed to be absorbing all the oxygen, making every breath an ordeal. "Stop staring at me," she told him without opening her eyes. She felt his body shift on the double lounger, the fine hairs on her skin were like antenna that telegraphed his nearness.

"I can't." Romain pressed his mouth to the valley between her breasts, his one hand calming her as her body jerked in response. "Shh. Don't move, love. I just want to cover you so that you don't get too much sun."

"Use a towel, not your body," she told him in strangled tones.

"My body does a better job," he soothed, his hand going in gentle sweeps up and down her.

"Not to worry. I have lotion on," Pip said with a gasp, her eyes still closed, as she felt his mouth nudge the skimpy bikini top aside.

"You never used to wear a suit when we sun-bathed," he muttered, his hand whorling on her middle, his teeth closing on the strap and tugging it downward. "But I never allowed that wonderful skin to get burned." His words had a guttural sound as the top was freed from her body. "So white." He took her breast into his mouth, kissing it with his tongue and lips, his body tenting over hers and protecting it from the sun.

"Romain!" She pushed at his head with her fingers, but as the hot river of feeling spilled through her, her hands held him rather than rejecting him. "Someone will see." The words dribbled from her mouth.

"There's no one here. Abdul and Ersa were here, but I sent them away, too. We are alone." He leaned back from her, his body hovering over hers. "Does that bother you?"

"Maybe," she managed, trying to still the tremor in her body that his stroking was evoking.

"We need the time." His mouth moved from her ear down her neck to her shoulder. His strong, white teeth nipped at the tender skin. "I want to talk."

"We're not doing that," Pip said, out of breath, as he tickled the skin of her abdomen with his lips.

"No? I thought we were communicating rather well." Romain lifted the scrap of material covering her lower body, his eyes riveted to the triangle of reddish hair. He pressed his lips to it, bringing an anguished moan from Pip.

"Please, Romain . . ."

"Please? That is what I'm trying to do. Please you." Romain clasped her hips, his teeth nibbling the sensitive skin of her inner thigh.

"Romain!" she couldn't seem to do more than mumble his name.

"You used to know how to please me. Do you remember?"

"Yes." As though they had a life force of their own, her fingers began a feather touch exploration of his back and shoulders. When she heard the hoarse groans issuing from his throat, it made her bolder. All in one fell swoop she threw away the reasons she should be talking to Romain instead of loving him and allowed the glory of touching him to take over.

"Philippa! Pippa!" It was his turn to groan her name as she touched him, writhing in the delight that she was bringing to his body. "Don't stop, darling. You've driven me mad since the very first moment I saw you in California."

Breath left her as his body sank onto hers, the welcome heaviness firing her blood like a torch to paper. Her hands stopped their gentle teasing and dug into him, holding him to her.

Daylight whirled in a kaleidoscope of color as Romain released the lever of the lounger and their bodies followed its contour to flatness. Except for the canopy shading their upper bodies, they could have been lying on a king-sized bed in one of the bedrooms.

Sanity flashed through Pippa as she thought of what she was doing, how much of her life she would hand over to this man if he made love to her again. "No," she pushed at him feebly.

"Yes, my sweet, yes. I want to give myself to you, even

if you throw me away again. Take me, please." Romain looked down at her, the planes of his face harsh in the sunlight slashing through the trees. His eyes had a self-deprecating softness to them.

Her arms slid up his chest and clutched him around the neck. "I never threw you away."

"Even if you do, I want you to let me love you now. I need that." His voice was muffled against her skin as he slid down her body, his mouth moist and open on her skin.

"I want it, too," she said sobbing, giving in to the need to love Romain once more.

When his tongue entered her lower body in ultimate joining, her body arched, cries issuing from her throat, causing his blood to course through his veins like lava.

"Romain . . . I can't . . ." Pip felt her body turn to liquid flame as he ministered to her.

"Wait, my precious, I'm not through loving you." Romain's voice was strangled with desire as he kissed each toe and slowly began the lovely journey back up her body.

"I want you," she told him strongly, her hand clenching on him.

"And I want you." Romain entered her and every electric charge in his body exploded as he began the slow sure strokes to bring her to the brink of sensuous love. When Pip cried out, his own body burst into shards of passion that cast both of them away into a world that only they could enter.

Some moments later when Romain was caressing her and soothing her with whispered words, Pip felt a strange release in her body as though something that had belonged to her had slipped its mooring and joined with Romain, as though some essential part of her body had left her and adhered to him.

"I don't want to move." Romain shifted and lifted her

over his body so that her curling red hair fell like a curtain around them. "And I want you to stay here with me."

"I . . . I don't want you to go away." She smiled at him, feeling replete and relaxed, more than she'd done since she left him. ". . . But I still feel we should talk. We solved all our problems this way—instead of talking—when we were married."

Romain's head shot up, his hair mussed, his eyes slumbrous yet angry. "Are you saying what we had together was bogus, a sham?"

"No!" Pip pushed herself to one side, wriggling free of his hold and sitting up, facing him, feeling his gaze as though his hands were touching her. "We're still quick to misunderstand one another, as always." She swallowed as though a rock were caught in her throat. "I'm saying that we are divorced, and by all that's sensible we should let well enough alone, but we've made love and that changes the perspective . . ."

"It damn well does," Romain snapped.

Pip took a deep breath, but didn't look away from him. "Since you seem to want to resurrect our relationship, I find that there are things that I've been burning to say to you for some time."

"Begin anywhere." Romain gave her an ironic smile and reached for the gold case of cheroots sitting on the iron table near the lounger. He shook one into his hand, studied her for a moment, sighed, and returned it to the case. "That's one thing I recall you disliked a great deal."

"Because of your health," Pip shot back, seeing some of the sexual tension leave his body, his eyes wary but not angry.

"So you always told me," Romain whispered, his finger reaching out to trace a gentle course from her throat to her navel. "We can talk now, but don't think that's the end of it, Philippa. It isn't."

170

"Ah, well, what do you think we should discuss first?" She ignored the last part of what he said.

"Why you left me," Romain said abruptly.

Her eyes slid away from his, feeling comfortable naked with him, yet not willing to bare her soul. "I was young."

"Yes, too young to be married," Romain observed in grating bitterness.

Her head swung back to him. "But not too young to know that I loved you." She made the admission in a flush of blood to her face and neck, but not flinching from his stare.

"I knew that you loved me, but I should have been more careful with you. You were fragile and I was damned intense."

"Yes," she sobbed a laugh.

"We didn't get out of bed for days." Romain watched the blood fluctuate in her face, his eyes running down her body. "That hasn't changed either."

"What?"

"You still blush all the way to your breasts."

"Oh," she frowned at him when he laughed. She could feel the blood pumping through her like a cataract. "You're getting off the subject."

"I think I'm right on target."

"Romain."

He shrugged and gestured for her to continue.

She looked off into the gardens surrounding the pool area. "Some of the things I'll tell you will hurt you. Maybe a few things will make you angry enough to throw me out of here."

"Go on." His clipped British accent had an acid ring.

"When I left you, I was confused and disoriented. I didn't know myself. I felt as though your love for me was fading even if you didn't see it. I felt inadequate as your wife and as a Dharanian. I was homesick and unsettled,

171

but I thought, with all that, I would still be back in Dharan in a few months."

"What?" Romain shot to a sitting position.

She looked back at him, feeling a smile slip on and off her face. "That's the truth. I didn't leave you at first to stay away from you. I wanted to get my head straight. I didn't doubt my love, though I doubted yours at the time of my leaving. You had become cold with me."

"No!" Romain barked. Then he pounded his fist against the soft cotton cushion of the lounger. "Maybe it did look that way. I was trying to be more controlled with you. I knew I was eating you alive, but I couldn't seem to help myself. The more we made love, the more I wanted to." He looked up at the oak tree that cast a filigreed shade over some of the patio. "I thought by the time we'd been married a few months I would be in control of things, but it didn't work out that way. I couldn't be away from you more than a couple of days without hurting." He shot her a look. "That's basically why I didn't come after you. I felt you had a good reason to leave me. I was all over you."

Pip felt hysteria rising in her as she laughed out loud. Then she clamped a hand over her mouth when he looked hurt. "I'm laughing at me, not you. When you went away for a day or two on business, I never slept. I couldn't, when you weren't there. I needed you there and wanted you to make love to me all the time."

"Philippa!" Romain reached for her, but she put her hand up to stop him.

"Let's get this said, Romain." She swallowed. "I really don't want to talk about what I'm going to tell you, but I have to."

"Go on." His strong brown hand touched her thigh.

"When I returned, Uncle George and Aunt Grace welcomed me as I knew they would. It was so comfortable those first few weeks just to lie there and do nothing.

When Uncle George suggested that I come to New York with them, I was glad to go." She sighed and took another breath. "It was while I was there that I discovered I was expecting a child."

"What?" Romain's body sagged in shock.

"I lost the child." Pip felt her whole being draw inside itself. Hiding had become a way of dealing with the agony she'd experienced when she'd lost the baby. "A daughter, the doctor said," she repeated dully, her hands threaded together.

Romain stared at her, seeing the beaded moisture on her upper lips, the tremors she tried so hard to control, running over her body. "You should have called me." He felt as though his body was being assaulted by small sharp razors. She'd been alone! Without him! "How far along?" His voice was harsh.

"About four months, maybe a little more. It's amazing how they can know the sex of an early fetus, isn't it?" Her matter-of-fact tone was belied by the trembling of her lips that she couldn't stop.

"Yes." Romain felt a towering anger. He wanted to curse all the gods and all the fates. He had lost a child that would have been the image of Pippa! He knew it! "Were you very ill?" The words tore from him.

"No," she said too quickly. Then she looked down, shivering for a minute, welcoming the towel that Romain put over her shoulders. It was a very warm day, the pool was heated, but she felt the familiar frostbite of the soul that she'd hoped had left her for good. "I was ill, but they said it was more emotional than physical." She looked up at him, knowing that her smile was a dismal failure. "It was a great shock losing the baby such a short time after finding out that I was going to have her."

"It must have been." Romain knew he sounded stilted, but he had the feeling he was on the brink of breaking apart.

"I was in the hospital for three weeks, then I convalesced at home. I wouldn't let Uncle George call you. I was going to do that myself, but I kept putting it off. It seemed like such a monumental task." She gave a shaky laugh. "I rehearsed what I was going to say to you, but it all seemed so inadequate. Then, when I was on my feet, I began to look for something to do, anything to keep my mind off the child." She paused for a moment, catching her breath. "I'd think I'd hear her crying at night. I was sure I was going mad. I was desperate for something to take my mind off the loss. Luckily, at the right time, I met Lou through a friend I'd had at the university in California, and we went into business together. I plunged into the new work like a drowning person grasping a lifeline, all the while telling myself that I would call you the next day. After a time, it became harder and harder to know what I would say to you, the words I thought were right began to sound shallow. There was not only distance between us then, there was a chasm of communication. We hadn't spoken in months. We were fast becoming strangers."

"I picked up the phone a hundred times to call you," Romain said through his teeth. "I wanted to give you time . . . then I was too proud to call."

"I know the feeling." Pip looked at him at last, steeling herself against the opaque hardness of his glance.

They stared at each other for long moments.

"I stopped using birth control after we married."

"I know, Romain. We talked about it, but I never considered having a child. I didn't want to do anything to stop one coming because I sensed that you wanted a child."

"Yes." He'd wanted Pippa's child very much, but he hadn't realized how much until she'd told him that she'd lost a baby. He felt scorched with pain.

Pip tried to smile. "Children were far from my

174

thoughts. Our stormy marriage was enough to concentrate on for a few years."

"I agree." He struck the palm of his hand with his fist. "Why the hell didn't I think of you being pregnant?"

"I didn't think of it either. I wanted to finish school, but it wouldn't have mattered. I could still have gotten a degree and taken care of the child. I was sure of that when I was in the hospital fighting to keep the doctors from taking her."

"Pip!" Romain reached for her, cradling her to him, the towel swathed about her.

"I don't know why it didn't occur to me that I might have a child." Pain and disbelief laced her voice. "It was so stupid." Pip had gone over and over it the long weeks she convalesced, bitter regret making her shun the lovely meals that her aunt and uncle had tempted her with. She had ignored the weight loss and plunged into the new business. Her dedication and punishing hard work were the reasons that Lou had offered her a partnership, or so he'd told her more than once. "I stopped trying to figure it all out because I didn't come up with any answers," she told him dully.

She shivered again and Romain moved swiftly, lifting her into his arms and striding toward the sauna.

"You're cold."

Ten minutes in the boxlike structure and she felt warmed through. Conversation had lagged between them, but Pip didn't care. She felt as wrung-out as a dishrag. Her feelings about the lost child had been bottled up inside her for so long. Now the dam had burst in her soul and all the energy she'd employed to buttress herself against pain had flooded away.

Romain finally spoke to her after they dressed and were walking down the long, tiled path that led from the pool to the house. "Would you like to go to the country inn tomorrow and just rest here tonight?"

175

Pip looked at him blankly for a moment. "I'd forgotten about that."

"I know."

She was taken aback that he would still want her to accompany him. She had seen the stunned look on his face when she'd told him about the child. Dharanians were very proud and caring of their children, and she knew that Romain would have been that type of parent. She felt a momentary wrench of grief as she thought of the little girl who would have been old enough to be bounced on her daddy's knee. He had been furious at first, she'd seen that. Now the mask that he was able to drop at will over his features was in place. She didn't know what he was thinking at the moment.

He put his arm at her waist when they crossed the Japanese bridge that had been built over a free, running stream. Was there something more that she wasn't telling him? He wouldn't allow any more secrets.

He accompanied her into the house and to the third floor, then went toward his own suite of rooms, his mind in turmoil. He had thought of fatherhood, naturally. He wanted children, and more than one. He had been an only child and had been lonely. His uncle had named him his heir and as such he thought of succession. There were cousins who could succeed him if he were childless, but naturally he wanted a son who could carry on the traditional role of ruler of Dharan. Somehow at the moment his thoughts kept going to a fragile girl child with red hair and turquoise eyes, whose heart-shaped face was as clear to him as though she'd walked in the door. "A daughter," he groaned, closing his eyes and pressing his hand to his forehead.

"Has the Lord Romain a headache?"

Romain spun around and saw the compassion in Abdul's eyes. Even this old friend had two daughters! "What are you doing here? I sent you and Ersa away."

"Would my lord like a massage?" Abdul ignored Romain's question with the ease of an old retainer.

Romain nodded without speaking and preceded his friend and retainer into the room next to his bedroom that had been set aside for just such a purpose.

Romain lay face down, his cheek cradled on his folded arms, his mind on Pip and how she'd been when they had begun to pull away from each other in Dharan. Why hadn't he seen it? Damn fool! He'd seen it but found it easier to put off finding out what was bothering her, rather than facing it.

It tore him apart when he recalled what she'd said about returning to him, that she'd had every intention of doing so after she'd straightened out her thoughts. Why had he been such a blind fool. Why hadn't he gone after her? Talked to her?

"The Lord Romain is very tense today," Abdul said blandly, ignoring Romain's glower. "It is good to have the Lady Philippa back with us, is it not?"

"Yes."

"I feel that the people of Dharan wish her back as well."

"Do you?" The sibilant menace in his question seemed to have no effect on Abdul.

"Yes. I have told my wife to tell the tribe that our brave lady who saved my brother's grandchild may be coming back to us."

"You what?" Romain jackknifed off the massage table, his naked body poised and ready for mayhem.

"I felt it would be good for the people to know this."

"Men in our country have lost their heads by being less presumptious, Abdul," Romain said through his teeth.

"This is true." Abdul placed the emollients back on the shelf and lifted the soiled towels into his arms.

"What the hell are you doing back here anyway? I sent you away."

"You did, Lord Romain, but I returned to make sure all would be well for the dinner tonight. I was sure that you would want to go to the inn tomorrow. Shall I return to drive you?"

"No, damn you," Romain snapped, watching the man bow, then leave the room.

He went into the bathroom for a quick shower, his mind dwelling on Pippa. No matter what happened he should have been notified right away! What the hell did she mean not telling him? My God, she had been so hurt and frightened, and he hadn't been with her. He stepped out of the shower, smacking his fist against the tile wall, barely feeling the shock of pain up his arm.

He threw himself, naked, on the bed, trying to sleep but every time he closed his eyes he saw Pip holding a child, the baby smiling and laughing. He shot to sitting position, then to his feet, dressing like an automaton in hunter green cotton velvet jeans and shirt.

He stared at himself in the mirror, not really seeing his image, his nerves vibrating like a taut violin string. He slammed the bedroom door when he left, the sound reverberating in the stillness.

He strode along to her section of the wing, aware that he should have called her first, not knowing what he would say to her, but very sure he had to be with her.

He was outside her door, lifting his hand to knock when Ersa came through the door, bowing when she saw him. "What? You, too? I thought I told you and Abdul not to come back until the king returns."

Ersa made the traditional sign of obeisance, steepling her hands in front of her face. "We are leaving soon, Lord Romain. There was much for us to do." Her smile touched him, her self-confidence unshaken by his glare.

"There was something to be said for the old days when there were slaves."

"As you say, Lord Romain," Ersa said serenely, slipping by him.

He walked around her and through the opening, stopping on the threshold when he saw Pip, staring at her as she pirouetted in front of the mirror, frowning at herself. He remembered her wearing something similar in Dharan. She was swathed in a gold lace sarilike garment from head to foot, gold open-toed sandals on her feet, staring at her image as though she couldn't believe what she saw.

"Scheherazade, I presume."

Pip whirled around to face Romain. "It was silly of Ersa to put out such an outfit. I should change."

"No."

"You like it?" She knew from the look in his eyes what he felt before he nodded.

"I was surprised to see Ersa," Pip mumbled, feeling ill at ease.

"She and Abdul are leaving again."

"Oh."

"Shall we go?"

Pip stepped forward and took his arm.

They dined in the small alcove off the library on a table set up by Ersa. Neither she nor Abdul made an appearance, so Pip assumed they'd left.

"This was a good idea."

"Yes, but we have to serve ourselves." Romain gave her a twisted smile as he led her to the kitchen and proceeded to read the instructions propped up on the counter.

"Is dinner complicated?"

"Not at all. Ersa left the food and all the cooking instructions. I hope you like casserole."

"I like anything," Pip told him.

"I remember."

"Are you saying that I'm a glutton?"

"Would I say that?"

"Yes."

They laughed together, their hands reaching out and entwining before either thought about it.

"This is fun," Pip told him as they carried the casserole and salad to the table some time later.

"Isn't it?" Romain reached out and offered her a bit of lobster from his fork after they were seated.

"Umm"

"I do love it when you do that."

Pip felt herself redden as he put down his napkin and reached for her hand, taking her small finger into his mouth and sucking gently.

"Umm," Romain imitated the sound.

"Silly." She felt out of breath.

"Yes."

"Romain, we can't stay at that inn too long. I mean, I have to go to work on the show for your uncle."

"We'll work when we come back from the inn. All right?"

"Yes."

"Tell me about your plans."

"Not when you're doing that to my finger."

"Doing what to your finger? I'm having dessert. Help yourself to the fruit and cheese. I prefer this."

Not even in the crazy, love-filled days of their courtship had Romain been this carefree, leaving himself open to ridicule, letting her orchestrate her own reaction to him. He had always been in full charge of his emotions and, often, of hers, too.

"Shall we have brandy in the living room?"

"First we clear the table." Pip leaned over and placed the palm of her hand on his mouth. "And don't tell me that this job belongs to Abdul and Ersa. We can do it, then they won't have the messy job when they return. Come on, lazy." Pip lifted their plates and turned toward the kitchen not knowing if Romain would follow. When was the last time anyone told Lord Romain that he should pick up cutlery and cart it to the kitchen? Never! Pip bit her lip to keep from giggling. In a minute she would have to turn around and see his face. It would be a thundercloud!

"Sassy brat!" Romain's free hand cupped her buttocks and squeezed gently.

She laughed out loud, barely setting her dishes on the counter without mishap. She faced him, feeling her eyes widen at his nearness and the sensual amusement in his eyes. Not a thundercloud, but a very dangerous Adonis was in front of her!

"Testing your luck?"

"You could say that," she chuckled, feeling at ease in the face of blatant sexual potency. He gave off a charge that would light the sky over San Francisco, Pip mused. She felt she had to take pride in the nerve it took to be his wife, even for so short a time.

"Who knows? You might get lucky and get away with ordering me around." His lazy look was a hurricane cloaked in blue sky. Beautiful, but so dangerous.

"True. Did I tell you that you're doing the pots and pans?" She whirled to the sink, beginning to wipe the counter with a sponge.

Romain's hard smile touched her all over, lingering on the quiver of her shoulders, the rounded enticement of her backside. "Making fun of me, are you?"

"Yes," she whirled to face him again, brandishing the wet sponge in her hands.

"Clean sweep fore and aft for me? Or the counter?" He barely concentrated on the words he used, only wanting to sustain the carefree mood she was in, hypnotized by the amusement in her turquoise eyes. She looked fragile, lovely, and unafraid. His throat tightened as he recalled the flashes of fear and hurt in her eyes when they lived together. He was worried now at how thin she was, but her indomitability made his blood pump faster. "Couldn't we use the dishwasher, princess?"

"Of course, but it's better to do the pots and pans by hand."

"And I'm elected."

"How astute of you." She couldn't keep the laughter bottled up any longer. It rolled out of her until she was gasping as she saw his mouth curve upward, his baritone amusement joining hers. How long had it been since they'd laughed like that together? "This doesn't get the job done," she said and gasped, touching his nose with the damp sponge.

He watched as she turned to the sink, filling it with soapy suds, then placing the few pots and the casserole dish in it. "Good idea," he told her, stepping behind her, and slipping his arms around her waist before she could step aside. He sensuously pressed his hips against her. "Great idea. I think we should offer to do the pans every night."

"This was supposed to be your job." Pip's knees turned to rubber as she felt the sexy hardness of him. "I was going to clean up. Remember? This is not time efficient—I don't think."

"Not true." He nibbled at her neck. "Think how rapidly we'll get the job done with twice the manpower, or is it womanpower?"

"Whatever." Pip swallowed as his arms came up under her breasts, lingering there. "Work," she managed through flaccid lips. "We won't get anything done this way."

"Oh, yes, we will," Romain said huskily.

"Pots and pans," Pippa breathed, her body writhing slowly against his as though he'd given it a signal. She had no control over it.

"I'm doing them," Romain assured her, feeling the

silky heaviness of her breasts on his arms. "Lovely work."

Pip kept her eyes on the casserole dish as she scoured with the cleaning pad, but she couldn't have said if the dish was clean or still soiled when she put it on the draining board. She finished in euphoric delight, seeing prisms of joy, as Romain reached for a drying cloth, dried his hands, and began a warm, slow exploration of her breasts. Slowly she edged her body around so that she could look up at him, her wet hands in the air, inhaling a ragged breath at the hot look in his eyes.

"I'll dry them for you, Pippa." Romain reached for a bottle of lotion on the sink, poured some into his hands, and rubbed her wet hands with the lotion. "There. I don't want them to get rough." He dried them with a towel, seeing the question in her searching gaze. "What worries you?"

"We went too fast the first time. We're doing it again."

Romain shook his head. "No! Not the first time and not now."

"Romain, you must see that the same sort of misunderstanding that . . ."

He put his mouth over her lips, urgently, effectively, blocking her words. He lifted his head. "Don't denigrate what we had. We made blunders, we know that. We'll communicate and not just in bed, but I won't stop loving you. I won't let that happen again. We'll talk but we'll love, too."

She felt caught in the tidal wave of his words. "Time," Pip said faintly, wanting what he said to be true but knowing that they needed the hard, brick-by-brick building of a relationship if they were to have anything at all. "Being practical doesn't spoil a relationship."

"These words come from one of the most impractical women I've ever known!" Romain teased her, kissing her nose.

"And you would know, you've had a stable of them." Her tart reply had him grinning, the dimples, so rarely seen, in strong evidence now.

"Darling, how you talk," he drawled. "You never wanted to discuss the women who were in my life before you. Have you been curious?"

"Yes," she blurted, having the strange sensation that a hole had been made in the wall she built around her emotions.

Romain threaded his fingers through hers. "Then why don't we talk about it over some very old brandy my uncle always keeps for visitors."

"You certainly aren't going to get out that hundred-year-old cognac!" Pip tried to laugh, but she felt a moment of panic. She still didn't want to hear about the streams of gorgeous women he'd had in his life. She didn't have the same childish self-consciousness about Romain as she'd had when they were married, but by the same token she wasn't about to test her emotions by hearing about his "lovers." She freed herself from his hold outside the living room. "Why don't we just discuss us now, not the past?"

"The present and future are often colored by the past," Romain said cryptically, his smile running over her.

"Not always," Pip protested weakly.

Romain sat down next to her, then scooped her into his arms. "We'll talk about everything. That way we won't have veils between us. I feel that I know more about you since our meeting again in California than I did when we were married."

Pip looked up at him and studied the hard features so close to her own. "That hurts to hear it, but I agree with you. I think we were uncomfortable with one another much of the time."

Romain felt his chest contract at her words. "We had a damn good sex life. Many people don't have that."

"You're growling like a bear."

"I feel like one."

"Poor baby." Pip pouted.

"Don't try to sidetrack me." He grinned when he saw the wrinkle of distaste on her face. "You're not going to hear horror stories. I wasn't that much of a Don Juan, Pip. I had mistresses. I enjoyed them, yes, but I was never committed to any woman until I met you."

"When I met you, you were dating a French model."

Romain's eyebrows rose. "Yes. Darienne Flaubert. You never told me you knew about her."

Pip wrinkled her nose. "At the time I read about her I didn't know you, and when we met, I didn't recognize you from your pictures. Your affairs were often in the gossip columns, with photographs of you kissing gorgeous ladies."

Romain exhaled, releasing her, but not moving away from her. "Ah, yes, of course. Well, Darienne was my latest when I met you, but she faded into obscurity as soon as I saw you."

"She still is one of the most beautiful women in the world."

Romain nodded. "So I understand, but I didn't date her when we were apart because she would have reminded me too strongly of when we met."

"I avoided anything that reminded me of that."

"To get back to the point, the women I knew before our marriage were ones who had the same sophisticated viewpoint I did about being together. We enjoyed each other with no commitments."

Pip nodded, trying not to let him see how his words knifed into her. Her traitorous mind let her see in glorious color Romain making love to beautiful women.

CHAPTER ELEVEN

They left the next day for the inn before the king and his entourage returned from the hospital. Pip hadn't gotten around to even the bare groundwork of planning for the benefit. She hadn't even called Lou to tell him she was going away with Romain, but she hadn't felt she could explain any of it to Lou or anyone else for that matter.

She sat next to Romain in the powerful Ferrari and tried to analyze what they'd said to each other far into the night. She had felt confused and shaken by some of what they'd discussed. She was even more taken aback when Romain followed her to bed at four in the morning.

"Not to worry, darling. You need your sleep. I know that." He had slipped into bed with her, pulling her close to him. "Sleep," he'd ordered gently and she had.

When she'd wakened that morning he was already dressed and downstairs. She freshened up, many of the things they'd talked about last night running around her head like loose marbles. When she'd gone downstairs, she'd found him in the kitchen, pouring coffee.

"Sorry. I don't get too much beyond juice and coffee, but there is toast and the vitamins." Romain gestured to the counter.

"Vitamins? You?"

"For both of us." He'd taken hold of her upper arms. "You need a little tender care, ex-wife."

"And you're going to do that?"

186

"Don't be so disbelieving. You might be surprised."

Now as she sat next to him in the luxury car, she shot covert looks at his profile.

"You're not in a tumbrel cart going to the guillotine, Philippa."

She went bolt upright in her seat, her body straining against the seat belt. "I . . . I'm just thinking."

"We made some painful strides last night, talking about each other—our pasts, our fears, and hopes."

"Yes. We're all talked out."

"No, Pip. We're just beginning. I'm back in your life and you're in mine. I'm sure we won't agree on everything—"

"On anything, you mean," she muttered.

"On everything we do and say," he repeated, "but I still think we have to take some time to get to know one another."

She nodded, feeling too enervated to argue with him. She didn't have the same high hopes for their future, but she felt that they should have some time to sort things out, she reasoned, ignoring the kernel of hope that was growing inside of her.

The car ate up the miles of highway into the New York countryside until they came to a small town with an inn sitting on a hill like a quaint jewel.

"The lake and inn share the name of Camellia. Do you like it?"

"Yes." Pip looked up at the lovely Victorian building and inhaled the clean sharp air.

They were shown to an upstairs room, carrying their own small amount of luggage.

Pip gasped with delight when she saw the high four-poster bed with the lace canopy. "Two steps up to the bed . . ." All at once it registered that there was just one bed.

"Yes, Pippa, one bed. I don't intend for us to be apart,

187

not for the time we're here. If we decide that we don't belong together, it won't be because we didn't try to patch our lives."

"But doesn't that make things more complicated? If we live together before we're sure, I mean?"

"Perhaps." Romain shrugged. "But if we separate, we'll never know all the small things that wedged between us in our marriage. Will we?" Romain quizzed blandly, putting his bag on the huge trunk at the end of the bed and beginning to unpack.

"Why do I have the feeling I'm a puppet on your string?"

"You're being fanciful," he dismissed, his accent clipped and very British.

Pip's mouth opened, closed, and opened again. "You're pompous," she finally blurted.

In the act of hanging a shirt in the old-fashioned armoire, he turned, studying her, narrow-eyed. "Self-confident I am, but not pompous; otherwise, wouldn't I have brought a caravan of camels with jewels, dancing girls, and other trappings?"

"Don't be so damned literal. You know what I mean. I feel railroaded."

"You came of your own free will, and by car."

"Stop that. I hate that twinkle in your eye." Liar! she told herself, it turns you into marshmallow. "You know what I mean," she blustered, her hands curling into fists, her body heating in agitation.

"Out of control, are you?" He approached her after the last of his things was put away and his bag stowed in the bottom of the armoire, and put her small case up where his had been.

"Yes! No! Wait, I can do my own unpacking." She tried to reach around him, but Romain ignored her and opened the bag and began lifting her underthings and nightgown from it.

"Lovely. I like the apricot color with your hair. Not too many women with your hair color would have the style sense to realize that it's a good color for them," he mused.

"Thanks for the vote of confidence," Pippa said tartly, yanking the garment from his grasp, irked by his lazy laughter. "Romain, you know what I mean . . ."

"Don't belabor the point," Romain interjected.

"You sound like Mr. Chips," she told him, irritated at the interruption.

His lazy smile ran over her. "Sharpening your claws again?"

"You would be incensed if anyone dared to interrupt you."

Moments passed before he nodded. "You're right about that. I'm sorry. I'll try not to do it again." He leaned over and pressed his finger on her agape mouth. "You'll catch flies."

Pip's mouth snapped shut. "You don't make that many concessions to anyone. Why wouldn't I be surprised?"

"As you can see, we have a long way to go with each other." He raised an eyebrow, his face a lofty mask.

She realized, in flash of rare insight into her former husband, that she had hurt his feelings. "I didn't mean—"

"This time together could be uncomfortable for both of us," he cut in, "but I happen to think it's worth some small inconveniences, don't you?"

"Yes, of course, but I would hardly call sharing a room after a long separation a minor inconvenience." It could be more like a mini atomic bomb, she finished silently.

"I assume we're civilized enough to handle a sophisticated situation. I know I am."

"So am I," she snapped. "But—"

"Good, it's settled."

"There you go again! Interrupting!" Pip fumed.

"Oh? I'll try to do better."

"Please." Pip turned her back on him, wanting to smack him for chuckling. She grabbed her carefully folded clothes and flung them into a drawer.

"I recall you being neater than this," Romain said blandly, stepping around her and sorting her things and folding them.

"And I don't remember you ever lifting a piece of clothing except to put it on," she shot back.

"You're a bit testy today. Is it your cycle . . . ?"

Pip whirled, her chin up. "That is not your business."

"It was once."

"Not now." Her menstrual cycle had always been erratic, but it had seemed to please Romain to keep a record of it in the early months of their marriage. She bit back the sigh as she recalled how nothing had seemed too small or insignificant when they first married. They had spent whole days talking and making love. Laughter had been the order of the day. She recalled how they had spent one day in the Louvre in Paris, and Romain had delighted her with his knowledge of art and the artists who painted the masterpieces. Halcyon days!

"Would you like to take a nap? Or does a walk sound good?" The emerald glint in his eye touched her like a brand.

"A walk sounds fine. Then you can get me some food. I'm hungry." A nap, indeed! He wanted a chance to get her into that high-poster bed, and it angered her to admit that he would have had minimal trouble doing it.

Romain threw back his head and laughed. "You have the appetite of a camel driver."

Pip couldn't stop her smile as she pictured the camel drivers who had come to the Hadji Oasis. It was the largest oasis in the desert area of Dharan and a meeting place for the nomadic tribes who came there to trade. More than once Romain had taken her, in the powerful

190

Land-Rover, to the oasis, and she had met many of the people who called Romain "lord." Pip had found the people talented, warm, and happy, and she had become friends with them. She had struggled with the desert language and often many of the conversations ended in laughter as she made a verbal gaff that delighted her hosts. She had enjoyed it very much and had been eager to return. The camel drivers were thin as rails and always shouting. They seemed to eat constantly, and when they weren't feeding themselves, they tended the bad-tempered beasts that they used for hauling, both human cargo and the sundries they could sell or barter. Both camel and camel driver often had the same vinegary sense of humor. "Your appetite isn't so bad," she volleyed back.

"I lived among the nomads when I was young, as you may recall. I was in charge of a camel. Not that one ever treated me as you were treated by one," Romain said and laughed.

"That beast hit both my new desert boots when he spat at me. If I could have reached, I would have punched him in the eye."

"I remember lifting you away from the camel and the driver when he began laughing, and you shaking your fist the entire time. I think there are stories told about you around the campfires, other than the one of your bravery saving the child of course."

"And you were laughing, too." Pip smiled reluctantly.

Romain nodded. "It was funny. What I don't think you realized at the time was how much the people gathered at the Hadji admired your courage. They know the temperament of the camel." He guided her toward the outer door. "Here's your key." He handed her one, then locked the door behind them with the other, before returning it to his pocket.

Once downstairs they nodded to the innkeeper, then left the inn for the sunlight and crisp cool air.

They walked along the quaint, tree-lined streets in town. Then they retraced their steps to walk through the small park that edged the lake.

"Are you cold?" Romain looked down at the red-cheeked, sparkling-eyed Pip and thought he'd never seen her look more beautiful. Her hair shone in the sun, crackling with health and swinging on her shoulders and her skin had a satin bloom. When he saw two young men eye her from head to toe, he bristled with jealousy.

She shook her head. "The air is nippy for April but it's so fresh."

Romain nodded. "We're very high. If you remember, we drove up some really impressive roads to get here."

Pip nodded.

They strolled along the narrow strip of beach, pausing at short intervals to skip stones across the cold, placid surface. When they came to the private beach sector they took a path leading to the road again.

"Look, there's a house for sale." Pip pointed through some pine trees.

"Yes. Shall we have a look?"

"And get shot for trespassing?"

"I shouldn't think they'd mind if we looked."

Pip felt his hand at her back urging her into the wide, landscaped yard. "It's pretty."

"And private."

They strolled around the yard, glancing in the many windows and admiring the great room facing the lake that was all windows and would be open in the summer with screens.

"How do." An older, hunched-over man, who looked cadaverous in his thinness, approached them around the house. "Thinking 'a buying on the lake? Name's Burnett, Latham Burnett." He put out his hand.

"No. We're just looking." Pip told him as he shook her hand.

"Yes, we're interested in this area. I understand the skiing is very good, and it's very private here."

"Yes to both," the phlegmatic Mr. Burnett answered. "Can't hardly count the strangers on one hand. Most folks around here are kin to others. Nice home, isn't it?"

"Yes." Romain handed him a card. "Would you give this to the caretaker and have him contact me?"

"That's me. I live two places down the lake. Would you like to see it?"

"No."

"Yes," Romain overrode her objection, seeming not to see when she gesticulated to him.

They walked through the spacious, four-bedroom home with the library, living room, and front yard leading to the docking area and the water.

"Very nice. I'll get back to you, Mr. Burnett, after my wife and I have discussed it."

Pip was silent while they were retracing their steps to the road. Once out of hearing of Mr. Burnett, she turned to him. "Weren't we being a little cavalier with the man? Letting him guide us around that lovely house when we had no intention of buying."

"You did like it, though?"

"Very much. It's roomy, but each bedroom has privacy away from the other. I like the master bedroom suite. And the kitchen is wonderful."

"And I liked the large lot and frontage on the lake, the privacy from the road. Yes, I think I'll get in touch with the realtor."

"Romain, when will you have time to stay here? Most of your business is done from the California office."

"I'll come here when you're with me," he answered cryptically.

"Romain, we came here to talk, and we haven't finished, so how can you come to the conclusion that I'll be with you when you return here?"

"I'm an optimistic person."

They made their way toward the inn, both of them silent, lost in thought.

"I didn't think to ask you if there was someone in your life in New York." Romain dropped the words like a bomb between them.

"I've dated and there have been a few that have interested me." Pip knew her voice was stilted, but she couldn't tell him that usually her relationships faltered because at some point she always compared them with Romain. No matter how hard she tried to prevent it she would draw back from the man and feel a smothering indifference. "How about you?"

"We talked about me. Remember?" Romain thought of the parade of females who'd marched through his life and how he'd hoped that one of them would blot Philippa from his heart. Some almost succeeded, but she was always there. He'd hear a laugh and spin around, thinking she was behind him. He'd see someone with the same graceful gait in the city, and he'd stare at the woman until she disappeared. The worst times were when he saw hair like hers, or on the rare occasion her eyes.

They entered the inn and went straight to their suite.

"I'll order some fruit juice for us," Romain said abruptly.

"Wouldn't you prefer something stronger?"

"Not now." He turned away from her and called room service. Then he faced her again as she sat on one of the high-backed chairs near a window. He took the opposite one to hers and leaned forward, his hands hanging loosely between his knees. "None of this is going to be easy. I'm sure both of us will want to call it quits before we come to some conclusion."

"Yes."

Romain's mouth twitched. "Do you think it's better to bury the past and go on as though we've just met?"

"I think it's better, but I don't know if I could do it."

Romain was silent for a moment. "I'll tell you how I feel. I think we should work at resolving our differences even if it means working through unpleasantness."

Pip exhaled. "I feel that way. It might dissipate this everlasting wondering about who you're with and where."

"And did you do that?" Romain pounced, triumph thinly masked.

"Yes."

"I used to picture you with other men. It made me crazy."

Pip laughed.

"That's not funny."

Pip took note of the menace in his eyes, but she couldn't stifle the mirth that bubbled through her. "I can picture how Abdul would try to tempt you with gourmet food and the nectar of the gods to woo you from your temper."

"Don't forget the dancing girls," Romain shot at her.

"Did Abdul supply those?"

"No, I managed that by myself."

"No doubt." Pip shot to her feet, irritated enough to slap the smile from his mouth, but restraining herself. "Excuse me, I feel soiled."

She marched to the bathroom and slammed the door behind her, unable to still the anger that quivered through her body. "Nothing's changed," she muttered to herself as she stripped the clothes from her body and flung them at the wall. "We still come out of our corners like two boxers, jockeying for position, aiming for the jaw."

She stepped under the shower, letting cold water stream over her body until she shivered, but still feeling so heated inside she was sure she would boil over. The last person I need in my life now is Romain. And that's what I'm going to tell him, she fumed after soaping her head and body. She stared at herself in the full-length mirror. And you can bloody well stop melting every time he looks at you. If you don't stop him now, you'll be a ninety-year-old woman still pining after a man you can't tie down. She glowered at her steam-clouded image, remembering his comments about the dancing girls.

When she reentered the bedroom, her mouth already open to speak, Romain strode past her into the bathroom, his brusque "pardon me" touching her like a lash.

"Well," she sputtered, arms akimbo, staring at the closed door. Damn the man! And she had rehearsed her speech so carefully. It would have stopped him cold!

By the time Romain came out of the bathroom, she was dressed in very tailored teal blue silk dress with leather shoes in a toning color. Her hair was pulled back in a tight french twist.

"Very chic," Romain drawled. "Tasteful but not gaudy."

"How kind of you," she said sweetly, wanting to smack him.

"Don't try it, darling. I'll retaliate." Romain's silky voice branded her.

"I don't know what you mean." She turned her back on him on the pretext of freshening her already glossy lips.

"If you punch me in the face as your eyes tell me you want to do, then I'll throw you on that bed, tear that dress off you, and make love to you until all your makeup is gone and your lovely long hair is wrapped around my neck and not twisted at your nape."

"Barbarian," Pip mustered the word from a dry throat, her heart hammering against her ribs.

"We have a dinner reservation in ten minutes."

Romain reached into his breast pocket, removing a black cheroot from a gold case and lighting it.

"I hate to eat when someone is smoking," she struck out at him in the only way she could think of at the moment.

They left their room and proceeded down the stairs. "I seem to remember that." He inhaled deeply on the thin cigar, then ground it out in a tall ashtray outside the restaurant.

She lifted her chin. "I think it's a good thing we're going back tomorrow afternoon. I don't deal well with fruitless pursuits."

"Poor baby," Romain teased, holding the door so that she could precede him.

She hesitated, the infinitesimal hairs on her body standing straight out as a frisson of anger rippled over her body. She had to steel herself not to run from him and hitchhike back to Manhattan.

Dinner was good country fare. Baked sole stuffed with crisp, tender carrots, celery, and a soupcon of onion was preceded by spinach salad garnished with hard-cooked eggs, mandarin oranges, and walnuts all in a sweet-and-sour dressing. The homemade bread was scones, a type of Scottish roll, and crunchy crusted rye.

"The food is delicious," Pip blurted, unable to stand the silence between them.

"Very." Romain looked at her. "It hasn't been a very successful time between us, has it?"

"No." Pip's heart plummeted at his words. She hated having him aver what she'd been thinking.

"It would seem that we both think this is a failure."

"I suppose." Pip felt as though she were falling down a deep well.

They didn't linger over dinner, yet neither was anxious to go back to their room. In unspoken agreement they left the inn and took a short, meandering walk along the lake. The silence between them was shattered by the sound of a screech owl.

Pip shivered in the chill dampness of the spring air.

"We'll go in now." Romain removed his jacket and placed it around her shoulders. "Don't be stubborn," he said through his teeth when she tried to shrug it off and give it back to him.

They retraced their steps to the inn without speaking.

Pip ran many reasons around in her mind on how to tell Romain she wouldn't be sleeping with him as she changed into her nightgown in the bathroom. Her dentist would have been ecstatic over the time she spent on her teeth. She brushed her hair until it hurt. When she returned to the bedroom, the lights were out, and she could hear Romain's deep breathing when she climbed onto the high bed. She felt thwarted and frustrated. She took deep breaths as she fought the temptation to grab the pitcher of ice water on the night table and dump it over his sleeping form.

Sleep was slow in coming because she was so tense. Each time she turned over to get a more comfortable position she felt the heat from Romain's body. Even though he didn't appear to waken, there was a restless reaction from him each time she moved. How could he sleep when she was so disturbed? He was an insensitive clod! She gnashed her teeth at her stupidity, but she couldn't dispel the affronted feeling.

Finally she fell into a dream-filled sleep, waking more than once. Cold woke her, but her body found and cuddled to his warmth. She fell back to sleep before she could question the sudden comfort that relaxed her.

Sunlight slashing into the room opened her eyes. She knew she was alone even before she heard the shower.

There was a strangers' politeness between them as they passed in and out of the bathroom and dressed in record time.

Pip found the fluffy omelet she chose for breakfast as hard to swallow as a rock, as she fought the tearing grief she felt at the thought of parting from him. At the same time she felt a palpable sense of urgency to be rid of him before all her defenses crumbled and he would see into her soul.

Romain dabbed his mouth with a napkin while watching her and seeing the myriad emotions in her face. How beautiful she was and how deadly to his peace and happiness! Nothing in the world had fazed him until Philippa, but she ripped him apart emotionally. Before her, his responsibilities to his country had come first and he had taken on monumental tasks for his government long before he was out of his teens. Not once had he felt threatened or coerced by friend or enemy. The challenge had buoyed him, thrust him beyond his talents into new endeavors. He'd loved it. Before his marriage to the beautiful woman across from him, life had been dictated by him, orchestrated and enjoyed by him. Philippa had brought chaos, imbalance, anger, frustration—He became aware of her puzzled stare. "You said something? Sorry. I have a great deal on my mind."

"Of course. The business," she said acidly. "I was wondering if you had intended to leave this afternoon."

"This morning will do as well," he interrupted her brusquely.

It took very little time to pack their things and leave the inn.

Pip felt a pang as they drove out the driveway to the main street of the town, but she didn't look back. "Mr. Burnett will have expected to hear from you."

"I talked to him this morning," Romain answered noncommittally.

"Oh." Pip fought to keep the disappointment from her voice as she imagined the people who would subsequently buy the lovely house on the lake and live there. Perhaps there would be children. . . . She bit down on her lip to mask the groan that rose in her as she saw a laughing boy and girl cavorting in the yard near the water. Tears stung her eyes. Pip looked out the window on her side of the car but she couldn't see the pine-strewn hills that threw giant shadows on the sunny land around them.

They drove for miles in silence.

Pip didn't know when the motion of the car and the fatigue of her own thoughts fused into sleep.

Romain glanced over at her as her head lolled on the back of the seat. He reached out an arm and scooped her into the curve of his shoulder where she settled with a purr of satisfaction. "Just as you did last night, my pet." He kissed her forehead, then focused his attention again on the winding road that would lead him to the New York throughway, then to the city itself.

The squeal of the brakes and the muttered imprecations penetrated Pip's sleep. Blinking, she awoke and moaned while she rubbed her stiff neck. She straightened and blushed as she realized that she had been cushioned in the curve of Romain's body and that he must have driven that way for hours. "Sorry. I didn't mean to fall asleep that way."

"No problem. You were tired. You are too thin and you certainly work too hard."

"I like my work." Pip slid over to her side of the wide bench seat. "And I do it well."

"I am not questioning your ability. I just think you should take time off now and then."

"And what do you call what I just did?"

"Certainly not relaxation."

"No. It wasn't that." Pip stared out the windshield at Manhattan traffic.

Romain jammed on the brakes as a driver cut in front of him, harsh words issuing from his mouth in Arabic.

Pip roughly understood him to say something very unflattering about the other driver's mother. "Romain, I think it might be better for me to stay in my apartment. . . ."

"My uncle will have returned to his house from the hospital. He'll want to see you."

"Yes, and I have every intention of visiting him on Long Island, but I think I would prefer my own place this evening." She struggled to keep her voice even.

"I think it is only a courtesy to return to his home when you know he's expecting you, but it will be as you wish."

"Why is it that you feel you must talk like Colonel Blimp when you are trying to bring me around to your way of thinking?" She was irritated. With him she was always in the wrong! "Save your diplomatic smugness for someone else!"

He shot her an angry look. "Stop being childish."

"I'm always childish when I argue with you, or so you think. What does that make you? A dirty old man?"

"Pippa, stop it."

"I won't." She was out of breath and in tears. "Take me to my apartment."

"So be it." He wanted to stop the car and put her over his knee.

"And you can save your fury for the Dharanians. I don't want it."

"No Dharanian woman would act as childishly as you."

"If she did, you'd probably cut off her head."

"Our women are certainly as well thought of by their families and spouses as American women are."

"I know that," Pip mumbled.

"You have such a poor opinion of me, Philippa. It's amazing that you married me the first time."

"Now who's talking like a child. You sound like a martyr."

"And you're being irritating."

"Ohh, what's the sense in talking to you."

Pip stared sightlessly at the wildness of Manhattan traffic. It was the rush hour, but Romain wove through the traffic with ease and panache.

Pip recalled the pictures he had shown her of when he had driven in the Gran Prix in Le Mans, France, and the Mille Miglia in Italy. Then she hadn't been able to stem her fear at the thought of him crashing in one of the high-powered races. Even now her skin prickled with icy perspiration at the thought. "You don't drive anymore, do you?"

"What?"

"Drive. You don't race as you once did?"

"No. Well, that is, I drove in Mille Miglia last year, but it didn't hold the same thrill it once had." He recalled how he'd felt when a woman had kissed him after the race and he had seen Pip's face instead. The woman had whispered "animal," and smiled at him when he'd lifted his head. He could still remember how disgusted he'd been with himself. He shook himself from his discomfiting reverie and pulled up in front of her apartment house.

"There's no need for you to come in with me."

"Just go in and unlock your door. I'll bring your bags."

"I can carry the smaller case."

"Philippa!" Romain snarled at her.

She left the car at a run going up the steps to unlock the outer door with her key. She held it open for Romain after ringing for the elevator.

They rose in silence to her floor.

He took the cases into her room, faced her, and inclined his head. "Good-bye Philippa."

CHAPTER TWELVE

Pip resumed her life like a robot. She responded to all the stimuli of her work with determination, but not with the same verve. She completed many small tasks she had been putting off and even began devising the formula for the benefit funded by King Haddad of Dharan, even though she felt an ache every time she picked up the folder. To her Dharan was Romain! Romain! Every hour of the day it seemed she had to forcibly eject him from her mind. She shook her head and stared down at the file in her hands. She told herself she was doing well and shrugged off the twelve-hour days she was putting in. "Hard work never hurt anyone," she muttered the maxim of her Scottish ancestors over and over to herself when she would begin to flag. At least with the long work day she fell asleep the moment her head hit the pillow, and for that she was grateful.

April disappeared into May. May became June. Pip felt slowed and heavy, even though she was pushing herself more and more. Each time she looked in the mirror her cheeks had a more hollowed-out look. "You are a strange lady, Pippa Stonely," she told her mirror one morning as she was applying a heavier base of makeup than usual. "You are beginning to look like the lead singer in a Punk Rock group with those black shadows under your eyes, but still you gain about a pound a week in weight."

That morning she had an early appointment with a client. She felt hazy and bemused through the entire meeting. Because she was feeling tired, she took a taxi from the client's office back to her own, a mere four blocks away. "I'll have to up the vitamin C and B 12," she muttered to herself when she paid her taxi.

"Try selenium, lady. My wife takes it. Says it keeps her from jumping off the Brooklyn Bridge. Got three boys," he pronounced glumly before shooting away from the curb back into traffic.

"Couldn't hurt." Pippa blinked at the retreating cab before turning to enter the building housing the offices of Rafkin and Stonely. By the time she'd taken the elevator to the tenth floor, her knees felt rubbery and she was choking with thirst.

"Hi, Pippa," Marylee Evans, her secretary, called to her as she walked toward her own office.

"Hi." Pip turned to greet the ginger-haired girl with the wide smile. It puzzled Pippa to see two images of her secretary. As she fell she seemed to hear Marylee call her name, but not only couldn't she answer, she felt divorced from the earth.

Pip opened her eyes to see Lou Rafkin, her partner, bending over her. She realized almost at once that she was lying on the lumpy couch in her office. "What—?"

"Don't move. You passed out, lady. You've been working too damned hard." He hauled in a deep breath, shaking his head. "We have medics coming who are going to take you to the hospital. I'll be going with you."

"Don't be silly," Pip croaked. "There's nothing wrong with me. I was just dizzy for a moment."

"Stop it, Pip. You've been out for over ten minutes. I want to know why."

"So do we." Lois and Marylee said in unison as they bent over her, their faces creased with worry.

"Just have Lois go with me, then," Pip capitulated.

"Someone has to be here when Lothar calls and King Haddad will want a report today. The work is in my briefcase . . ."

"Shut up, sweetheart. You scared the hell out of me. I've never heard Marylee scream that way," Lou told her gruffly just as the medics pushed their way in the door.

In short order she was on her way to a small private hospital in Manhattan.

"It's the closest, and they have room and all the facilities," the medic riding with her in the ambulance explained to Pip and Lois.

Once there she underwent extensive testing that both tired and irritated her. She felt sure the tests were unnecessary. A good night's sleep and she would be fine.

Later in the privacy of her small room she and Lois carried on a desultory conversation, but Pip had a hard time keeping her eyes open.

A tall spare man pushed open the door, staring at Lois until she rose to leave, telling Pip that she would just be outside before closing the door behind her.

"What's the bad news?" Pip asked lightly, not liking the grim look on his face.

"My name is Dr. Braverman. I understand from your friend that it's Miss Stonely and you are unmarried." At Pip's nod he looked down at the chart in his hand, then back at her, his cold expression not changing. "It is not too late for an abortion, but I think you should have considered it earlier. It certainly would have been better than working yourself into exhaustion to abort the fetus."

Pip stared at him, swallowing several times. "Are you telling me I'm pregnant?"

"Are you telling me you didn't know?" Dr. Braverman's eyebrows rose.

"I'm telling you that I'm willing to do anything that will protect the child and bring it to term." She could feel her whole being tighten in a protective cocoon around the new life. Oh, yes, she wanted the baby, and she was going to do everything that she could to protect it.

The stern face relaxed and he pulled a chair closer to the bed and seated himself. "Good for you, and I'll help you get well." He looked down at the chart in his lap. "You have an iron deficiency that diet will help and vitamins will aid, but you need more rest, fresh air, mild exercise." He looked up at her, his lips pursed. "A business colleague by the name of Lou called and said that you've been working long hours." At her nod, he continued, "That will have to stop. I don't say you can't work, but I'd like you to develop a new regimen, say, a six-hour day, an exercise schedule that's not too arduous, of course, and vitamin therapy—the works. What do you think of my idea?"

"You have my word it will be done," Pip said fervently. "When can I go home?"

"Tomorrow, unless something exotic turns up, which I don't foresee. How does that sound?"

"Wonderful."

"Do you have your own ob-gyn?"

"Yes. Dr. Wales."

"Good choice. I know her very well. I'll apprise her of the situation. Good luck to you."

The next day both Lou and Lois were there to drive her home from the hospital.

"Your apartment looks like a florist's shop," Lois told her fondly. Pip sat between Lou and the model in the front seat of his car. "The staff has been worried about you, not to mention all the clients who have been concerned."

Pip's head swiveled toward Lou. "You didn't say anything to the king's secretary about me, did you?"

"No. We talked, but you were not mentioned." Lois patted her knee.

"Thank you." Pip couldn't help the sigh of relief that

escaped her. The last thing she needed was having inquiries made about her stay in the hospital, inquiries that could reach Romain's ears. For the time being she wanted to hug the knowledge about having a baby to herself. It was such a special time!

"I like flowers." Pip turned her head and smiled at Lois, relaxing again. Since the doctor had told her yesterday about having a baby, she had been in kind of a euphoria. She had a part of Romain she would never lose—his child! She would have to tell him, she realized, but she would take a few days to hug the news to herself and dwell on the thought of being a mother. Besides, she wanted to think carefully about what she would say to him before she faced him with his impending paternity.

"You should tell him soon," Lou said gruffly, reading her mind. "If it were Lois, I would want to know at once."

"I'll remember that, O, Learned One." Lois smirked. Then she leaned across Pippa and tapped his arm. "Don't be dictatorial with her, Lou. She knows what she's doing."

"I'll tell him in a week or so. I want to tell Aunt Grace and Uncle George first." She couldn't explain to Lou and Lois that she needed time to figure out what she would say to Romain.

Lou nodded. "I've already arranged for a full-time housekeeper for you. Her name is Danville. She's a widow who has been looking for full-time work."

"Thanks, Lou. How much is this going to cost me?"

"Never mind, the firm is taking care of it."

"No way. I'm taking care of it. It's nice of you, but I want to handle this myself. I'll cut back on other things, but I want to take care of my own expenses."

"Independent lady," Lou growled.

Lois chuckled and kissed Pip's cheek. "You bet we are."

Lois and Lou took the few things she had up to her apartment, made her a pot of tea, extracting a promise from Pip that she would go right to bed.

After they left her, Pip went through to the bedroom, stripped off her clothes, and showered the grimy hospital feeling from her hair and body. She felt tired but refreshed when she finished. Climbing between the crisp sheets on her bed was so welcome, but it was also an effort because she felt so fatigued. She was asleep almost at once.

She awoke thinking the alarm had gone off. Groggily she stared at her bedside clock. Seven! She blinked and yawned trying to orient herself. It took a few moments to realize that it was not the morning. She'd slept for six hours and it was seven in the evening. What she'd thought was the alarm clock going off was actually the doorbell ringing. "All right, all right, I'm coming," Pip muttered, swinging her feet to the floor, pulling a dressing gown over her nakedness, and stumbling out of the bedroom. "It sounds as though someone is leaning on the bell," she muttered to herself as she crossed to the door and opened it the length of the chain. "No!" she gasped, horrified.

"That's a fine way to greet someone at your door," Romain drawled, placing one of the suitcases he was carrying at his feet. "Would you mind opening up? These are heavy and I'm crushing the flowers."

"Flowers?" Pip asked blankly, unhooking the chain and swinging back the door.

It was so obvious to him she didn't want him there. She didn't even try to hide how she felt. But he wasn't going to allow her to cut up their life as though it were nothing. He could feel the bones in his face tighten.

Pip stared up at his grim face. All the pleasant wooing had vanished. He looked like Romain again, tough as old boots, determined and unswayed. Why had she opened the door? Why had she let him in the apartment? She cursed her stupidity. "I'm tired and I don't feel like entertaining. Why didn't you call . . . ?" Her voice trailed at the white heat in his face. She had the hazy sensation of smelling brimstone.

"I'll put these in the spare bedroom," Romain told her, hefting his luggage and taking it down the short hall to the small room she used as a guest room.

"You won't fit in there," she muttered through tight lips. "The bed's too short and narrow, and when you throw your arm in your sleep, as you always do, you'll hit the wall," she talked to herself, feeling helpless as she stood in the center of her living room.

Romain returned to the room, his eyes narrowing on her. "Shouldn't you put those in water?" he indicated the white roses she still clutched in front of her like a shield.

"Good idea." Pip had to steel herself to walk past him into the small kitchenette that was separated from her living room by a long counter. The electricity that ran over her skin told her that Romain was behind her. She shoved the delicate rose buds into a glass vase she hauled from the cupboard above her head and turned to face him. "This will do." She held up the vase as though she would get him to move away from her with it.

He took the vase from her hand and placed it on the counter. "Why are you looking so pale?' His hands came up to grasp her upper arms. "You had obviously been in bed when I arrived. Have you been ill?" He felt her flinch under his hands and his grip tightened bringing her closer to him. "Tell me," he demanded in a hoarse voice, fear filling him. She was ill! He knew it! Icy despair touched him. No! He wouldn't let anything happen to her. "Pippa, is something wrong?"

She heard the pain in his voice and pushed back from him, feeling the edge of the sink dig into her back. "No, no. I'm not ill. I was resting. I've been working too hard . . ."

"I know that," he said gruffly, his eyes still going over her, some of the ice leaving his veins. "You're sure you're all right?"

"Yes, I'm fine." Tears stung her eyes as he nodded and stepped back from her.

The phone rang as he opened his mouth to speak.

"Excuse me."

"Of course," Romain answered her just as formally, inclining his head and following after her as she lifted the phone in the living room.

"Yes, Aunt Grace, how are you? Fine, just fine. Well, maybe a little tired. You are? Oh, wonderful, I can't wait to see you," Pippa sobbed, then coughed to cover the emotional moment. "No, not really, I'm fine. Romain is here. Would you like to speak to him?" Pip babbled, then held the phone out to him before her aunt could respond. She needed time to pull herself together and get her blood to stop thundering through her veins like a torrent. She closed her eyes, her back to Romain as he carried on a low but distinct conversation with her aunt.

"It will be nice to see you. I'm sure my uncle would be crushed if you didn't stay with him. No, I insist. I will apprise him of your arrival." He pulled a gold case from his pocket with his free hand. It was one that Philippa had given him on the anniversary of their first meeting.

When she turned to interrupt and tell him that she wanted her aunt and uncle to stay with her she saw the case. Her entire system went on hold. She found it difficult to catch her breath as she recalled how delighted he'd been with the gift and that she'd remembered the date. "Darling, darling," he'd crooned to her, "you've made me so happy. I'll have you with me every time I reach into my pocket."

He'd swept her into his arms and carried her up the

210

stairs to their bedroom where they'd made passionate love to each other for hours. It had seemed eons later that Romain had shown her the pocket watch he'd gotten her, the fob in the shape of a heart and encrusted with diamonds and turquoise. That, and her wedding ring, had been the only jewelry she'd taken with her when she'd left Dharan. She inhaled a shaky sob, her hand pressed to her mouth. She mustn't think of those times. She had to keep her wits about her. Her child was the chief concern now.

He snapped the gold case open to the pad, extracting the gold pen that was magnetized to the case. "Yes, I have the arrival time . . ."

"They've always stayed with me," Pippa blurted, coming out of her reverie.

"Would you like to say good-bye?" Romain handed her the phone, the palm of his hand over the mouthpiece. "I'm sure you would want them to have every comfort and amenity. They could use some spoiling, don't you think?"

"Yes," she rasped, snatching the phone, making small talk with her beloved aunt but not trying to dissuade her from going out to the Long Island estate to stay. "Yes. I'll meet you at the airport and . . ."

"Abdul will pick you up and take you to the airport, then you can visit with them here before he takes them to my uncle."

Pip made her good-byes in a red haze, anger spilling from her the moment she hung up. "Just what do you think you're doing? Coming here like Attila the Hun and taking over my apartment and my aunt and uncle! It's time for you to leave." She raised her chin defiantly.

"No. I'm staying. Whether you speak to me or not, I'm staying." Romain's eyes glittered with combat. Then his gaze slipped away from her and shot around the room. "Where did you get all the flowers and plants?" His head swiveled back to her, and he saw the convulsive swallowing of her throat. "It's not your birthday." He fired the words at her.

"I know that." She tried to rally, throwing words around her head like marbles in a can, rattling but signifying nothing. Her mind had turned to mush. She looked up into his eyes and sighed. "Romain, why don't you come back tomorrow and we'll talk?"

He studied her deeply, seeing her uncertainty, and a tinge of fear in her eyes. Romain took a deep breath, tamping down his ire. They were going to make a new beginning, reprising the best of times, discarding the worst, he vowed to himself. He reached out and grasped her hand, pulling her with gentle words toward the couch. "Don't pull away," he told her with a smile. "I'm not going to eat you, Pippa. Though I can remember a time or two when I tried."

"Romain!" Pip could feel her body heat from the toes upward, fighting the melting feeling that was turning her body to honey at his words. "Why are you here?"

He faced her on the couch, his one arm along the back, his one leg almost touching her. "I've come to try and play it your way."

Caution and curiosity warred within her. Now what was that high-tech mind of his fabricating? Romain not only thought faster than others, he could compute what they might be thinking and have an answer and resolution ready before they voiced their thoughts. It had been a constant surprise and irritant the way he had been able to read her when they were man and wife, and she had worked hard to develop the ability to shield her mind from him—at least some of the time. He had penetrated that barrier more than once. She forced her mind to what he's just said. "You have?" she asked.

He spread his hands wide. "I've capitulated. You've mentioned more than once that my life had been smothering to you, that I haven't paid enough attention to what you want and need, or how you want our life to be." He let his hand fall to her hair, looping one of the long strands around his finger. "I guess I'm saying that it's time to turn our lives around. You're in charge, Pip. You orchestrate how we'll live, what we'll do, whom we'll see. How does that sound?"

"Dangerous," she pushed the word from her dry throat. "Give me the night to think about it."

"Pip," Romain admonished, irritation in his voice. "We both said we should give our marriage a chance. And putting it off is not the best way to do that. When we tried it on my terms, it didn't work. Now we'll do it your way."

"My way," Pip repeated lamely. "Whatever that is," she muttered, watching him as he looked around the room again, his face changing as he took note of the other flowers and plants then back at the white roses he had brought her.

Romain frowned at her, feeling cold jealousy that a selection of men might be behind the assortment of flowers. "Who sent these?" His arm made an arc as he gestured toward the multicolored blooms.

"I like the white roses." She tried to smile at him as she lifted one of the fragrant buds from the vase to her nose.

"Pippa!" The soft command echoed in the room.

"The office staff, mostly. Some came from clients." Pip rose to her feet and crossed the room on the pretext of sniffing the fragrance of a bouquet of carnations that sat on a windowsill, the rosebud held in front of her like a barrier.

"Why?"

"I was ill. No, not ill, just a fainting spell." Pip swung around, mouth agape as Romain cried out and jumped from the couch.

"What the bloody hell do you mean? I knew something was wrong. Give it to me straight, Pip." Blood congealed in his veins, his heart thudded against his breastbone. If she was ill, he would take her to the finest clinics in Europe. No! He wouldn't allow her to be ill. There were miraculous cures in some of the Asian hospitals. No! It made his hands shake to dwell on what she could have. "Tell me."

"I fainted in work yesterday."

"No!" he shot back hoarsely. "You never faint."

"I did yesterday." She faced him, braced, determined to take her time in relating her news, until she noticed the pain etched his face. His bones pushed through the flesh in a grinding effort for control, his color fading to putty. "Romain, don't. I'm not ill."

"Swear it," he ground out, his teeth snapping together on the words.

"I swear," Pip whispered, her hands reaching out to him in comfort.

"No. Don't touch me. I'll explode if you do," Romain said in a strangled voice. "Why did you faint?"

"I'm . . . I mean we're—ah—going to have a baby."

Romain stared at her not believing he'd heard her correctly for a moment. He shook his head. "God, I didn't take precautions." He hit the palm of his hand with his fist. "No. You can't, Pippa. You're not strong enough. You had trouble last time."

Pip shook her head. "Don't be ridiculous. I fainted because I've been overworking and not sleeping well at night."

"Quit your job."

"I'm thinking about taking a leave of absence."

"Please do that," Romain grated, his hands clenching and unclenching at his sides. It struck him like lightning that he had lived without her all those months when they were separated because he knew she was alive and well in

214

the United States. Now, at the thought of her life being at risk, he knew that he could not leave her. "If you don't let me stay here, I'll camp on your doorstep. Oh, my darling, this is such wonderful news—"

Pip saw the sheen of perspiration on his upper lip, the lethal glitter in those green eyes. "I wouldn't expect you to live on my doorstep, but perhaps—"

"When were you going to tell me? Or wasn't I going to be told?"

"Of course you were going to be told. I wanted to tell Aunt Grace and Uncle George and then you, probably tomorrow or the next day."

"Your order of importance intrigues me." His hard drawl prickled her skin like morning dew, a muscle jumping at the corner of his mouth.

"It's not as though we're married." Pip's defiant words dribbled away at the look of molten fury on his face. "It's my baby," she whispered.

"And mine."

"I don't want to argue with you. I'm going to bed." She spun on her heels and marched toward her bedroom.

"Fine. I'll see you in the morning, but you'd better believe me, Pippa."

"About what?" she answered him, not turning to face him or able to quell the quaver in her voice.

"You damn well know."

"If I were you, I wouldn't choose to stay where I'm not wanted," Pip shot at him, lifting her chin and sailing into the bedroom.

"You're not me." Romain's whisper reached her just before she slammed the door.

"Thank God for that," she said childishly, plunking herself down on the bed and pounding her fist on the quilt folded at the foot.

Her head fell back against the pillow and she curled herself into the fetal position. "How am I going to handle having him around again? It will be like trying to put a hurricane in a five-pound bag. He'll go crazy in such a confined area, and I'll go insane waiting for the explosion." She pushed her face into the pillow. "And how I'll hate it when he leaves me," she groaned.

She fell asleep, hugging her quilt to her, dreams invading her rest almost at once. Romain was there, the white djellaba he often wore when he went into the desert, flowing out behind him as he seemed to zoom toward her. Alien mists floated around him as he gestured to Pippa to come to him.

"No," she called out, even as she felt herself being propelled toward his waiting arms. "No." She was swept into the mists, calling for help, the sounds she made drowned in Romain's laughter. She was suffocating, smothering . . .

"Philippa! Pip! Wake up. Lord, you're buried in your sheets." Romain half laughed, half groaned as he struggled to unwrap her body mummied in the sheets. "What a dream," he muttered as he freed her head.

"What? What happn'd?" Pip gasped, perspiring, out of breath, and shaking.

Romain caught her close to him, cradling her body, rocking her back and forth. "A nightmare. What was it about?"

"You," Pip sobbed, clutching his shirt convulsively. "You had me wrapped in your djellaba, and you didn't hear me telling you I was smothering because you were laughing and . . ." she gulped a breath and pressed her face into his chest.

"It's all right now. I'll keep you safe, even from me." His heart squeezed inside of him as he massaged her shaking body. He hated what she told him, but he was damn well going to rid her of all her fears. No matter what it cost him he would stop the tremors that racked her body—permanently.

216

She pushed back from him and looked up at his face. "I was being stupid."

"Dreams, especially nightmares, can be very real." He pushed the damp tendrils back from her forehead. "Now get over here to a chair and I'll remake your bed."

Pip was so awestruck by the picture of Prince Romain of Dharan getting clean, dry sheets from the linen closet and remaking her bed that she said nothing.

"Now get back in here, and I'll cover you and stay with you until you're asleep."

"There's no need." Pip felt flustered, her gaze sliding away from him as she climbed into bed. When he tucked the blankets around her, she stiffened. Wasn't he going to leave? She would never sleep with Romain in the room! He was holding her hand! She had no sensation of her eyes closing, her body relaxing and curling against him as fatigue took her and she tumbled into sleep.

"You've been afraid too long, my Pippa," Romain told her as he kissed her forehead and tried to release his hand from her grip.

"No," Pip groaned, pulling at him in her sleep.

It was Romain's turn to groan as he lay down beside her, cuddling her body close to him. "I'll be having the dreams now, darling." He turned on his side and scooped her into his arms, hearing her satisfied sigh with ironic amusement. "One of us is going to sleep well." He laid his head on top of hers, trying to fight the hardening of his body. "Potent lady, you'll keep me awake tonight."

It was dawn when Romain finally slept, but he felt no chagrin, only a deep sense of the rightness of holding Philippa again. It was as though someone had sutured the missing half to his being again. "You're mine," he mumbled into her hair before his eyes closed.

Pippa awoke feeling refreshed and very cozy, catching the cool breeze that fluttered the curtains at the open window. It was so warm in bed she dreaded the thought

217

of getting up and going to work. Memory flooded back and she recalled that she didn't have to work today, that she was going to take a few days off and then go back to work for short periods each day.

She pressed her hand to the flat of her abdomen and became aware that another hand was already there. Romain! Last night flashed before her eyes. She thrust away from his hand and stumbled out of bed, feeling vertigo as she whirled to face him.

Eyes blinking, Romain came awake, at once knowing where he was. He saw Pip swaying with one hand over her mouth. "Morning sickness," he pronounced tersely, leaping from the bed and catching her up in arms. "It's all right, Pip, I have you."

"You're not a doctor, oh, aagh . . . I hate to be sick," she sagged in his arms, retching when they reached the bathroom.

"There, you'll be better now," he soothed her, wiping her face with a damp cloth.

"Never." She croaked. "You've made me sick. This hasn't happened before," she whispered through dry lips, her head bobbing on his shoulder as he lifted her into the shower and stepped in beside her, washing her down with speed and ease and drying her just as fast before carrying her back to bed.

Pippa clutched his shoulders and thought about all the times he made love to her in the shower. He hated her now, she thought sadly, her mouth sandpaper dry. Wouldn't he have made love to her in the shower if he did love her, she pondered fuzzily.

"Not to worry. You just stay here and I'll get you something to drink." Romain tucked her into bed again and strode from the room.

"Sure, abandon me now that I'm sick and ugly," she sobbed, tears rolling down her cheeks onto the quilt that was tucked under her chin.

"Here we are," Romain said cheerily a few minutes later, placing a tray on the bedside table, then coming to help her sit up so that he could put the tray on her lap. "There you are. Crackers and tea."

Pip took a bite of cracker, then another and another until she'd finished them and half the cup of tea. Feeling better, she sank back against the pillows with a sigh. "I never eat things like that for breakfast."

"Ungrateful brat," Romain said and laughed at her. "I went out and purchased several books on pregnancy and the chapters on morning sickness recommend tea and dry toast or crackers."

"You bought books? On being pregnant? This morning?" Pip gaped at him, the teacup poised in front of her mouth.

"Yes, several. Do you want to see them?" Without waiting for an answer Romain left the room in that smooth, powerful way he had, and returned in seconds with five hard-bound books and three paperbacks. "Would you like to read them?"

Pip looked askance at the stack of books he put next to her on the bed. "You haven't read all of these?"

"I've speed-read all but one, but I intend to go back over them, of course."

"Of course." She closed her eyes. "No one likes a speed-reader, didn't you know that? They are graded on the same scale as a wiseacre."

"I'll teach you to speed-read."

"You told me that when we were married, but . . ." she paused, realizing all at once that what she was saying would put them on a more intimate plane than she wanted to be.

"Yes? Continue," Romain urged, sitting down next to her on the bed and moving the tray to the side table again. "You were saying that I was going to teach you speed-reading. And that I failed to do it. Another way I

219

let you down, I see." Romain settled his length at her side, stretching out his legs so that they were touching hers. Then he lowered his head to press his lips to the valley between her breasts. "Something else I will rectify."

His lips and breath feathered over her breasts causing an ecstasy that had Pip quivering. "Nothing to fuss about," she wheezed, her eyes falling shut, her body in somnolent awareness of his heated closeness.

"Don't be silly," he breathed, his lips questing under and over her soft globes, pausing a moment at the nipple. "How did you happen to end up with the most beautiful breasts in the world, my pet?" Before she could answer, he began to caress and suck gently on the rounded firmness, eliciting a groan from Pip.

The tender, pulling sensation had Pippa arching her back in delight.

Romain lifted his head, easing back from her, his hair mussed where Pip had clutched his head, his breathing harsh and erratic. "No! Don't, Pip. I have to stop."

"Why?" She felt cheated and irked as he straightened the sheet around her and sat back. He was close to her but no longer touching her. It gave her a feeling of satisfaction to see that the hand he ran through his hair was shaking.

Romain took some deep breaths, his eyes emerald fire as he looked at her. "You delight me, love. You're still the same quintessential voluptuary you've always been, but we have to be careful. One of the books said that it was usually safe for a couple to have intercourse when the woman was pregnant, but that there could be times when it wasn't. When the doctor says it's safe for you, then . . ."

"Don't assume," she snapped at him, feeling frustrated. "I may not be in the mood then. Besides, we're not married, nor do we have a relationship."

"What we had just a moment ago was a tropical storm and you know it." Romain's eyebrows met over his forehead in a resentful bridge, his green eyes glittering battle. "So don't try to negate it."

"I'm going to brush my teeth." Pip looked at him pointedly until he muttered an Arabic imprecation, lifted the tray, and strode from the room.

She lingered in the bathroom, polishing her fingernails and toenails, giving herself a steamy facial. She was loath to leave the bathroom and face Romain. She didn't want to have words with him again. They argued about anything and everything!

She opened the door cautiously, her chin up, prepared to do battle with him if she must. She saw clothes laid out on the bed, cotton jeans and a blouse, even undies. "It's a good thing he didn't put out a bra. I wouldn't have worn it," she told her mirror image. She had finished dressing and had made up her face with a very light hand, just a touch of lip gloss and skin moisturizer and eyeliner. Her color hadn't come back completely, but she didn't want to bother with liquid makeup and blusher. When she was brushing her hair, it sunk in that Romain had been very quiet for a long time.

She opened the door to the bedroom and knew almost at once that he had gone. She felt bereft and flooded with grief. "Damn you, Romain Al Adal. You come into my life, turn it upside down, and leave." She curled her hands into fists, looking around her living room with stinging eyes. "I could kill you, but I will not let it get to me. I'm feeling teary because I'm expecting. Pregnant women do that. I won't miss you," she spoke through her teeth, her one hand curled protectively over her middle.

She saw the note sitting on the coffee table. Pippa almost crumpled and discarded it when she recognized his handwriting.

Her hands were shaking as she read it. "Pippa, I'll be

back in an hour. Have to get clothes. I've made an appointment for us at your doctor's. Found the number in your book. We're lucky to get a cancellation. Romain."

"The . . . the buffoon!" Pippa sputtered, relief and anger warring through her. "If he thinks that part of reprising our marriage is for him to run it, he has another thing coming. I'll—I'll make my own appointments," she blustered, pressing the note to her breast, the sun blinding bright as it shone through the windows.

CHAPTER THIRTEEN

The gynecologist confirmed that Pip was to have a child and told Romain, who later joined them in the examining room, that there was no worry involved with intercourse.

"Thank you," Pip told the doctor stiffly, glaring at Romain, who lounged at ease in the chair next to her.

After getting several prescriptions, which Romain took and placed in his wallet, and a diet and exercise regimen, they left the office.

Pip wouldn't look at him! How dare he throw questions at Clare Wales as though she were on trial and not the doctor Pip had known for a long time.

"Your doctor is very attractive," Romain drawled.

"And if you say quite bright for a woman, I shall kick you in the knee."

"When did you ever hear me make a sexist remark like that?" Romain touched the tip of her nose with his finger.

"Who gave you the right to give my doctor the third degree? I trust her and like her," she said and glared at him, arms akimbo.

"Stamping your foot?" Romain chuckled. "My, my, you are getting tough."

"Tougher than you know, buster." Pip lifted her chin and sailed past him to the car.

"You mustn't be jealous, darling. I'll be faithful."

"Ohh. How dare you think I'm jealous? And I happen to know that Dharanian men aren't known for their fidelity." She stared at him stonily as he opened the car door for her.

"Wrong. They are faithful to the women they love," Romain whispered in her ear as he helped her into her seat, then shut the door even as she opened her mouth to retort.

She glared at him through the windshield as he went around to his side and slipped under the wheel.

"Tch, tch, mustn't pout. New mamas must be serene."

"I am a very serene person," Pip said through her teeth.

"Good. Tomorrow your aunt and uncle will be coming. Do you mind them knowing that I'm staying with you?"

"You're not staying with me."

"I am." He turned on the ignition of the powerful car and shot away from the parking lot with a blare of horns from the irate drivers he zoomed around to get to the street.

"Don't drive like a maniac," Pip told him as she was thrown against her seat belt.

Romain cursed roundly in Arabic. "Sorry, darling. That was foolish of me when you're in a delicate condition."

"I am not in a delicate condition. Clare just pronounced me fit as a fiddle."

"But overtired. Remember that." He reached over and squeezed her thigh, loving the feel of the soft but smooth muscled flesh. "You make me angry when you say we won't be together while you're pregnant. We will be. I don't want to camp on your doorstep, but if I have to buy the building where you live in order to be close to you, I'm prepared to do that, too," he told her softly.

"Plutocrat."

"I prefer the term 'determined' because that's what I'm going to be with you."

224

"And I say I'm going to be in charge of my life."

"I have no quarrel with that. In fact, I recall telling you that you would be orchestrating both our lives." He lifted her hand to his mouth, his tongue tracing her palm. "And that was before I knew about the child. Now there is our baby and I won't be shut out of that."

Pip inhaled deep shuddering breaths, angry with him and angry with herself because she accepted the justice of what he said. She remained silent as Romain steered the Lamborghini through Manhattan with the same panache that colored all his movements.

When they reached the apartment, he managed to find a parking place in front. He shut off the engine and turned in his seat and looked at her. "Would you consider living in my apartment here in town? I do have underground parking there." Hard amusement laced his words.

Pip bit her lip. "I think we have more to discuss than underground parking."

Romain shrugged, green eyes glittering irritation. "I know that." He bit back his anger, his one finger touching her shoulder. "Not much has changed. We can still flare at each other over the smallest things."

"Yes."

"I'm not leaving you, Pip. We can go on from there any way you choose. However you orchestrate our being together is fine with me. I told you that and I meant it. I intend to bend over backward to see that you have a comfortable, safe pregnancy. Will you meet me halfway?" Romain hadn't realized he was holding his breath until he saw her nod and he exhaled deeply.

She watched him come out of the car and to her side. She knew Romain too well to try getting out by herself. He made no effort to hide his contempt for men who did not perform the courteous amenities.

He tucked his hand under her arm as they went up the

steps to her building, loving the softness of her body that was so close to his. "Since Dr. Wales says you're very healthy except for working too hard, I think you should plan certain times of the day for complete rest." He grinned down at her. "Would it tire you too much to go out to dinner? We could come home early."

We! Pip heard the pronoun like an alarm bell in her brain. He was moving ever closer to her! Soon she would come to depend on him, need his presence. Now was the time to tell him to bug off, disappear, call back in ten years. It didn't matter that it seemed like eons since she'd done anything so frivolous as go out to dinner when it wasn't business. No, now was the time to be resolute and keep Romain from getting too close. "Dining out sounds wonderful."

"Good." Romain felt like shouting with laughter. He was dizzy with triumph just because Philippa had told him she would like to go out for dinner.

Once in the apartment, they were silent with one another again. Pip felt a wariness, a need to protect the peace, however nebulous, they had between them.

Romain watched her move around the small rooms straightening up, her body graceful and only slightly concave in the middle. It had been the greatest relief of his life when the doctor had said that the fainting spell did not portend any damage to Pippa. He had been fully prepared to push for an abortion if the need arose, even though he sensed that she would have fought him on that. He needed her alive and well. It was important to his heartbeat that she be more than able to bring a child to term. He wanted her to have his baby, but he neeeded her alive and well even more. He felt the planet drop from under his feet at the thought of losing her in death.

That evening when Pippa entered her walk-in closet to choose the dress she would wear, it gave her a start to see Romain's suits side by side with her clothes as they once had been. Despite the roomy wing they had had in the Dharanian royal complex, so that each of them could have had a separate suite, Pip and Romain had stayed together in one grouping of mammoth rooms. Romain had insisted that some of her clothes hang with his as some of hers were in his closet. Pip remembered how she had enjoyed this simple intimacy between them. In those days she floated through the moments and hours, coming alive only when Romain was with her. They had never slept apart when they were married even when they were angry with one another. That had been one of the pacts they had made when they first married. Now, as she stared at the fine pin-striped business suits he favored, the memories threatened to swamp her. "We were so close, yet so far apart," she mumbled, fingering the silky material of a pair of trousers. "You were a fool, Pip. There was so much you could have discussed with him, but you held back, letting the irritations sour."

"Do you always stand in closets and talk to yourself?" Romain's sardonic words startled her.

"Only in the months with an r." Pip bit her lip when he laughed, her body turning to goose bumps at his nearness.

"Shall I join you?"

"I'll be right out." Pip grabbed something off a hanger and tried to push past him.

"I think you'll be more comfortable if you wear something other than cotton sweats." His arm went around her and he pulled her back against him, lifting the clothing from her hands and waving it in front of her.

"Oh." She could tell by the lopsided smile Romain gave her that he knew she'd been trying to escape him. "Sweats are very popular in New York."

"Perhaps, but I'd like to see you in this when we go to Chez Mere." Romain lifted a midnight blue silk sari from the hanger, letting it drift through his fingers. "What do you think?"

Pip nodded, knowing the garment became her. Her partner, Lou Rafkin, had brought it from India when he'd vacationed there last year with Lois.

"Great. I'll wait in the living room for you." He kissed the top of her head and released her.

Pip watched him stride from the room, the fine gold thread running through his hunter green silk evening suit shimmering in the lamplight. It clung to his well-formed body as though the master tailor had sewn it to him. She knew that Romain had his dress suits made by Alvani of Italy and his business apparel designed on Savile Row. Even his sports clothes were the best Americans could fashion. Romain was so used to having the best of everything that he took no notice of it at all. That was what had baffled her about him when they were married. More than once he'd gone to less fortunate countries with money and supplies, sometimes taking her with him. His capacity for work among the poor in countries such as Ethiopia and Sudan was incredible. With the zeal and good humor of a dedicated missioner he'd roll up sleeves, sweep away red tape, and begin to help. It had struck her more than once when he'd let her accompany him that Romain as the tireless worker in the dust and dirt was a bizzare foil for the man who led the jet set in fun and business.

When he shut the door, it jerked her from her reverie. "Damn him, I let him choose my dress," she fumed, weighing the idea of putting the sari back and getting another outfit. "No, I'll wear it, but because I want to, not because it's his choice."

She grimaced at her reflection when she was through, touching perfume to her wrists only, barely noticing how the sari delineated every inch of her form right to the gold slippers that picked up the gold thread in the dress.

She had swept her hair up on the sides and let it fall loose down her back. She wore braided hoops of gold in her ears, but she was ringless and wore nothing at her throat or wrists.

Pip turned away from the mirror, took a deep breath, crossed the room, and opened her bedroom door, pausing there, feeling an alien shyness with Romain.

He saw her at once and rose from the couch, his throat tightening. "You're lovely," he said huskily. "In the old days you would have been in the marketplace in Dharan, and I would have given my fortune for you." His voice was a sibilant caress, making Pip shiver. "Do you need a wrap?"

"Not unless we're walking." She smiled up at him, feeling confidence flow through her at the admiration in his eyes. He had always been able to lift her up that way, and though caution dictated she be wary with him, she thrust it away. Tonight she was with Romain and she was going to enjoy herself! She could worry about the consequences tomorrow.

He reached out and took her hand. "We'll be taking the car." He tucked her hand under his arm, and they left the apartment and took the elevator to the ground floor.

Pip was startled when she saw Abdul open the door of the Rolls and bow to her. "Good evening, Abdul."

"Good evening, Princess."

"Abdul has never accepted our divorce," Romain told her when he followed her into the back of the limousine.

"I don't see why. Divorce is as common as marriage in Dharan. His two brothers have put wives aside," Pip said, using the term for divorce that the Dharanians preferred.

"To him you are the Princess Alida, chosen one of the prince," Romain murmured, inhaling the delicate air of her perfume. "Ahh, you still use Joy."

"Once a year I splurge, but I'm very stingy with it. I'll

229

only use a drop or two. That way it lasts a long time." She laughed, turning to look at Romain. Her smile faded when she saw his scowl.

"There is no need for you to economize on anything. You have a substantial settlement."

"Which I return every month."

"And which has been invested for you in Dharanian holdings. You are a rather wealthy woman in your own right."

"No!"

"Yes."

Pip reeled, speechless at what he'd told her. She hadn't wanted his money, preferring to make it on her own. Not once had she ever considered keeping the checks he'd sent her because she'd had a small annuity from her parents' deaths that she'd kept for emergencies. That money had kept her head above water after the miscarriage of her baby and allowed her to take time to hunt for a job. Her aunt and uncle had been upset with her when she'd used the annuity, but she'd been adamant in refusing their help. She'd wanted to be independent, to discover the person she really was, and she'd done that. It had never occurred to her that Romain would invest the money she had returned.

They drove through the kaleidoscope of the late spring New York evening, the steel and glass caves giving off the surrealistic sheen of another planet.

"I've always liked New York at night," Romain murmured, taking her hand in his and kissing the palm.

"You didn't tell me that Abdul was going to drive us." Pip accepted his change of subject with relief, needing a chance to think over what he said before she could reply to it. She couldn't keep the money he'd invested for her, yet she sensed she would have an atomic quarrel with him if and when she attempted to give it back. She smothered a sigh and tried to put it in the back of her mind. She wanted to enjoy the evening. She felt a fluttering in her heart when he continued to caress her fingers with his lips.

"It's more romantic this way, don't you think?" Romain pressed his mouth into her palm. "Abdul driving with you and me in the back, I mean."

It took all of Pip's self-control not to run her hands over the crisp black hair as Romain bent over her, his mouth insistent on her skin. "Very romantic." Pip coughed to clear her throat.

Romain moved closer to her so that their bodies were touching. "It will always be a mystery to me how you can be in such great shape physically and still be like a velvet pillow to hold."

Pip laughed.

He lifted his head, his face very close to hers, "Do you know how I've longed to hear you laugh?"

Pip stared up at him, dumbfounded at the volcano in his eyes, appalled at the answering warmth at the core of her. The man had too damn much power!

"I will never let you leave me again, pet."

"Even if our reprising isn't successful?"

"It will be."

She chuckled. "The Al Adal supreme confidence surfaces."

"Yes." He leaned back against the seat and pulled her into the curve of his arm. "And did you know you were the only person who has ever been able to get under my skin, Philippa?"

"No one could do that."

"You could and did. You couldn't have done a better job on me with one of Ahmed's scimitars." He referred to the old man who was a blacksmith at the oasis in Marib.

His face was noncommittal, his voice sardonic, but Pip felt as though someone had just massaged her with ice. The words worked their way from his throat as though they were jagged edged iron. Had she hurt him like that? Ridiculous! Romain was the most complete person she had ever known. No one could penetrate the aura of self-assuredness that was so much a part of him. She lifted her hand to his cheek just as Abdul opened the door. "I never meant to hurt you," she whispered hurriedly, then pushed at Romain to get out of the car.

"Damned poor timing," Romain grumbled at his serene chauffeur as he stepped from the car and turned to take Pip's arm.

"Thank you for the lovely ride, Abdul." Pip patted the man's arm.

"It is always a pleasure to serve you, Princess."

"I'm going to stake you out on the desert, Abdul."

"So you have told me, many times, lord."

"This time I mean it."

"Inshallah." Abdul bowed and went around the car to slide behind the wheel and drive away.

"If it is the will of Allah," she translated looking up at Romain who stood close to her. "You can't win," Pip chuckled.

"Damn him. He thinks because he's been my mentor since childhood he can still run my life." Romain winked at her when she laughed again. Then his lips twitched. "You would think he was our chaperon."

"He knows how dangerous the Al Adal men are with women."

"And do you?"

"I most certainly do."

Romain threw back his head and laughed, seemingly unaware of the feminine eyes that turned on him as they entered the French restaurant called Chez Mere.

They were led to the table discreetly shadowed by potted ferns, more private than its counterparts. When Romain heard Pip giggle, he looked at her one eyebrow raised.

"Just once you should be given the second best table in the house." She bit her lip to keep from laughing.

He shot a look around the crowded restaurant, taking in the line of patrons waiting to be seated, then gazed back at her and shrugged, hard amusement on his face. "Maybe one day." A sharp shake of his head sent the attendant, who would have seated Pip, away and he seated her himself.

"Maybe never."

"That, too."

The fare was simple but beautifully prepared. Succulent prawns broiled over hickory and served with wild rice from Minnesota and a salad of tomatoes, celery, carrots, and endive in a light vinaigrette dressing.

When Pip refused dessert, Romain ordered a fruit tart and fed her from his plate. "It's good for you," he crooned, taking the piece she'd bit into and putting it into his own mouth and chewing.

The intimate gesture made her feel hot and cold at the same time, perspiration beading her upper lip. "Romain, stop. I think you're taking giant steps when you should be taking baby ones."

All at once he leaned forward, his tongue touching above her lip. "You seem warm. Are you feeling all right, Pip?"

"Yes," she said hoarsely, aware he hadn't responded to what she'd said.

"Good."

They left Chez Mere and Abdul appeared the moment they stepped outside. Pip was glad to step out of the cool, spring wind into the cozy car.

Again Romain pulled her close to him and tucked her head under his chin. He kissed her hair, then shifted her easily so that he could touch her ears with his tongue.

Pip felt a feather of excitement and lifted her chin so that he could have better access to the sensitive skin. A

233

groan was pulled from her throat as his mouth continued the slow, moist questing.

"Darling," Romain murmured, his other arm coming around to clamp her to his side.

How long they rode like that Pip didn't know. She was in a vortex of emotion that masked time and space so that she didn't know if Romain had been kissing her for minutes or hours, if his searching fingers had been on the pulse point of her body for eons or seconds.

"Ahem, Lord, we have reached our destination," Abdul said in his expressionless voice as he held open the passenger door.

"Fool," Romain snarled at his attendant as he helped Pip from the limousine.

"Good night, Abdul."

"Good night, Princess."

Romain ushered Pip up the steps of the old apartment building muttering to himself. "I should retire the old fool."

Pip gasped when he lifted her in his arms in the elevator and held her in front of him so that their eyes were level. "You would miss Abdul."

"Not if I had you."

Pip felt hot all over at his words. "I like being this tall."

"Do you, darling?" Romain's voice was husky, his lips touching hers, lifting, touching again. "I would find it lovely work to keep you off your feet forever."

"Romain," she whispered, feeling hot and helpless.

He carried her into the apartment, not releasing her when he locked the door behind them. Then he carried her straight into the bedroom. "I'm going to buy a vault underground where no one can find us."

"I'd get claustrophobic." Pip felt a fluttering in her heart as Romain let her stand, then began tossing his hand-tailored clothing every which way. In a flash of déjà

234

vu she recalled other times when the two of them were so eager for each other that they literally tore their clothes from their bodies. Her breath caught in her throat.

"I'll buy a mountain then. We'll live on the very top," he paused, his face tightening. "I'm taking a lot for granted. Will you let me love you?"

Pippa knew she should deny him, but she couldn't. The slow nod of her head seemed to fire him. She was fascinated by the green flame in his eyes. His tough, muscled body seemed to clench into sensuous awareness, an answering simmer beginning in her own. She began to unwind the sari.

"Let me."

She nodded again, the sexual enervation entering her body wouldn't allow her to speak, yet she felt a power that energized her as nothing had done for a long time. She pirouetted slowly as Romain unwound the cobwebby material from her body. Then she faced him clad only in silky panties and the gold high heels. She saw him close his eyes for an instant as though he fought for control. Caught in the web of excitement that emanated from him, she gazed at his hardening body feeling a dizzy delight at the thought of being locked to it in a fevered embrace. Romain wanted her. She wanted him as much if not more.

"You are Venus." Romain told her in a choked voice, his one finger coming out to trace the curve of her breast, then to wander down, his palm flattening on her middle. "Our child."

"Yes," she breathed, reaching up and nudging the shirt that was draped over his one arm to the floor. When she pushed at his shoulders, his eyes widened for a moment, then narrowed in sexy amusement. "Getting me into bed, are you?"

"Yes, and I don't think it will be too difficult."

"You never had a problem there."

"No."

Stripped of their clothes they stared at one another in torrid assessment as though counting every pore. They fell onto the bed, together as if pulled by the same love string, now very close but not quite touching. Languorous eyes stared into passionate ones. In sensuous laziness they began a tentative exploration of one another, questing everywhere with their hands and eyes but not kissing.

"How can such simple gestures blow me apart like this?" Romain gasped as her hand slid down his middle and grazed his manhood with gentle fingers.

"I don't know," she answered in dazed acceptance, not pausing in the tactile search of his body. Pip felt drawn into a love spell as the remembered wonder of their joinings filtered through her.

"Darling." Romain cuddled her close to him, pushing her back on the cover, staring down at her. "I am going to love you inch by gorgeous inch." His mouth forayed down her form, intruding in the most intimate way, arching her body as she gasped out his name again and again, her soft cat sounds making passion percolate through him.

Hot color flooded her body as it recalled only too well the fierce lovemaking of their marriage. The thought that this was the way they had settled most of their differences in the past rather than ironing them out flashed through her mind, then flooded away as his caresses turned her to molten wanting, dissipating all but their mutual passion. For a moment she struggled against him as she felt herself being swamped by emotions, instinctively knowing that she was being hooked, gaffed, and boated by the strong tide of love that had always been between them.

"Darling . . . what?" Romain lifted his head, his eyes glazed, his hair mussed where she had run her fingers through it.

"Romain, I . . ." She fought to bring the words from

236

her tight throat. She struggled against the seduction of feeling that glittered in his eyes. "This never settled anything."

"It did for me. I wanted you then. I want you now."

She opened her mouth to retort that wanting wasn't everything, but his hand covered her mouth in gentle reproof.

"Please. Don't." He pulled her more fully against the contours of his body. "It's been so long."

Pip's protests fell silently from her lips, her body instinctively moving closer to him.

His mouth possessed hers in open hunger, attempting to lock away all objection, set aside any difference, and fire her with passion. "You're so lovely. You were always beautiful, but now you are so very special." He punctuated each word with a kiss, his mouth sliding over her face and neck as though it would kill him to leave her now, fixing at last on her mouth where he drew the very core of her into him.

The wariness that had had her pulling back from him melted as though it had never existed. Every reason for avoiding this man dissipated in a furnace of emotion as she clung to his muscular body, arching hers to be closer to him as she felt his thumb rub in gentle rhythm over her breast.

He paused for a moment, on fire for her, but wanting her to make the decision in their lovemaking. He stared down at her in hungry awareness as the rosy tip flowered into his hand.

"Yes."

Her simple declaration fired him like no sensual stimulation had ever done, and he had to fight for breath and to keep his body from exploding. His mouth dropped to her body once more and he knew that the groans heard were his and Pip's. Every feather touch that Romain made on her body had his own libido bursting through

237

his skin, his body hardening and throbbing against her, tormenting and delighting him. He felt her legs slacken and part against him and he felt choked by a love such as he had never known. It was as though all the feeling that he'd had for her in their courtship and marriage had doubled, tripled countless times. He wanted to take all of her, but he held back letting her steer their course, his breath rasping in his throat, his control thready and nebulous. "Darling?"

"Yes, Romain. Please, now," she breathed.

Romain needed no further enticement. He parted her legs gently, his body sliding between them. He felt her body withdraw, heard her gasp, as though she wanted to protect herself against his hurricane invasion. Then he felt the quiver of surrender as her sexuality took over and controlled the moment. Her response had been the same, perhaps even to a lesser degree when he had taken her as his virgin bride. Then she had been eager, unafraid, confident in their love.

Her hesitation made him take her a little wildly as though he wanted to pierce the barrier of self-protection she'd tried to put between them and destroy it. When he heard her hoarse moan, he stopped at once, fearful that he had hurt her.

"No, Romain, don't stop."

"My angel." He groaned against her breasts as he began to move in slow cadence, each gentle thrust entering her more deeply, at the same time giving more of himself to her. "Pippa!"

She wanted to respond to his cries of delight, but she couldn't summon up enough to do so. All her energies and concentration were on the beauty building within her and on her desire to touch every portion of Romain's body. He was so wonderful!

Passion spiraled them upward as though they were

caught in a cyclone that pulled them from earth and whirled them to that other place where only lovers go.

"Darling!" Romain cried as they slowly settled to earth again.

"Yes," Pip answered in dreamy content.

"I want you to marry me."

Pip stiffened, lifting her head from his shoulder to turn and stare at him. "Romain, it's too early to . . ."

"No!" His gruff interruption had her blinking. "I don't want to hear your Yankee logic about why we should be parted. It doesn't fit our lives at all."

"I might have been born in New York, but I grew up in California." She shot back in inane irritation.

"Don't split hairs." It infuriated him that she could argue against their being together when they'd just had one of the most beautiful love experiences that two people could share.

"Don't be so arbitrary." Pip could feel her own temper edging upward.

"And don't try moving away from me. I won't let you."

"Going to keep me by force?"

"If I have to, yes."

Pip felt her mouth slacken in surprise at the mule look of him. "This is the way you want to reprise our marriage? With force?"

"Damn it Pip, that isn't what I meant and you know it. I just don't want you pulling away from me, that's all."

"I would hardly call what we just shared as divisive," she told him loftily.

"Stop talking like a damned librarian. I know it was perfect. That's what I'm trying to tell you."

Pip tried to smother the giggle that rose up in her throat but she couldn't. It escaped threatening to overcome her.

"What's so damned funny?" Romain rolled over so

that his body was tenting hers, his mouth tilting in answering amusement, but his eyes still watchful.

"You sound like a little boy who's lost his teddy bear."

"No, I'm a man who's going to make damned sure he doesn't lose it." His mouth came down hard on hers.

All retorts that Pip would have made fled her mind as she felt her love for him build in her soul, spreading throughout her body. She reached up and clasped him tightly.

CHAPTER FOURTEEN

The following days were euphoric for Pip, especially having her aunt and uncle with her and sharing her good news. Even the many warnings she gave herself about her relationship with Romain being a tenuous one, that there was no permanency connected with it, couldn't dampen the heady delight that she experienced with him. Though he had not mentioned marriage again, Pip knew that it was on his mind and that Romain Al Adal was like a dog with a bone once he had an idea in his head.

Most evenings they dined at home, but there were other times when he took her to business dinners. One day they even flew to Washington to participate in a gala dinner the President of the United States had given for members of Middle East delegations. Pip had basked in the obvious pride and warmth in Romain's glance, and she couldn't keep the happiness from showing as he kept her by his side the entire evening.

Pip was touched by the way his uncle had shown the same warmth toward her and at one point steered her away from the others for a moment.

"You have done wonders with Romain. I thank you for it."

"I have done nothing, sir," Pip protested, then gritted her teeth when she blushed as he looked at her knowingly and chuckled.

"You are right, of course. You don't want to discuss

your intimate life with me. That's as it should be, but I thank you for what you've done anyway." The smile left his face for a moment. "Romain has not been close to many people."

"What do you mean, sir?" Pip whispered.

"We will talk another time," he said and patted her hand, turning away.

Pip stared after him, puzzled and uneasy.

The following week Romain came home even earlier than he usually did. It had surprised her how often he was home before six in the evening, seeming very content in her small apartment. He didn't allude again to their moving into his own very large three-story suite at the Quillon, a hotel the Dharanian company owned in downtown Manhattan. He smiled at her and held out his arms to her.

Pip stayed where she was, frowning at him. He was pale and there were lines of fatigue around his mouth. "What's wrong?" Pip felt a flutter of fear. Was he ill?

"Damn it. They've loused up." Romain sounded American for a moment. "I have to fly to Paris and talk to our people there. Would you like to come with me?" He crossed the space between them and scooped her into his arms, his mouth fixing on hers in moist and tender possession. Romain lifted his head, his eyes narrowing on her as though he already knew her answer. "It isn't necessary for you to do work for Lou at home. Let someone else do it and come with me."

"You know I love my work and I have a stake in the firm—"

"Yes, yes, please don't go over that ground again about how important it is for you to be your own person. I sometimes would like you to put the same importance on our life together." He strode away from her, leaving her open-mouthed and angry. She jumped when he slammed

242

into the bathroom, the sound reverberating through the apartment.

That night they were quiet as they shared their dinner. As had become their custom since Romain had taken up residence in her apartment, she made the entree and Romain had tossed the salad. Though they sat together and watched television for a while, their conversation was stilted. How different it was when they retired and turned to each other with the deep hunger that transcended all barricades and all silences. It burned away all but the powerful love that they couldn't deny.

Romain left for Paris two days later. There was still a starchiness between them so that their parting kiss had a reserve that made him want to shake her.

Pip found the apartment empty and uncomfortable without him and more than once she went to the closet just to touch his clothing and press her face into his jacket to catch the illusive scent of that hard-muscled body. "Damn the man. He's made me want him again!" she murmured. You've always wanted him, a voice deep inside her scoffed. "So? You don't have to rub it in." Pip answered the voice out loud.

Later in the day she decided she'd had enough of being shut in the apartment. She'd gone over the plans for a magazine spread that Lou had sent her for a fashion show time and time again and had come up with no fresh ideas. "Damn you, Romain, you've taken away my ability to think," she grumbled to herself, throwing down her pencil and going to shower and change into her business clothes.

Going back to the offices of Rafkin and Stonely after the span of three weeks gave her a strange alien feeling as though she were an intruder there now. That feeling was soon dispelled by the exuberant greetings of the staff.

"I know you shouldn't be here, but I'm so glad you are," Lois said and sighed. "Lou has been climbing the walls with that Botanical Gardens show out in San Francisco. Maybe you can cheer him up."

When Pip entered Lou's office, he looked up, scowling. Then he jumped to his feet and came around and hugged her.

"Lois says you're driving everyone up the wall."

He shook his head wearily. "True, but I can't figure out how to be in two places at once. I have to oversee the Metropolitan Museum show, which is complicated enough, but this one . . ." he snapped the chart he'd been holding. ". . . is driving me out of my mind."

"Let me go out for you, Lou." Pip didn't realize what she was going to say until the words fell out of her mouth. "It would be a big help to me. Romain's out of the country, and I really don't have enough to do." She shrugged, not able to meet his gaze.

"Missing him, are you?"

"Like mad," Pip admitted with a sigh. "Let me do it. I had an appointment with the doctor this week, and she says I'm in great shape. If it weren't for Romain making such a fuss, I would have come back to the office."

"You should shoot him or marry him again."

"Shooting him might be more merciful," she told him glumly, grimacing when he laughed. "We argue at the drop of a hat as we always did."

"Lovers always argue." He looked at her thoughtfully. "You're sure the doctor said everything's fine."

"Oh, yes, and I could take a day or two and visit my aunt and uncle."

"All right." He laughed again when she hugged him.

Later that day she called her aunt and uncle. "Yes. I should get there on Thursday. I'll take a shuttle from San Francisco. I love you, too."

She packed very lightly, taking only silk dresses and a jacket that would coordinate with the three outfits if the city turned chilly. She was pleased with herself at the lightness of her bag when she took a cab to the airport. "Oh, I should have called Abdul to take me." She cringed as she thought of the reproachful glances she would get from the loyal servant on her return. Abdul considered it his duty to be their attendant in everything. She sighed as she thought of the long, involved explanations it would take to free her of his reproach.

"Maybe I just won't tell him," she murmured to herself.

"Would you like me to help you with your luggage, madam?" A friendly flight porter took them to the baggage area for her.

Soon she was on the plane and taking off for San Francisco.

Pip slept much of the way, eating very little of the food that was offered her.

Lois had arranged for her to stay at the Aurelia, an older hotel in San Francisco but one which had the patina of old money.

The room was good-sized and furnished in antique rosewood with a canopy bed that she had to use a step stool to get into.

"I wonder what Romain would think of this." Pip laughed to herself as she lay spread-eagled on the bed with her eyes closed, recalling the time they'd been at Camellia Inn. She promised herself she would just take a short nap since she'd scheduled an appointment with Bridger White, the coordinator of the show, at the botanical gardens where it would be held.

As her eyes fluttered open, she knew she was late. When she looked at her traveling clock, she groaned out loud. She'd slept for two hours, not the half hour she'd promised herself. She jumped out of bed and dialed the Waverly Botanical Gardens that had been donated to the city of San Francisco by the Waverly family some fifty years previously. Much of the money that supported the

245

gardens came from the family and their influential friends. "Bridger? Yes, it's Philippa Stonely. I'll be a little late. Oh, dear, why do they feel that way? Oh? Surely you explained that we have no intention of damaging any of the plants. Lord, they think the crowds may harm the flora? Well, wait until I get there. We'll talk to them. We'll work something out." Pippa crossed her fingers, talking more confidently than she felt.

She hurried through her toilette, fixing her hair and face then calling down to the desk to reserve a taxi. She liked the aqua-colored cotton suit she was wearing, but she could feel a tightness at the waist even though the skirt was one of the stretch band ones that she found in the back of her closet. "It will have to do. I don't have time to fuss."

The taxi cab ride to the gardens took her through some of the picturesque sections of the city by the Bay. She requested the driver to take the winding Lombard Street to the bottom because she loved looking at the homes on it.

At her destination she dashed through the gate, ignoring the amused stare of the guard as she loped down the curving avenue that would take her to the greenhouses. On the way she passed a building with a sign out front proclaiming it the conservatory and saying that in the month of July it would host a rock group. Pip skidded to a stop and looked at the domed structure that was at least four stories high and huge.

Walking now, she entered the garden greenhouses that were more like a modern glass building.

A harried silver-haired man, tall and distinguished, rushed toward her. "I hope to God you're Philippa. The Waverlys and the Hares are here, and they are adamant that our plans will somehow kill off all the plant life." He wiped the perspiration on his brow.

"Would they be averse to us using the conservatory if we could get it?"

Bridger blinked at her as he pumped her hand. "Good idea, but it's usually booked solid," he answered slowly. "Let me make a call before you speak to them. We could use the ammunition." He spun away from her on the run.

Pip looked around at the high-vaulted glass-walled area, entranced with the climbing and growing foliage, and she was mesmerized by a collection of cacti near the far door. She was leaning down to read some of the tags when she felt a hand at her waist. Startled, she swung around almost tipping over into the cacti.

"Whoops. I didn't mean to scare you. I'm Drew Waverly. I saw you talking to Bridger and assumed you were the person they sent us from New York to butter us up and change our mind." The insolent words were accompanied by a glinting amusement in his eyes.

"You have a nerve," Pippa told him, but she couldn't smother her own mirth. "I would have looked lovely sprawled among the cacti, and I assure you I would have endeavored to take you with me."

Drew Waverly threw back his head and laughed. "I'm going to tell the family that they must give way at once. We have a most formidable Easterner at our heels."

"Bet on it." Pip smiled back feeling relaxed.

Bridger bustled up to them a few minutes later, glanced from one to the other, then back to Pip. "About that thing we discussed, Miss Stonely, we may have a cancellation. They are just handling it now."

"Wonderful." She turned and looked at Waverly. "I suppose it's time to meet the rest of your family."

"Don your armor and draw your sword." He grinned when he saw Bridger's tight-lipped distaste.

Though Pip smiled at the words, she felt it would take a great deal of confidence to deal with the ten or so haughty people standing in the far section of the greenhouse.

"So . . ." she told the group an hour and a half later, after hearing from Bridger that they had the cancellation, ". . . we can have the show in the conservatory and have a walking tour through the gardens after the show with ample ushers present who will keep an eye on the flower collection." She knew that she had them before Drew came over and shook her hand.

"Will you have dinner with me to seal the bargain?"

"I'm sorry I can't do that, but thank you anyway."

The next day when Pip left the hotel to walk to Bridger's office, a Porsche pulled up to the curb with Drew in it, urging her into the car.

"Don't you have a job?"

"Of course I do. I'm president of the Waverly Bank and my offices are here in town. I am also divorced with no children. There is only minimal insanity in the family, and I'm taking you out to lunch."

Pip opened her mouth to refuse then shrugged. "I'm not sure how long my meeting with Bridger will be."

"Here's my card. Call me at the office, and I'll come by and pick you up. I know a lively little Italian restaurant that serves a pasta salad that will make your taste buds dance. Then we'll walk across Ghirardelli Square and eat ice cream."

The meeting with Bridger went well, and because everything was straightening out, he looked on her as some sort of a savior.

Lunch with Drew was fun. The restaurant was a sidewalk cafe, and they sipped white wine and watched all the smiling San Franciscans pass by. Later they strolled around the famous square eating Italian ice cream.

"Will you dine with me tonight?"

"No, I don't think so. I have an early date at the gardens, and I'll be working all day. Then the day after tomorrow I'll be going south to visit my family outside Los Angeles."

"Then all the more reason you must dine with me tomorrow." He looked down at her. "You are the most interesting lady. When do you expect your child?"

Pip stiffened, finishing her ice cream, wiping her hands on a napkin and discarding it before she answered. "Then you can see why I don't wish to go out with you."

"I like children, and since you don't have a wedding ring, I assume you are not encumbered."

"Drew, I am not interested in a liaison with anyone at the moment, and—"

"I'm still taking you to dinner tomorrow night."

Pippa worked so hard the next day that all she wanted was to climb into bed and sleep. When she called Drew to cancel their dinner date, there was no answer, so she left the message on his machine before going to bed. It was six o'clock and she had eaten little that day, but she wasn't that hungry. She fell asleep immediately.

Pip swiped at the buzzing, sure that a bee was circling her head. Her eyes felt sticky when she finally opened them, and realized that the phone had been ringing. She fumbled the receiver to her ear. " 'Lo," she muttered, then listened. "Hello? Hello? I'm glad you hung up, Drew. I'm still not in the mood to go to dinner." She yawned and sat up in bed, stretching. "But I am hungry." She looked aghast at the clock. It was nine! She would have to hurry and change if she wanted to dine. She dialed the restaurant she'd seen off the lobby and made a reservation for nine forty-five.

She hurried through her shower but took time to shampoo her head which gave her a lift.

She donned a silky paisley print shirtwaist that swung sensuously around her legs. She kept the belt loose at her waist. She pulled her hair up on top of her head and fixed button diamond earrings that her aunt and uncle had given her one Christmas to her ears. She picked up the clutch purse that matched her snakeskin low-heeled pumps and was preparing to leave the room when someone knocked. She flung open the door. "Drew, I don't want to—" Air entered her lungs in shocked recognition. "Romain! What are you doing here?"

"Who the hell is Drew?" He edged her back into the room, fury smoking out of every pore. He looked a six-foot-three-inch vengeful devil, black hair and black eyes in satanic anger.

"I—I don't have to answer your question, and please stand out of my way. I'm going down to dinner. I have a reservation."

"Not with Drew," Romain thundered, making her jump.

"I won't be eating at all if you keep shouting. You'd spoil anyone's appetite bellowing like that."

"Has your appetite been poor?" Romain took hold of her arms and stared down into her face.

"No. I didn't eat lunch because . . ."

"What? You know you should have regular meals. Promise me you'll never do that again."

Pip opened her mouth to tell him to rocket to the moon when she noted the white lines etching his mouth, the muscle jumping in his cheek that always telegraphed his pain or agitation. "All right."

Romain exhaled, pulling her forward into his arms, then releasing her and turning with her toward the door. "We'll eat now. I know this hotel has a fine restaurant."

"Even if it hadn't, I wouldn't go any further to eat." Pip sighed, her stomach growling.

"You wouldn't have to." Romain pressed the button for the elevator and let his other hand feather over her waist. "I would order dinner sent to our room from any restaurant you chose."

Pip stared at him, shaking her head. "Of course you

would, and even if they were closing, you would just hand the chef a thousand-dollar bill to carry on. Right?"

"If that's what it takes." Romain said with a nod. "And stop getting your damned democratic principles ruffled."

"Despot."

"Some of the time."

"All of the time."

"If that's what it takes to keep you healthy, to paraphrase you Yankees, 'you ain't seen nothin' yet'."

"That's southern not northern," Pip shook her head, preceding him out of the elevator, and walking straight into a man's vest.

"There you are. They said at the desk that you must be out." Drew looked down at her smiling. "Why do you look horrified, my pet?"

"Only I call her that," Romain observed softly, sending a shiver down Pip's back.

Drew looked up and past Pip and assessed Romain who stared back at him. "And you must be Pip's bete noire," he remarked casually.

Romain's smile had a evil gentleness.

The men were almost equal in height with Romain a hair taller. Drew was a slimmer-built man but no less muscular.

Pip felt she was witnessing a face off between wolves. "Ah, we seem to be blocking the elevator here, and since I have a dinner reservation at nine forty-five, I have to go." She shot away from the two men, her eyes on the gold, scrolled letters above an archway off the lobby that proclaimed it the Peacock Grill. She marched right up to the maitre d', and before he could even give his customary greeting, she gave her name and demanded to be led to her table.

"This way, please," the maitre d' looked slightly offended at her hurried actions.

"Thank you." She followed him to a table in the corner far from the music and close to the kitchen.

"No," Romain snapped at her back. "We'll take that table."

The terse words stopped the maitre d' in his tracks. His haughty look turned conciliatory when he faced Romain, then his mouth dropped. "Mr. Waverly. Sir, would you like your regular table?"

"For the three of us, Marcel."

"I want my own table," Pip muttered to the maitre d'. "They'll give me indigestion."

The maitre d' heard the last word and stared down his nose at Pip.

Drew raised his eyebrows.

Romain gave a hard laugh as he seated her, then placed himself at right angles to her and across from Drew. He removed one of his cheroots from a gold case and rolled it between his fingers.

"Oh, dear," Pip murmured, recognizing the gesture as one of anger.

"Drew Waverly, isn't it?" Romain quizzed silkily, passing his gold lighter under the cigar.

"Yes. What's yours?"

Pip looked from one to the other and hid behind the two-foot-long menu.

"Romain Al Adal, and Miss Stonely and I are married."

Pip ducked around the menu. *Were* married," then ducked back again as Romain gave her a frosty stare.

"Ah-ha. So you could be the father of the child."

"Not could be. I am. Not that I care to discuss our private business with you."

"Pip gave me to understand that she's a free agent."

Pip peeked around the menu. "I did?"

"She did?" Romain grated, simultaneously.

252

"Yes. And since I love children, I consider myself in the running."

"There is no contest, Waverly. Remember that."

"What running?" Pip gasped, almost lowering the menu. "This is not a derby and I'm not Secretariat."

"Did you know the horse? Wonderful animal. My family has always owned race horses." Drew smiled at Pip.

"So has Romain's. Tell him about Desert Shamrock who won the steeplechase at Aintree," Pip offered helpfully, raising the menu again when Romain shot her a sharp-eyed look.

"I did not come here to talk of horses."

"I'm starved." Pip smiled at the hovering waiter who ignored her.

Romain looked at the waiter, and he was at their table in an instant.

Pip opened her mouth to order when Romain lifted the menu from her hand.

"She'll have poached salmon with lemon, no butter or oil of any kind. With it she'll have a fruit salad with yogurt and honey sauce. One baked potato with butter. And fresh spinach boiled for one minute only and served with almonds, no dressing. The food must be prepared perfectly." Romain leaned forward to emphasize what he was saying.

Both the waiter and the maitre d' bowed to him obsequiously.

"Of all the . . ." Pip sputtered.

"I agree. Can't be too careful in a pregnancy." Drew chimed in, earning an icy stare from Romain.

"I need no help with my wife's diet," Romain fired at Drew.

"Ex-wife," Pip muttered, her hand hovering clawlike over the delicious tray of canapes the waiter placed in the middle of the table.

"Eat, darling," Romain commanded.

"She's right, you know," Drew faced Romain, his hands pressed palm down on the table. "You really have no more rights with her than I do."

"Neither of you have any," Pip mumbled before sliding a very hot stuffed mushroom into her mouth.

"You certainly don't have any privileges with my wife, not even that of friendship." Romain's hard glance touched Pip, then Drew.

"Umph-ahh-ohh." Pip's eyes shot around the table, looking for something to put out the fire in her mouth. In her agitation with the men she hadn't taken note that the mushroom was blistering hot.

"Let us handle it, Philippa." Drew patted the hand she was trying to flap in front of her mouth, his eyes still on Romain.

"Pip usually speaks for herself," Romain stated, his eyes fixed on his adversary.

The waiter brought the drinks that Romain had ordered.

Before he could set them around, Pip reached up and grabbed the nearest and took a long deep swallow. It took away the pain for a moment, then a different type of burning took over and she began to cough.

"Pippa, for God's sake, what the hell are you doing drinking that? It's Waverly's Irish whiskey, and a double at that." Romain wrenched the almost empty glass from her nerveless fingers.

"I think I would take care of her better than that. I wouldn't let her drink during pregnancy." Drew flicked his finger at the waiter ordering another drink.

"You . . . have . . . nothing . . . to say." Pip coughed, smiling weakly at the waiter when he handed her an orange juice with two lime slices in it that Romain had ordered for her.

Drew patted her hand. "There, there, mustn't be upset."

Pip flirted with idea of kicking him in the knee, but she was too intent on her burned mouth to do it.

"She isn't upset," Romain drawled. "She's wondering whether to hang us or draw and quarter us."

"Don't be ridiculous." Drew looked down his nose.

"Draw and quarter," Pippa wheezed. Her dinner could not be savored with the inside of her mouth so tender.

Romain handed her his glass of ice water. "Sorry, I didn't notice you were in extremis."

"Burning one's mouth is not amusing," Pippa said loftily.

"Then pay attention to what you're putting into it next time."

"Was Madame La Farge your grandmother? You have the same compassionate nature," Pip sniffed, edging the water glass back toward him, glaring at him when he captured her hand.

"No, she was not a relation; nor do I knit while people are losing their heads; nor do I want you to dump ice water in my lap."

"A crude supposition on your part." Pip gave up when she couldn't wrest the glass from him.

"Of course it is," Drew said stoutly, patting Pip on the hand.

"Twit," she breathed, then stiffened when she realized that Romain, who was sitting much closer to her, had caught what she said.

All at once his manner toward Drew changed. Urbanity, that was second nature to him, flowed.

Dinner was an ordeal for Pip. Drew was now eyeing Romain warily as though he sensed the change in him, and it made him uneasy.

Romain took every opportunity to brand her as his own. He leaned over and kissed her lips often, he squeezed her hand. He even tickled her thigh under the table, so that Pip jumped.

255

She was relieved when they left the restaurant, until Drew insisted they go to a club he knew.

"We'd love to, wouldn't we, darling?" Romain laughed at her.

"No."

"She'd love to go," Romain said easily, then almost lifted Pip off her feet as he led her to a limousine.

Tadwilliger's was for dancing! Pip looked at the sea of people gyrating on the huge dance floor and decided that she had a headache. Before she could say anything, Drew led her out to the floor and began a very restrained two-step.

"Why didn't you tell me he was coming out with us tonight?"

"Because I didn't know, Drew." Pip had to almost shout to be heard.

"Are you going to marry him again?"

"May I cut in?" Romain swept her away from Drew before she could answer.

"I don't want to dance. I'm tired," Pip said petulantly.

"Fine." Romain hooked an arm around her and led her from the floor, whispering something to the maitre d' and pushing some bills into his hands.

"You can't just leave Drew that way." Pip looked over her shoulder as Romain led her to the street and signaled to the limo.

"We just did."

CHAPTER FIFTEEN

Pip stood in the shower rehearsing all the scathing epithets she was going to throw at Romain as soon as she was in her nightgown. On the drive back to the hotel and up the elevator she hadn't spoken to him, going directly to her room, then to the bathroom, aware he was at her heels.

Finally when she was in her nightgown and somewhat calmer, she went out to the bedroom. "Romain," she began, then stared open-mouthed at the bed. He was under the covers, turned on his side away from her. "Romain! What are you doing?"

"Huh? What? Oh. Jet lag. Need sleep." He turned over on his side again and began a light snoring that told her he was sound asleep.

"Damn you! How dare you zip into my life, zap it, then fall asleep. Poor Drew." She glared at his supine form for a few minutes. I should smother you with my pillow, she said to herself. "Oh," she touched the soreness of her mouth, glowered at Romain again and slipped under the covers. Tomorrow she was going to tell him to get out of her room and find his own. Yawning, she closed her eyes and was asleep at once, feeling oddly comforted.

She felt a feathery pressure at her ear, then on her face. She snuggled deeper into the warmth at her back, hearing a groan, but not worrying about it.

257

"Wake up, darling."

"Okay." She turned over and slipped her arms around Romain's neck and pressed her mouth to his still without opening her eyes. She welcomed his open-mouthed pressure on hers, the intimacy of the kiss sending sparks through her body. The kiss deepened, and Pip could hear her own purr of satisfaction. When she felt his mouth slide across her cheek, then heard him chuckle, she came fully awake. Her eyes flew open and she pushed at his shoulders. "Damn you, Romain."

"What's wrong? Isn't that the way we always woke each other?"

"When we were married."

"Let's marry again."

"Romain . . ."

He let his hand feather over her bare buttocks, her nightgown now bunched around her waist. "Your derriere is velvet, sweetheart."

She had planned to tell him to leave her room. Instead, her hand rose to run through the softness of his coal black hair. "We always seem to be doing this."

"What better thing to do, my love?"

"Don't we need more for marriage?"

"We have more, much more than we had before. Do you deny that you have mixed socially with my business associates many times and enjoyed it? That you have as good an understanding of my business than many of my colleagues?"

"I do understand your work and find it interesting, and I have enjoyed meeting your business friends socially."

"They think you're wonderful. They admire your quick intelligence as much as I do."

His earnest words rivered through her like lava, making her feel proud. "Thank you."

"It was the truth, not a compliment. You are an asset

to me as my wife and an astute business woman. I want you at my side in all segments of my life."

"Romain," Pip gulped, feeling tears sting her eyes. "You feel that way in this country, but in Dharan . . ."

"It will be the same. My people know you and know how caring you are of them. They will never forget that you put your life at risk for a peasant child. They know how you have worked alongside me in Ethiopia and Sudan. They admire you as I do, and they love you . . . as I do."

"Romain." Pip closed her eyes, snuggling closer to him, wanting to believe that all would be well between them.

"You are my life, Philippa Stonely Al Adal."

"Not yet, but soon." The words fell from her flaccid mouth as Romain began to quest her body in sensuous slowness, his mouth like a moist brand that set her on fire wherever it touched.

Their lovemaking exploded around them.

Pip could feel Romain's struggle as he tried to control his passion so that she would be pleasured as well. "Don't wait. I'm ready."

"Darling!"

"Please, Romain. I am."

The tide of passion pulled them in and they were tossed on an ocean of feeling that had Pip gasping and clutching to Romain as though he were the last and only lifeline she had.

Romain rolled onto his back taking her on top of him, stroking her quivering body into quiescence. "Pippa."

"Yes." She snuggled her face into his neck, her eyes closed in bliss as he continued to caress her.

"Who is Drew Waverly?"

The question caught her off guard. "He's a man," she told Romain inanely.

"That I know. How long have you known him?"

"Two days." She yawned, her eyes fluttering shut again.

"Two damned days! And already he feels he can discuss our child with impunity!" Romain felt choked in a flash fire of jealousy.

"He likes children."

"So do I. That still doesn't give him the right to think he can order your food."

"I order my own food." Pip yawned again. She was just too lazy and content to remind him that he ordered her food not Drew.

"Pippa, I don't want—Pip? Pip, are you asleep?"

"Noo," Pip managed the one word before she fell down into the deep well of sleep.

Romain turned her face up to his, smiling when he saw how her mouth parted in sleep. "Even asleep you make my libido climb out of sight, angel. And I damn well am not going to let some sophisticated Bay area bimbo try to get close to you. You belong to me and I won't let you go." He pressed a light kiss on her parted lips, feeling his heart thud against his ribs at her vulnerability. "You are the lady of my heart, darling. You are going to have our child, and I'm going to be with you every step of the way." He cuddled her closer, pulling the comforter around her shoulders. He fell asleep feeling more contented than he'd been since they parted, his whole being committed to keeping her with him for all time.

Sunshine opened Pip's eyes. She felt comforted and warm, the nightmare quality of her other wakings without Romain dissipated. She knew at once who was holding her and she wriggled her backside in joy.

"Don't do that unless you want to play," he whispered in her ear.

"I like games."

"So do I."

She edged around to face him still cocooned in his arms. "Begin."

Romain's mouth covered hers almost before the word was spoken.

Pip felt the usual curl of delight begin deep within her and spread through her body.

His face fixed to her skin as though it were home, and he slid down until his tongue could invade her body in the most wonderful way. When he heard her gasping cries his own body leaped in response, his mind whirling with the power that she could engender over him. Only with Pip did he want to give and give. With other women in his life he'd felt a lazy satisfaction from what he received. With Pip his whole happiness was in giving to her, making her climb to the apex of sensuous enjoyment and explode in sexual love. That was more stimulating to him than anything on earth.

Pip felt an other worldly sense of being able to step outside herself and observe the two lovers writhing under the quilt. She felt objective yet committed and was delighted with the way Romain stroked her body with his tongue and hands. Watching, she felt a rush of irritation with the other Philippa! Why did she lie there enjoying Romain's ministrations so much when she could be attacking him in sexual play. As the two parts of her joined together again, Pip became the aggressor.

Romain lifted his head dazedly as he felt her push at him. "What is it, darling?" He shifted his weight. "Am I too heavy?"

"No," Pip told him, pressing him back and lying atop him. "It's my turn. I want to love you now," she told him in her most sultry voice.

Romain blinked, then lazy heat filled his eyes. "Be my guest."

"Thank you," she told him touching the firm male nipple with her lips. She was inordinately pleased with her-

261

self when Romain couldn't stifle the moan issuing from his throat. In slow, exquisite discovery she let herself go from the manacles that she had fastened around her feelings, she opened the floodgate of emotion that she had dammed up. Now every impulse was directed to the only man she had ever loved. It was torture to know she should hold back when all that she wanted was to melt into him as she had not done since the early days of their marriage. Each centimeter of his beautiful, strong body she touched and pressed in tactile delight. She urged him to turn on his front, and she began massaging and kissing and the erotic joy she wanted for him began firing her as well. "You have nice buns, Romain," she told him silkily, with a sensual bravery that was new to her. She chuckled when she felt him stiffen, then look over his shoulder at her in wry passion.

"In control, are you?" he queried her huskily.

"Yes."

"Then I must tell you that I'm delighted my buns please you, pet." Before she could answer, he turned, catching her body as she started to slide off the bed, laughing when she squealed in frustration.

"I was just getting going," she gasped, laughing, now flat on her back.

"Were you? And I was just reaching the end of my tether."

She reached up a finger to trace under his eye. "Do you think you're too old to be a father? You have laugh lines here and here."

"Brat. I'll show you how old I am." Romain's eyes glittered over her before he fixed his mouth to her, their passion reigniting on contact.

When Romain penetrated her it was as though it was the first time, and they both cried out in the ecstasy of joining that seemed new, yet greater than it ever was.

They lay entwined, their breathing slowly settling back to normal.

"I saw hurt in your eyes when I said that about your laugh lines." Pip trailed her fingers over his abdomen, feeling satisfaction when he flinched in sensual awareness. "I'm sorry."

"Do you think I'm still too old for you?" The question was forced from his throat. "Do you think I'm too old to be a father?"

"Still? I never thought you were too old for me."

"And I'm damned well not too old to be a father."

"You answered your own question."

"You were a baby when I married you."

"I knew what I was doing."

"I pushed you into it, then tried to keep you in a cocoon, away from anyone who might influence you against me."

"You didn't do that. You've never been that type of person."

"I didn't want to be that way with you, but you made me crazy." Romain kissed the corner of her mouth, his one hand coming up to brush the hair back from her face. "I wanted you at my side, no matter where I went. I was so fixated about you I risked your health by taking you into places that had fever."

They were turned on their sides now, looking into each other's eyes.

Pip saw the anguish in his and shook her head. "You never endangered me when we took supplies to hungry people. You helped me grow. Oh, Aunt Grace and Uncle George taught me early to be aware of the needs of others, but it wasn't until I went with you that I saw, in a very graphic way, how much people need people." She kissed his chin. "I liked going with you to the camps in Ethiopia and Sudan. I felt useful, needed."

He grimaced, closing his eyes for a moment. "When I

263

realized that some of the camps had fever, I almost went out of my mind with worry. I was scared witless that you would pick up bacteria." Romain stroked her hair. "I wanted to box you in, wrap you with ribbon."

"You make me sound like a present."

"To me you were the greatest gift I'd ever been given." Romain told her, then gave an embarrassed twitch as she stared at him open-mouthed but silent. "Your aunt and uncle were very gracious when I spoke to them on the phone." He changed the subject but didn't release her from his arms.

"You've spoken to them since your arrival here?" Pip quizzed, aware he had tried to divert her.

"Yes. They're helping me with the plans."

"Plans? For what?"

"Our wedding."

"What?" Pip could feel her mouth fall open. Breathing was difficult. "You're joking."

At the slow shake of his head, she pressed one hand against her mouth trying to pull back from him, but he didn't release her.

"Romain, don't be ridiculous. We aren't going to hurry it."

"And we haven't, but I think we know we want to be together, don't we?"

"There has to be more than that. It isn't enough to know you want to be with another person." She swallowed painfully. "Will we want to stay together is a better question. Will I fit in your life? Will you fit in mine?"

"We will."

"Romain, we were sure the first time." She sighed shakily.

"And I'm just as sure this time, but there will be exceptions in this marriage. I have already told my uncle that you will be dictating what our lives will be like and that as much as I love the company and the work I do, it will take second place to you."

"You told the king such a thing?" Pip felt as though her eyes were bulging in her head. "How could you! He's the head of your government!"

"I know that." His gentle derision was emphasized by tiny kisses over her face.

"That's awful. Dharanian women wouldn't speak in such a fashion . . ."

"I've told you that things have changed a great deal in my country so will you stop that babbling and just concentrate on our upcoming nuptials. After we are well and truly tied again you may orchestrate our lives however you please, just as Dharanian women have been doing for centuries. Though I must say they aren't quite as direct as you. You'll see. We'll be happy."

Pip wanted to argue with him, point out the many flaws in his premise, but he had such a vulnerable look about his mouth, she refrained.

For a time they lay there, arms around one another, lost in thought, then, in mutual accord they rose from the bed.

Romain stared at her nude form. "You have the most delectable body, and I want you every time I look at you. Your tummy is rounding so wonderfully," he exhaled a deep breath. "I don't dare touch you. We'd be back in there again."

Pip gave a shaky laugh, feeling both sad and happy. How much she wanted to be his wife again! She hadn't realized how deep the feeling ran until he mentioned that they would marry once more. Yet she couldn't forget how their relationship had deteriorated when they had been wed.

Romain went to the phone to order breakfast sent to their room.

While he was talking, Pip went into the dressing room,

standing for a few moments with her back pressed against the door and her eyes closed. "Oh, Lord, could we make it?" she whispered to herself. "To be with Romain for all time would be so wonderful." For a few seconds she pictured them hand in hand with a baby toddling in front of them. She closed her eyes in bitter-sweet reaction, her heart twisting within her. She couldn't shake the picture of them together in marriage from her mind. Eyes opened or closed, she saw them with their baby. Like an automaton she donned her dressing gown.

"I was hoping to join you in the shower," Romain told her huskily.

She stared at him. "You're still tanned everywhere," she remarked a little crossly.

"Yes." He laughed at her.

"Damn you," she said gently.

"I'm more than willing to lie in the sun when only you are with me," he said lazily, reading her mind.

"I can see your breasts through that material." He leaned down and took her one into his mouth.

"Romain," Pip gasped, holding his head with both hands.

"No," Romain's voice cracked as he lifted his head to look at her. "Don't touch me. I know we don't have the time, but I plan on washing your entire body with my tongue one day soon." He turned away from her and stalked out of the dressing room telling her he was going to shower.

"You do?" Pip said weakly, leaning against the vanity, knowing her mouth was still agape, barely able to hear him as he hummed a tune in the shower.

Shortly after noon they left San Francisco. Pip looked out from her cockpit seat in the Lear jet taking them to Los Angeles and thought of the note she'd left for Drew Waverly at the hotel desk. It hadn't been too informative, but she'd made it clear that she didn't see herself in his life and vice versa.

"I hope you told him you're mine," Romain said, reading her expressive face.

"Or words to that effect," she whispered.

"Good." He could hear the relief in his voice. Damn, he'd been scared when he'd seen how Waverly looked at her, but he'd damn well duel the devil himself for Pippa. She was the world to him!

She sighed, thinking of her uncle and aunt and feeling as though she was strolling through a fantasy. She was going home to be married . . . again! To Romain! "Alice through the Looking Glass," she murmured, then jumped when she felt Romain's hand press her knee.

"Stop acting like a startled fawn. You're not going to a hanging, you're being married."

She turned to look at him. "What if we relive the parts of our marriage that we'd rather forget, the parts that were so painful we were almost destroyed?"

"Neither of us will do that. I want to save what's good. Do you?"

"Yes."

"Then we'll go from there."

"But what if . . ."

"Pip, we'll do what every other married person does who wants to protect the union. We'll fight the things that keep us apart and cherish the rest."

"I know I sound divisive."

"Apprehensive, maybe."

Pip sighed. "It seems too good to be true."

"We'll make it happen."

Pip laughed. "The Al Adal confidence again."

"Yes."

"Well, against such overpowering odds I'll have to cooperate."

"Good."

The California sky was clear and the Pacific Ocean looked serene and rolling as they followed the coast south.

In a short time they were circling the private field where Romain would keep the plane and in minutes they were on the ground and deplaning.

As usual there was a car waiting, but instead of the limousine Pip expected, a sleek red Ferrari awaited them.

"Wow." Pip smiled at Romain.

"Do you like it?"

"Who wouldn't?"

"Good," he told her as he led her around the front of the powerful machine to the driver's side. "Because you're the driver. Do you think you'll have trouble with the stick shift?"

"No," Pip breathed, looking at the car wide-eyed. "You'd rather drive. I know it."

"I love to drive, but so do you. I've just flown, so we'll split it up."

Pip stared at him. There had been times that Romain had let her drive his car when they'd lived in Dharan, but most of the time when they were together he had driven. When she was by herself, she had driven a Maserati and had been proud of her skill with the wonderful auto and a few times she had driven a Land-Rover they kept for the desert. She liked to drive.

"Stop looking at me as though I have two heads," he urged her behind the wheel, closed her door gently, and went around to get into the passenger seat. He looked over at her, smiling at the sidelong glances she shot his way. "Start the car, love. I told Grace we'd be there in time to take a swim in the pool and have cocktails with them."

"Oh." Pip barely heard him she was so intent on studying the dashboard that looked more like the controls of a 747 than a car. "Here we go," she mumbled, her tongue at the corner of her mouth as she turned the key and engaged the gears. She sighed with relief when she pulled away without jerking.

"Don't let the freeway throw you," Romain remarked as he saw her white knuckle the steering wheel approaching the ramp. "You're driving very well."

"Uh-huh." Pip concentrated on maneuvering, checking her rearview mirror, barely hearing Romain's soothing words. She said a silent prayer and pulled into the traffic, the powerful engine leaping under her hands. In short order she was passing the slower cars.

"You have the instincts of a race driver. Shall I take you out on the track one day?"

"You don't race anymore!" Pip stiffened, her insides wrenching with pain.

"As I told you, I did after you left me. The thrill wasn't there, but I did drive a few times."

"Always the Gran Prix, I suppose?"

"Yes."

"France, Italy, and Monaco?"

"Yes. Darling, I never got a scratch." He reached out covering her knee again.

"You were a wild driver when you were young. Abdul let me read your clippings." Her voice shook. "Were you like that when you went back to it?"

Romain drew in a deep breath. "Perhaps once or twice."

"Damn you, Romain." Pip sobbed, biting her lip, the car leaping ahead.

"Slow down, love," he whispered, putting his hand on her shoulder. "I give you my word I will not race again."

The car dropped back.

"I know it's wrong of me to want you to give up something you love—"

"I don't need that kind of distraction now that I have you again. My life isn't an empty vessel that needs filling.

You do that, and I assure you I won't miss driving one bit." He twirled one of her curls around his finger. "But I will still take you out on the desert track I have, and you can drive as fast as you like."

"As long as you're with me," she said and laughed shakily.

"Correct."

They drove the rest of the way in companionable silence, the tape playing love ballads, Romain's arm along her shoulder.

Pip felt an excitement at coming home, and as she drove up the winding drive, she felt eager and weepy.

"You love them very much, don't you?"

"Very."

"I like them myself. That's why I've had the Pink Palace, which is small and cozy, refurbished for them in Dharan. It will be theirs for their lifetime and will be kept in readiness at all times for them. They seemed to like the idea when I told them."

"Romain! Thank you." Pip stopped in front of the house and turned and kissed him.

His arms were closing about her as the driver's door opened and her uncle laughed.

"Can't you wait until your wedding tomorrow?"

CHAPTER SIXTEEN

Returning to Dharan was like a dream that had been wrapped and rewrapped inside of her, then put in the back of her mind. It was as though another person had been here not her, and that it had been eons ago and not years.

Pippa shrugged away her fanciful thoughts and stared out the window as the plane taxied to a stop on the flat, dusty plateau above Dharan City.

"Tears?" Romain leaned over her, taking the crystal drops into his mouth.

"I didn't know until this moment how much I missed being here. It's a beautiful country," she sniffed, laughing at her tears. "I love the desert and the desert people."

"And they love and miss you, my darling wife." He scooped her into his arms, looking into her eyes and not out the window as she had. He took no notice of the red carpet that had been rolled to the door of the plane and the white-robed palace guard that stood in review. "We'll spend about half the year here and the other half traveling or in the States." He frowned for a moment. "Of course we'll return to New York to have the baby."

"Romain! I assumed the birth would be here in Dharan."

"No," he answered abruptly. "I want you to be where you'll feel most comfortable. My uncle agrees with me and so do George and Grace. The child will have dual

271

citizenship no matter where he or she is born, so we'll be doing what's best for you." He lifted her from her seat and led her toward the open door of the plane, turning at the opening to give her a crooked smile. "Did I tell you that I thought our second marriage very beautiful, Princess Al Adal?"

"Once or twice." She sighed, feeling shy and adventurous all at once, wanting to cart him off to a desert oasis and make passionate love to him, yet not able to control the flush that crept over her skin at the look in his eye.

He turned around and saw the color guard, the band as it began to play and cursed roundly, making Pip chuckle.

"Why are you surprised? After all, you are His Royal Highness, the Crown Prince of Al Adal and Dharan." She couldn't check her mirth when he shot a mocking look her way.

"My orders were for no fanfare."

"Your uncle?"

"Who else?" Romain stepped down the short drop steps of the jet to the tarmac, his eyes crinkling against the glare of the hot sun. He scowled at the military figure who came forward to offer Pippa his arm. "Never mind. I'll take care of the princess," he told the man curtly.

The man bowed, his face expressionless as he melted back into the small group of guards standing at attention.

It startled Pippa when they played the national anthem of Dharan, and she saw Romain's uncle coming down the red carpet toward her, beaming. "I didn't know he was coming," she breathed.

"Neither did I," Romain responded, irritation in his voice. "Am I never to be alone with you?"

Pippa looked at her husband, smothering the laughter that bubbled up in her at the mule look of him. "He is the king," she told him, not able to stem the quiver of amusement in her voice.

272

"I know that," Romain said testily. "And stop laughing at me."

"I can't help it. You look so frustrated."

"That's the way I feel."

The king opened his arms to her and she went into them quite naturally, hugging him with genuine affection. "Ah, my child, you are here with us at last. Will you forgive me that I was not at your wedding ceremony?" Pippa stared at Romain, then let her hand slide into his. She felt him clutch at her.

The king slanted a glance at their entwined hands, looking pleased. "Perhaps I might have been able to come to the wedding, but I was en route to Dharan when I heard the news of your impending nuptials."

"I would have loved to have you there, sir," Pippa told the king, leaning forward to kiss his cheek, smiling at him when he beamed.

"We are to have a reception for you and Romain at the palace. Romain's mother and I will be hosting it." The king smiled.

"I'm trying to take my wife away to the desert for a rest, not have a three-ring circus." Romain glared when his uncle threw back his head and laughed. "She's in a very delicate condition."

"Haven't you been well, child?" the king quizzed, sobering at once. "Is the pregnancy difficult?"

Pip felt herself flush. "Don't listen to him, your highness. We'd be delighted to take part in a reception."

"We're not staying long." Romain muttered, following behind them as his uncle took Pip's hand through his arm, effectively freeing her from her husband, then leading the way to the limousine waiting for them.

Heat shimmered off the tarmac and sandy area bordering the runway like a fire storm of multicolored crystal.

"I talked to your uncle and aunt on the phone today, and they said the ceremony was beautiful and that you

273

looked lovely in your cream lace dress, child. It belonged to your mother, I believe."

"Thank you, sir. And yes, it did belong to my mother."

"She looked like a goddess," Romain interjected.

"I would hope you had more of a smile on your face than you do now."

"He did," Pip told the king, looking over her shoulder and blowing a kiss to Romain.

"We're still not staying." Romain stared at her lips.

The king ignored his nephew.

Pip glanced back again at her grim-faced husband before replying to the king. "It was lovely. Uncle George shot many rolls of film, so you'll be able to see much of it. And the flowers you sent made a glorious backdrop. My aunt had sprays of them everywhere. We were married in the old gazebo, and it was filled with the fragrance from the flowers."

"Good."

On the ride back to the palace it seemed to Pippa that the king was positively gleeful over his nephew. Romain had cuddled her close to him in the car and not all her whisperings and wrigglings had freed her from him.

When they entered their rooms in the palace, she faced him. "Don't you think you were a little impolite to your uncle?"

"No. He knows damn well I'm trying to get you alone and he's having a field day watching me try to do it." Romain's chin came out an inch.

"We're leaving for the oasis tomorrow," Pip soothed, trying to mask her laughter.

"Damn right we are. I wanted to leave today."

"The reception will be nice."

"It will tire you."

"No. As soon as I feel the least fatigue . . ."

"I'll get you out of there so fast," Romain promised

tight-lipped, pulling her into his arms. "I need you to be healthy and happy, then I'll be."

"I'm well and I've never been happier." She lifted her hands to his face, massaging the skin that was already lightly bristled with a beard. "We're married and together."

"For this life and into the next ten lives on this or any other planet."

"You made your vows to me yesterday. That sounds like another."

"It is. I'll never let you go again."

The smile died on Pippa's lips when she saw the white bracketing his mouth, the steely hardness of his eyes. For a millisecond she felt a frisson of fear, but it passed and she pressed herself close to him.

That evening she decided to surprise Romain and wear one of the many filmy desert garments in her closet that had been specially woven for her by Dharanian nomadic women. The one she chose was a pinky white diaphanous silk with rose-gold thread woven through it so that it sparkled hot pink whenever she moved. The dress was draped around her so that a short train swayed over the floor behind her.

She didn't cover her face because at the court of Dharan, not only did the women dine with the men, they also wore Western dress if they chose.

Romain came into the room as she finished putting the pink touches of makeup to her skin and outlining her turquoise eyes with a shimmer of rose gold that highlighted them. "My goddess," Romain breathed, "your hair shimmers like fire." He moved toward her, leaning down to kiss her mouth. "I've brought you something to go with it."

"Lisette told you what I was wearing!" she accused. "I wanted it to be a surprise."

"Believe me, love, seeing you now is doing more than

enough for my libido and blood pressure. Here. Will you wear them?" He handed her the open leather case with the rose diamonds nestled there, his eyes a green flame.

"Of course." Once more she felt a shiver down her spine at the look in his eyes.

They left the room, Romain's hand at her waist.

The reception was large! There was music and delicious food. As was the custom among Dharanians, there was no alcoholic beverage, but there was an array of food and drink such as would tempt the most diverse palate of the diplomatic corps who attended.

There was no receiving line, but Pip and Romain went from table to table greeting the guests with his uncle and his mother, Princess Lalia.

"May I speak with you, my dear? Perhaps we could go into Haddad's study." Romain's mother smiled, but her eyes were determined as she steered Pip away from Romain and down a hall to the privacy of the royal study. "I brought you here because there is something I must tell you, and my brother-in-law was anxious that the information come from me," the princess explained when she sat facing Pip, who stared back at her wide-eyed and a little apprehensive.

"My son was a loving, open child who sought the approval of his father, my beloved Hassan." Princess Lalia paused, taking a deep breath. "My husband loved me deeply, but he had been raised by teachers and mentors and kept from his own parents' love. He thought that was the way to raise a child and preceded to keep Romain away from him and when he was with him, being stern and aloof. His older brother, Haddad, admonished him about it, but Hassan was firm. The man who was so loving to me was cold and unfeeling to his son. Romain was close to me and his uncle, but there was little warmth in the relationships he had with others. He was cynical and rather hard except to his uncle and me." The older woman sighed, her face seaming to age.

"Yes," Pip prodded in a low voice.

"When Romain met you, he changed, becoming more loving, more outgoing . . . until you left him. Then he withdrew from people again, if anything he was worse than he had ever been, harsh and bloodless almost. Though he was not consciously cruel, the coldness was there. He seemed to die by inches."

Pip gasped, her one hand pressing her lips.

"I wanted to tell you this because I know that Romain is walking on eggs with you, wanting to be careful, determined that you will never know how much he needs you, that you are the only one he can be truly open with." She smiled at Pip. "He loves you more than life, and he needs you to show him how to love this wonderful child you have created. I sense he fears being like his father."

Pip had seen little of the vulnerable Romain his mother had described. "Sometimes I see a strange look in his eyes," Pip murmured. "It frightens me because it's like a hunger."

His mother nodded. "His need of you," she answered simply, rising to her feet. "Come, child, my son will be tearing down the palace looking for you."

"Yes." Pip smiled back. "Thank you. I love Romain and I'll take care of him."

"I know." His mother kissed her. "Thank you for giving my son the gift of love."

Later when Pip saw her husband, she took his arm and whispered to him. "Let's go to the Hadji tonight."

Romain's hand clenched at her waist. "Do you mean that?"

"Yes."

"We'll go tonight after the guests leave. I shall put you to sleep in the caravan, and I'll drive out to the desert."

"You should have a driver. You'll be tired," Pip protested.

"No. Abdul will be with us and the usual guards. We'll make the oasis by sunrise."

After the reception, Pip dressed herself in the light cotton jumpsuit that she would be traveling in and not all Romain's adjurations that she should wear sleep wear changed her mind.

"But I have a bed made up in the caravan."

"Romain, if I get sleepy, I'll crawl back there, but for now I'm riding up front with you."

They said good-bye to the king and left with the desert moon waning, stars winking like diamonds on black velvet.

Romain drove with the expertise that colored all his movements and the miles passed quickly. When he saw her swaying in the seat, he insisted she go back and sleep.

Pip remembered pulling the cover over her shoulders against the chill of the desert night, then she knew no more.

Sunrise came in a flash of green, orange, beige, and blue. Then the sun climbed into the heavens with instant warmth, the desert coming alive.

Romain opened the back and scooped her into his arms. "Say hello to the Hadji, Pippa."

She inhaled the fragrant air and looked around the section of oasis used by the royal family, the small palace, cool, quiet and private.

"We'll be alone."

"Yes." Pip saw the intensity in his eyes, but it didn't make her ill at ease anymore. She felt for the first time that she really knew her husband.

"You should sleep," Pip told him when they were in their mammoth suite of rooms.

"I will, if you'll sleep with me. I can't let you out of my sight, Pippa."

"I am a little tired." She had the fluttery feeling he was going to make love to her when he helped her off with her clothes, his hands lingering on her body. When he cuddled her close to him and urged her to sleep, she wanted him more than sleep.

She woke first and knew at once it was noon.

"Where are you going?" Romain muttered into her neck when she moved.

"Swim."

"Good idea."

The water in the pool was cool, and they frolicked like children.

When Romain carried her out of the water, she was laughing. He let her stand while he dried her, then led her back to their rooms to dress.

She watched him covertly, wondering if what his mother said about him being remote because he feared her rejection of him was true.

After they dressed in the very loose, light clothes of the desert, he led her out to the beautiful atrium filled with flowers, urging her to sit on the lounge chair.

"Romain, I hope you don't intend to treat me like a hothouse flower. I want and need to exercise and be active."

"As long as you don't overdo."

"I'm not going to overdo, just keep in shape. It isn't good for me or the baby if I become sedentary."

"What would you like to do?" Romain questioned her warily.

"I would like to go riding. I know my horse will be in the stable. Abdul always keeps her in readiness for me."

"But it's been some time since you rode a horse. Your doctor in New York said it would be all right as long as you were used to riding and didn't gallop."

"You asked my doctor? When?"

"Before we left California I called her. Come along and

let me dry you, then we'll go down to the stables." He took hold of her upper arms after he'd swathed her in warm towels. "There will be no endangering you. I won't allow it."

"I just want to go riding, Romain, not rocket over the moon." She saw the glittering remoteness in his eyes again and smiled. Pip reached out a hand and placed it on his chest and felt him flinch, her body prickling with the tight leashed emotion in him. "Romain, there is something I want to tell you, and I want to do it tonight." She pressed her two fingers against his lips when he would have spoken and shook her head. "Tonight."

He nodded, removing her towels.

She marched into the bedroom, feeling no embarrassment at her nakedness in front of Romain, knowing that her husband was right at her heels. She passed a mirror and sighed at her reflection.

"What's wrong? Aren't you well?"

She looked over her shoulder at him and smiled, then gestured toward the mirror where their nude images were. "I look like a baby tank."

Romain stood at her back, staring into the mirror, at her body from toe to forehead, his face softening, his heart racing. "You're exquisite."

She turned to face him pummeling his chest lightly with her fists, and grimacing. "Liar," she told him, her smile fading as she saw the look of astonishment on his face at her word.

"You were always lovely, Pippa. Now you're incredibly beautiful."

Words died in her throat at the hot sincerity in his eyes. "Every day I find out something different about you." She rubbed his lightly bristled chin. "But at last I think I'm beginning to really know you." She smiled at him when he slanted a curious glance at her.

"Surely it's no revelation to you that I think you the

280

most wonderful creature on the planet," he told her wryly, kissing her forehead, then striding away from her. "I'll make sure that Abdul has all in readiness for our ride this evening," he called over his shoulder.

Pip felt rooted to the spot by the depth of passion she heard in his voice, but she managed to speak. "Romain, tell him that I wish to ride to the tent this evening and that we'll be staying there overnight." She referred to the mammoth tent structure that was always in readiness for the king and in which she and Romain had spent a great deal of time when they first married. Some of her happiest memories of their marriage were there.

Romain paused without turning. "You're sure?"

"I'm sure," she whispered as he nodded once curtly and left the room. "After all, I have something to say to my husband," she continued to herself, smiling and stretching and feeling happy, carefree, and very, very sure of Romain.

They went for their ride that evening, an armed guard escorting them because they were going to the tip of the oasis where the tent was located. Though they would be ostensibly alone, a small army of nomads were constantly on watch.

The desert was as usual full of its own sounds, the night breeze was cool, but not yet with the coldness that deepest night would bring.

When they dined, again there was little sign of the servants, just a swish of clothing and the slap-slap of sandals. Food was served silently, then the attendants disappeared, and they were alone again.

"Romain, I like being by ourselves, but I don't really mind the servants around us."

"I do," he said abruptly.

Pip grinned at him openly.

"You're laughing at me again," he accused.

"Not really, darling. I'm just relaxed and beginning to

281

realize that when you get that strange look in your eyes, you just want us to be together, apart from others for a time."

"For always."

They went into the lounge after eating, sitting together on a large, soft couch, leaning back against banked cushions.

"Umm, lovely," Pip murmured, wriggling closer to Romain as he cuddled her in his arms.

"If you're sleepy, we'll go right to bed," he told her huskily.

Her temper flared for a moment until she saw the heat in his eyes. "Darling, I have something to tell you." She sat up Indian fashion, facing him on the cushions. "Romain, my darling, I love you because you're generous and loving, and because I realize how much you love me." She took a deep breath, looking right into his eyes. "I know you're going to be a wonderful loving father, too. Romain, don't be afraid of loving me too much because you could never love me as much as I love you."

"You talked to my mother and she told you about my father," he said in a strangled voice.

"Yes, and I thank her for it. I was worried about that look you get in your eyes. Now I won't, because I understand and there are no secrets between us now. Are there?"

"No," Romain replied, his throat working. "Sometimes I was sure I lost you because I was smothering you, and it destroyed me to think that I could do that to you. That's principally why I didn't come after you."

"I know," Pip inhaled. "I suppose we were both too intense. Maybe we needed to be apart to understand that our love reaches beyond the stars and is too big for mortal men." She half-laughed, feeling her eyes sting when he leaned forward and pressed his face into her lap.

"Philippa." Romain groaned, pulling her into his

282

arms, "Do you know how much I want to love you, every minute of the day and night?"

"Yes, I do," she said and sighed, rubbing her hair against his chin.

Romain looked down at her for a moment. "It frightened me when the love I felt for you grew more intense every day, and though I wanted to be alone with you all the time, I was aware that I was holding you too tightly to me. I worried about that this time. I didn't want to drive you away from me again."

"You didn't drive me away. My own insecurity did that."

"Shh. Let me say this while I can." He smiled down at her, his face open and vulnerable, his eyes moist, his mouth twisted. "I have always loved you too much, wanted to keep you in my sight and hold you to me." Romain gave a harsh laugh. "Even my uncle said that I was smothering you. Did you know that?"

"It's not true." She curled her arms around his neck, running little kisses along his chin.

"Oh, it's true, all right, but I'm fighting it." He pushed her head back gently on his arm, so that he could look into her eyes. "You are everything to me, Pippa—breathing, loving, laughter are all mixed up in you for me, so much so that I want to keep you with me always, that I want to make love to you all the time." His hard smile lifted one corner of his mouth. "But I also know that I want you to be the independent lady I fell in love with— and that I can hold you and not make love to you if that's the way it has to be."

Pip felt as though her whole being had melted in the wonderful realization of how much her husband loved her. "You mean that if I didn't want to make love for the rest of my pregnancy, you could stand that?"

Romain swallowed with difficulty, his eyes closing for a moment as though in pain. "It would be one of the greatest purgatories of my life, but I could and would do it to keep you well. My life is hell without you in it, Pippa. I can do anything that will keep you safe."

"Easing your discomfort with a lovely young girl from the desert," Pip tried to say it teasingly, but the words turned on her like razors and cut her.

"No," he thundered, his hands clenching on her. "There were plenty of women around to assuage my need of you when you were gone, but when I tried to make love to them, I saw your face. Finally, I stopped trying to bury your image with other women."

Pippa whispered, "You shouldn't have tried."

"The truth is," he said hurriedly, shaking his head, "I always felt married to you. I wanted you so much. I tossed and turned in my bed at night planning numerous campaigns to get you back because my life was empty without you and I knew that." He inhaled deeply, running his mouth over her hair.

"Then let's not put any barriers between us again. I love you, Romain," she told him, her being soaring out beyond the stratosphere, unfettered and joyous. "My love won't die. It will flower and flourish for all time, my dearest." She pressed her hand to his face.

"And you are well enough to make love?"

The harshness of his voice ran over her skin like a rough caress. "Yes, yes, please husband, make love to me."

"I want nothing more," he muttered, pushing her back against the cushions and beginning to disrobe her gently, his hands tremoring over her.

Pip, impatient with him, began an exploration over his skin, her mouth following her hands as she fondled the hard nipples on his chest, the crisp hair tickling her face erotically. She loved it when his body quivered in spasmodic reaction to her caresses, and she moved down his body in a moist and passionate quest.

"Philippa!" Romain called out to her hoarsely, pulling her over his body, his hand caressing her from neck to coccyx. "Darling, you're blowing me apart!" he told her in shaky laughter.

"That's the idea."

They came together in an explosion of spirit and love that had them both gasping and clutching each other.

"I love you," Romain breathed.

"Me, too." Pip yawned sleepily. "S'nice." Romain's chuckle against her skin was the last thing she heard before sleep claimed her.

They spent long, langorous days at the tent in the oasis. When they returned, the king sent a message to Pip to join him for lunch when Romain had to visit a distant group of nomads.

"My child, you've healed my boy. I know that his mother talked to you and that you now understand him better than you did. For many years his cynicism was overriding everything he did. He was hard and unbending, seeming not to care if he ever had love in his life. I have always known you were the one for him, Pippa child, and now you've saved him."

"And he has saved me." Pip pressed her hands against her rounding middle and smiled at the king.

They were in New York as planned when her labor began, and though Romain gave cool concise orders to everyone, including the staff at the private hospital where she was taken, Pip could see the beads of perspiration on his face. Though he was smiling and attentive when he spoke to her, nothing she said took away the tension in his body.

Their son was born in the early hours of the morning, thrilling Pip. "Isn't he wonderful, Romain?"

"Yes. He looks like you," Romain told her, smiling wanly, then wrapping her and the baby in his arms. "I'm so happy that you're both well and have come through this all right. I love you, Pippa. I will love you more each day we live in the thousand years ahead."

Pip turned her face into his neck and kissed him, feeling content. "Doing this again was a great idea, I think."

"Doing what again?" Romain asked, kissing her lips.

"Our marriage," Pip answered, looking at the two males she loved.

"A very good idea," Romain whispered, covering her mouth with his.